THE BAD NEIGHBOR

An Agent Victoria Heslin Thriller, Book 9

JENIFER RUFF

Greyt Companion Press

THE BAD NEIGHBOR

An Agent Victoria Heslin Thriller, Book 9

Copyright © 2024 Greyt Companion Press

ISBN ebook: 978-1-954447-34-9
ISBN paperback: 978-1-954447-35-6
ISBN hardback: 978-1-954447-30-1

Written by Jenifer Ruff
Cover design by Rainier Book Design

ALSO BY JENIFER RUFF

The Agent Victoria Heslin Thriller Series

The Numbers Killer

Pretty Little Girls

When They Find Us

Ripple of Doubt

The Groom Went Missing

Vanished on Vacation

The Atonement Murders

The Ones They Buried

The Bad Neighbor

THE FBI & CDC Thriller Series

Only Wrong Once

Only One Cure

Only One Wave: The Tsunami Effect

The Brooke Walton Series

Everett

Rothaker

The Intern

Suspense

Lauren's Secret

THE BAD NEIGHBOR

The Bad Neighbor is the ninth installment in an award-winning series featuring FBI Agent Victoria Heslin. While part of a larger narrative, each book, including this one, stands alone as a complete mystery thriller. A list of the Victoria Heslin books and other thrillers by Jenifer Ruff can be found jn the front of this novel.

1

Zoey

Then

After a week of driving from California to Virginia, Zoey Hamilton parked her Toyota in front of 6613 Mountain Meadows Road. She stared up at the white colonial with a mix of nerves and excitement. Her new home. A fresh start. A chance to leave the past behind her.

As thunder rumbled in the distance, Zoey climbed out of her car and got her first in-person look at the place.

The house had lingered on the market, its "As-Is" condition a deterrent to other buyers, but her husband had loved it at first sight. From California, Zoey had pored over online photos, committing every detail to memory, and finding a strange charm in the imperfections. Now that she stood in the driveway, the weathered exterior, the cracked, peeling paint, and the missing shingles were all expected flaws. But an ominous energy seemed to emanate from the house, something she hadn't sensed from the pictures. Zoey forced herself to shake off the strange feeling. Too late for second thoughts, anyway. The good outweighed the bad. The house had five bedrooms—five! If she and Chris got lucky, their first child would occupy one of those rooms next year, with more little ones filling the others in time.

Aside from the necessary renovations, the house was great, though not without a tainted past. Unfortunately, a criminal one. Not the kind of crime that left physical stains. No one had died within the walls. Nothing gruesome had occurred there. The crime was a white-collar case of embezzlement. The former owner had fled, taking millions with him. He was long gone, and Zoey wanted to forget he ever existed, so why was she even thinking about him now?

The front door of the house opened with a loud creak, and Chris emerged on the porch. In jeans and a t-shirt, he looked as handsome as ever. She'd missed him so much.

"You made it!" he called as he jogged down the front steps to join her.

After a celebratory hug and a deep kiss, their first at their new house, he helped her get their Labrador Retrievers, Finch and Wren, out of the car.

Zoey and Chris strolled around the yard, gusts of wind pulling at their hair and clothing as their dogs sniffed the unfamiliar territory.

The front garden was probably a showstopper once, before an entanglement of weeds took over. Zoey planned to tidy it up in the spring, introduce new plants, and put up birdhouses and bird feeders.

There was a lot to do. That was becoming more apparent with every passing minute since she arrived. But Zoey was good at getting things done. She liked to stay busy. With some help, they'd whip the house into shape while making it their own. She planned to write, paint, take long walks, and expand their family. Zoey pictured a future of laughter echoing through the home's hallways and children playing in the massive yard.

She squeezed Chris's arm, and he turned, offering a smile that seemed to touch her soul. In that moment, despite her weariness, her heavy eyelids, and the ache in her back and shoulders, her heart soared with a new energy.

When the first raindrops fell from the sky, Zoey and Chris ran inside together with their dogs.

Little did they know their world was about to fall apart.

2

Victoria

Now

At 6020 Mountain Meadows Road, FBI Special Agent Victoria Heslin stepped out onto her porch and pulled her blonde ponytail through the back of her cap. Inhaling the crisp fall air, she surveyed the yard. Fallen leaves and twigs littered the grass from last night's storm. As Victoria propped her leg on the porch railing to stretch, the distant whine of a chainsaw cut through the morning stillness—neighbors already at work clearing debris.

Veterinarian Ned Patterson, her fiancé, emerged from their house ready for their run. "I'm glad HR gave you the nudge to use or lose some vacation hours," he said, planting a kiss on her cheek.

"I know it was last minute, so thank you for switching your clinic schedule and taking some time off." Amidst their busy careers, Victoria valued the rare opportunity to spend quality time together.

They jogged down the road, past the sprawling estates of their neighbors, each home surrounded by several acres.

Keeping up with Ned always presented a challenge. With his long legs and quick turnover, he set a demanding pace, one she could barely match, but a reason she loved running with him. Staying in top shape was crucial for her job. She never knew when she might need to outpace a suspect.

"What do you think about driving into the city to visit a gallery this week?" Ned asked.

Victoria scrunched up her nose. "They're always so crowded. I mean, unless you really want to." The thought of staying home and doing nothing was far more appealing. "I have a list of books I want to read, and movies I think we'll both like. We can hike. You can do your cooking experiments."

"A staycation sounds good to me," Ned said, speaking as effortlessly as if he were at home, reclining on the couch rather than running. "We could have a barbecue one night. I'll grill. Invite friends. Your dad. The neighbors."

Victoria shook her head.

"No to which part?"

"The invite-the-neighbors part. I don't really know them," Victoria answered.

"Neither do I. It's been months since I moved in with you, and I haven't met any of them yet. That's the point of having them over. Or...is there something you're not telling me about the people who live here?"

"They're probably all nice," Victoria said with a resigned shrug. "And as long as I don't have to spend much time with them, they get to stay that way."

The words slipped out with more conviction than intended. As an introvert, she actively avoided unnecessary social situations, always finding excuses to avoid going out. On the rare occasions she had to make an appearance somewhere, she handled it well enough—or so she told herself. But the interactions never failed to leave her drained.

"Face it, Ned." She shot him a wry look. "I'm just a bad neighbor."

Ned shook his head. "No, you're not a bad neighbor at all. You don't do anything obnoxious or disruptive. No all-night ragers, blasting music, or letting the dogs do their business on other people's yards, right?"

"Well, no..."

"Exactly. Like I said, you're not a bad neighbor." He grinned. "You're just...not a particularly good one."

Victoria's lips twitched to contain her smile. "Ouch. Way to sugarcoat it."

Victoria had never interacted with her neighbors aside from the occasional wave from afar, but she had researched them before purchasing her house. She wanted to avoid any unwelcome surprises, especially the awkwardness of discovering she lived beside someone under a current FBI investigation. Or worse, someone she had investigated in the past.

Ironically, her neighborhood didn't get the all-clear she'd hoped for. The FBI was looking for Steve Johnson, who had lived on her street until he embezzled money and disappeared with it. His wife remained, living alone for years before moving away, leaving the house abandoned. The FOR SALE sign had come down just a few weeks ago. Victoria didn't know who had bought the house or if they had moved in yet.

Perhaps Ned's idea of hosting the neighbors wasn't so terrible after all. It seemed important to him. Victoria wouldn't raise the subject of the barbecue on her own, but if Ned brought it up again, she would agree and go into it with a good attitude.

They had reached the front yard of the recently sold house. Bright spots of color came from bird feeders and birdhouses that weren't there before. The new owners must have settled in. Victoria had been working so many hours recently, she'd missed their move.

"I think the new people might be the offenders that email mentioned," Ned said.

"I'm not sure what you're talking about. What email?"

"The one we got from the home owners' association recently. It was about the pond and toning down the lawn decorations for the sake of our neighbors and property values."

"Hmm," Victoria said. "I must have missed that one."

"If it's this house, it's not like they've gone overboard with plastic flamingoes or anything. The new folks must think we're a bunch of uptight sticklers."

At the common area at the road's end, Victoria and Ned veered onto a five-mile pine-scented trail that looped through the mountains. Leaves, damp from yesterday's heavy rainfall, swished beneath their running shoes as their conversation focused on post-run plans and the blueberry pancakes Ned promised to make.

They finished their run at the neighborhood pond. The sun cast dappled shadows on the still wet grass and glimmered across the water's dark surface.

The world seemed to have quieted to a gentle calmness, and Victoria took a moment to appreciate the beautiful morning.

A sudden commotion came from the woods, and Victoria whipped around.

Two yellow labs bounded toward them.

"Whoa, hello guys." Victoria laughed as the dogs pushed their noses against her legs and wagged their tails. They wore cute collars, one plaid and one with flowers, but no tags.

"Sit," Ned commanded.

Both dogs sat at his feet, looking up at him, tails thumping the ground.

"They listen well," Ned said.

Any second, Victoria expected to see the dogs' owner, but no such person appeared. The surrounding forest remained quiet.

Facing the woods, Ned shouted, "Anyone missing two dogs?"

No one answered.

Ned cupped his hands around his mouth and shouted louder this time. "Hello! Anyone there?"

Again, no answer.

"I've got a scanner at the house," Ned told Victoria. "If they'll follow us, we can see if they're chipped."

"Come on dogs, we need to find out where you belong," Victoria said. "Your owner must be wondering where you are."

"Let's hope so, or you'll want to keep them." Ned gave Victoria a sidelong look and a grin.

Despite his teasing, she knew Ned wouldn't hesitate to expand their large pack of animals if it became necessary. He loved animals as much as she did. Yet, Victoria was confident it wouldn't come to that. The dogs obviously belonged to someone. She and Ned just needed to locate that person.

3

Zoey

Then

I n the heart of her new kitchen, Zoey gripped a knife and sliced through the tape, revealing a box of wineglasses—a wedding gift from her aunt. They were often used and much appreciated.

As she lifted each fragile stem, a memory surfaced: her aunt's clear warning to reconsider marrying Chris.

Things had gotten ugly in the past, forcing Zoey to provide explanations to friends, family, and coworkers. Understandably, they were concerned about her well-being.

If Zoey hadn't loved Chris so much, if being with him wasn't everything she'd imagined and more, she might have heeded her aunt's warning and walked away. But love had anchored her, and she'd weathered the consequences. Now that they had moved, she clung to the hope she had nothing to worry about anymore. The worst should be behind them.

While the kitchen faucet dripped steadily, despite her attempts to make it stop, Zoey lined up the glasses on the cabinet shelves she'd scrubbed. Then she broke the empty box down with a forceful stomp and added the remains to the growing heap of flattened cardboard in the dining room. Finch and Wren circled the pile, noses to the ground, as if they might find treats hidden within the folds.

"There's nothing for you in there," Zoey told the dogs. She snapped a picture of the flattened cardboard and sent it to Chris with the caption, *Progress!*

His reply brought a smile to her face. Two thumbs up and *I love you.*

Zoey typed back, *I love you, too. Feeling like Wonder Woman today, getting stuff done.*

The Wonder Woman comparison was a stretch. Zoey's shoulders sagged under a dull ache from the long cross-country drive, and her throat felt scratchy, as if she were coming down with something. Yet she needed to stay busy because when she was idle, a lonely feeling of homesickness swept over her. Zoey supposed it was natural, and if Chris was with her during the day, rather than at his new job, she might not feel that way. She just wasn't used to being by herself for such long stretches. It wasn't even noon, and already she couldn't wait for Chris to get home.

Determined to cross more items off her to-do list until then, Zoey fetched a large bag of birdseed to bring outside. As she grasped the bag, a barking commotion erupted from Finch and Wren.

Zoey set the birdseed down and hurried to the front of the house. The dogs had stationed themselves at the door, their tails wagging as they pressed their noses against the frosted glass sidelights on either side. Clearly, an unexpected visitor or a wandering critter was out there.

Zoey pulled the door open partway, sticking her leg across the opening, wary of her dogs getting out. Despite their obedience training, she didn't trust them to stay in the yard.

There was no one there, but someone had left an enormous basket of items on her front porch, and a white Mercedes SUV was pulling away from the house. Whoever was driving hadn't waited long.

Zoey carried the heavy basket inside and set it on the kitchen island. There was a note handwritten in elegant, perfect script on a thick piece of stationery.

Dear Chris and Zoey,

Welcome to Mountain Meadows! We're thrilled to have you as our newest neighbors.

Best wishes, The Mountain Meadows Community.

Touched by the gesture, Zoey explored the basket's contents, first selecting a bottle of wine with a mountain range on the label. After tucking the wine bottle back into place, she scanned a collection of locally made bath soaps, chocolates, honey, jam, and crackers, all collectively arranged in a stunning display. In the front, a guidebook to the Virginia mountains listed the area's attractions.

Among the items, one made her pause. A pamphlet for a new neighborhood development called Lakeside Estates. The words, *Only two more homesites remain*, were emblazoned across the cover. Curious, Zoey thumbed through the brochure. The prices seemed reasonable until she realized they represented only the cost of each available lot. They didn't include an actual house. "Not in this lifetime," she murmured, tossing the brochure aside.

Returning her attention to the basket, Zoey imagined someone visiting local stores and handpicking each item. Nothing like this had happened when she'd moved into the buildings she'd previously called home in California. This was an unparalleled display of hospitality.

Zoey left everything as she'd found it, so Chris could appreciate the generous gift when he got home later.

In that moment, in her beautiful new neighborhood where people left remarkable welcome baskets on porches, Zoey felt optimistic about her future in Mountain Meadows. She wondered about the kind soul in the Mercedes who had delivered the basket and hoped she'd get to meet that person soon.

4

Grace

Then

If Grace Fairchild had to declare a favorite room in her house at 6615 Mountain Meadows Road, it would undoubtedly be her home office, the room where she felt the most organized and powerful. Her framed Edvard Munch painting, a more sinister version of *The Scream*, was a wedding gift from her grandfather. It hung on the wall facing the room's entrance, where it wouldn't escape any visitor's notice. Everyone in her family had coveted the small painting, yet it was she who came to own it. "Let there be no doubt you're my favorite grandchild," her grandfather declared when Grace opened the treasure, gasps of shock and envy from her relatives. So, it hardly mattered that she detested the howling, distorted face and the dark, depressing colors depicted in the painting.

The office itself was a masterpiece of interior design. Salvaged wood beams, crafted from a centuries-old barn, weathered but now polished so they gleamed, crossed the vaulted ceiling. The breathtaking view on either side of the tall windows—the apple orchard and the mountain tops beyond her guesthouse—could rival any viral Instagram snapshot. It had, in fact, garnered its fair share of online approval, which pleased Grace's parents as much as it did her. But at this time of day, the natural light streaming in through the pitched windows became a nuisance. With the touch of a button, five shades descended from the top of the windows and unrolled in silence to darken the room and eliminate the glare on her screen.

Grace adjusted her cashmere crewneck sweater and placed her hand on her protruding collarbone as she again focused on her search results. Her forehead wanted to crease, but her Botox would not allow it. Grace's current fixation was not one of her usual remodeling projects, social engagements, or charitable endeavors, but on the house next door, and more specifically, its mysterious new occupants. They couldn't possibly cause more turmoil than the previous owners, but Grace would feel much better once she had information on them.

The house had been a persistent bother for years. It had lingered on the market, diminishing the desirability of the surrounding homes, until it finally sold As-Is. A minor miracle perhaps, considering its condition. At first, all Grace knew was that the buyers had purchased the house under a trust, leaving their actual identities a mystery. Fortunately, it didn't take her long to find out who they really were. A friend of the realtor provided their names—Christopher and Zoey Hamilton from Redondo Beach, California. Grace was relieved at first. Hamilton was a solid name. She'd even considered it for her son's name, before settling on Handford instead.

Of course, her next step was to learn everything she could about them, to determine if these Hamiltons were what she considered "desirable" neighbors, a family from good stock, or not. Strangely, neither Christopher nor Zoey had any social media presence. They appeared to be private people. That could be a good thing. Unless it wasn't. There might be something more than a preference for privacy driving their discretion. Did they have something to hide?

Delivering the welcome basket a few days after the moving trucks arrived allowed Grace a thorough look at the house. She'd even peered in through the windows, recoiling and leaving the basket on the porch as two large dogs charged toward her. Though they were behind the windows, their raucous barking was more than she could bear. Still, she'd seen more than enough to realize the house was in even worse shape than she'd thought. No wonder no one else wanted to buy it.

Grace prayed the Hamiltons would quickly transform the exterior and clean up their yard, which remained a blemish on the entire neighborhood. So far, the only change to the outside was the installation of garish-colored miniature houses on poles in the neglected front garden—a sight Grace abhorred. The eyesores grabbed her attention every time she passed by the home, making her feel uncomfortable in her own neighborhood. She expected her new neighbors to help maintain and protect the aesthetics of Mountain Meadows. So far, the Hamiltons' efforts fell far short of Grace's standards. She needed to do something about that.

5

Victoria

Now

Victoria ushered the two Labrador Retrievers into her garage and filled a large water bowl for them. They lapped the water up, their tongues working side by side. After emptying the bowl, both dogs sprawled out on the garage floor, heads down but eyes open, clearly drained from their outdoor adventure.

Ned joined them a moment later with a handheld microchip scanner. Kneeling beside the female, he ran the device over her body, following the grain of her fur. The scanner emitted a soft beep.

"They're chipped," Ned said, rising to his feet as he stared at the scanner's digital display. "Her name is Wren. According to this info, she's registered to a woman in California named Zoey Hamilton."

"Really? That can't be right."

Ned scanned the other dog. Once again, the device emitted a beep. "Say hello to Finch. Same owner—Zoey Hamilton. Same California address."

"Finch and Wren. Their owner must like birds," Victoria said, thinking of the painted bird feeders in front of the house down the street.

Ned dialed the phone number on the scanner and listened with his phone against his ear.

Victoria heard the automated message even before Ned repeated it. "The number you dialed is no longer in service."

"Zoey must be the new neighbor," Ned said. "I'll take the dogs and drive over to her house. Want to come with me?"

Victoria thought about her plans to take a hot shower and enjoy a leisurely breakfast. Despite those plans, she said, "Sure."

"If these dogs belong to the new neighbors, you might like them. They're dog people."

Victoria couldn't help thinking she wasn't a fan of people who let their dogs run loose. Just as quickly as the harsh judgment arose, it dissipated with a pang of self-reproach. She'd made an assessment without context, a tendency that bothered her when others did it. There were other explanations. She had no grounds to cast judgment until she had the full story.

Victoria went into the house to grab a jacket. From over a dozen leashes, she selected two colors that coordinated with the labs' collars.

Ned lifted the dogs into the back of his 4Runner while Victoria climbed into the passenger seat. He backed out of the garage, headed down the long driveway, and through the double gates.

A half mile down the road, they turned into their new neighbors' driveway.

"Should we have brought them a house-warming gift?" Ned asked.

It was basic etiquette, and yet it hadn't crossed Victoria's mind until now. Her mother had also been a private, introverted person, yet she wouldn't have missed the opportunity to extend a kind gesture. Unfortunately, having passed away over a decade ago, she wasn't around to give Victoria gentle reminders. Victoria hoped returning the dogs, if these were indeed the new neighbors' dogs, would make up for the oversight.

At the base of a tree, a faded yellow tennis ball caught Victoria's attention. Another ball lay beside the bottom step of the front porch. A good sign the dogs belonged there.

There was a car at the end of the driveway, parked outside the garage. A blue Subaru Crosstrek with a California license plate and a bike rack.

"I wonder what kind of biking they do," Ned said, parking behind the Subaru.

"They? How do you know it's a 'they' who lives here?"

Ned shrugged. "I don't. But it's a big house."

"I lived in a big house alone before you moved in with me."

"True. Even so, it's sort of unusual."

Ned cut off the engine, and they climbed down from his SUV. The cool breeze chilled Victoria. She couldn't wait to get out of her damp running clothes and shower.

Straining against their leashes, the dogs pulled toward the front door and trotted up the steps.

"They sure act like they live here," Ned said.

"They were the same way at our house. I think they just want to go inside and lie down somewhere."

The front porch steps had rotted, and Victoria avoided touching the sagging railing.

"Whoever lives here might still be asleep and they don't even know the dogs got out," Ned said. "Not everyone gets up before dawn like us."

Victoria gestured to the security camera doorbell beside the front door. "Don't say anything weird. It might get recorded," she whispered.

Ned frowned. "I was going to stare straight into the camera and recite our grocery list, just to confuse them. But if you don't want me to..."

Victoria laughed at his random humor and bumped his hip with her own.

After a brief wait, a man of average height in his early to mid-thirties answered the door. He was good-looking, with thick dark hair, tousled and messy, and stubble around his jaw. He wore jeans, a well-worn long-sleeved shirt, and athletic shoes. The man didn't smile, and behind glasses with tortoise frames, his eyes reflected worry.

"Oh, hey," he said. After briefly taking them in, he looked past them, scanning the front yard and driveway.

"Hi. I'm Ned Patterson, and this is Victoria Heslin, my fiancée. We live up the street."

"I'm Chris Hamilton." His response was reserved, far from an enthusiastic greeting. "You and my wife Zoey are friends?" he asked Victoria.

"No, uh, Zoey and I have never met," Victoria answered, gripping Finch's leash as he pulled to go inside. "Are these your dogs?"

"Oh, yes, yes." Chris opened the door wider. "I'm sorry. Please, bring them in."

Victoria and Ned unclipped the leashes. The dogs rushed in and immediately plopped down on two cozy dog beds. Near their beds were metal water bowls and a woven basket full of dog toys. A coat rack shaped like a dog's bone hung on the wall beside the door. It said, *Live, Bark, Walk.*

Victoria expected Zoey to appear behind Chris any minute, curious to see who was there. It was early for visitors and rarely did anyone knock on others' doors in this neighborhood, regardless of the time of day, as far as Victoria knew. Yet there was no sign of Zoey.

Chris tilted his head, looking from Ned to Victoria. "Why do you have our dogs?"

"We found them in the neighborhood," Ned answered.

Offering no sign of the relief or gratitude Victoria had expected, Chris stared at his dogs as if considering his next words and coming up short.

"They came out of the woods near the pond," Ned added. "I'm a vet and they have microchips, so I scanned them. But your dogs are registered to

Zoey and a California address. You might want to get that updated as soon as you can, in case they get out again."

"Right. We will."

"Tell us if you guys need anything," Ned said. "We're right down the street. First house on the right behind the iron gates. And if you don't have a vet yet, I'm at your service."

"Oh. I think they do. Zoey had to take them. But, you know, maybe next time."

"It was nice to meet you," Victoria said.

"You, too. Really, thank you both," Chris said.

He appeared to look past them again, as if distracted. Victoria sensed something wasn't quite right.

She and Ned walked back to his SUV in silence. Passing the front garden, Victoria noticed the empty bird feeders swaying in the breeze.

Once inside the vehicle, Ned cast a glance back at the house. "Did he seem...off to you?"

"Yes, definitely. Almost as if he were hiding something."

Ned drummed his fingers on the steering wheel. "Maybe he had a late night and just woke up."

"More he never went to sleep," Victoria said. "He was fully dressed, wearing sneakers. And I wonder why Zoey didn't come down."

Ned started the engine, and Victoria caught a flash of movement in her peripheral vision. It was Chris. As he jogged down his porch stairs, he made eye contact with her, holding up a hand for them to wait.

Ned put the SUV back in park and rolled down his window.

Victoria leaned back against the leather seat, bracing herself for whatever news Chris was about to deliver. Instead of approaching Ned's side, Chris walked around the front of the vehicle to Victoria.

"I think I'm going to take you up on your offer," he said. "I can use your help with something now." He looked toward the road before he continued. "It's about my wife. Zoey. The thing is, she asked me specifically not to overreact but...I guess I'm just concerned because, well...I can't find her."

6

Zoey

Then

Zoey couldn't shake her homesickness, which made her feel disconnected from her surroundings. She had imagined a quiet house would be peaceful. Instead, the oppressive silence unnerved her. Rather than feeling inspired to write and create, she felt lonely, though not alone, exactly, which was creepy in its own way and something she didn't quite understand.

She stood in the center of the large back room, wrapping her arms around her chest to ward off a chill as she took in the wide windows, stone fireplace, and built-in bookshelves. More than any other room, this one held echoes of the previous occupants, Steve and Sarah Johnson. They'd left a large mahogany desk and a leather wingback chair, but the sense of their lurking presence came from more than just the furniture they'd left behind. It came from something Zoey couldn't pinpoint.

The air inside the room carried a faintly musty scent. Zoey traced a groove on the stone fireplace, resulting in a spot of soot on her finger. A faint creak from the hallway made her spin around, heart pounding. It was only the dogs settling into their beds. She shook off the paranoid sensation and wiped her finger on the bottom of her t-shirt.

Determined to at least eliminate the feeling the space still belonged to someone else, she started by vacuuming dust motes from the corners and beneath the furniture. The machine's loud hum was a welcome intrusion, filling the silence. Maneuvering the vacuum across the faded hardwood floors, Zoey cast a wary glance over her shoulder, as if she might catch someone watching her. The issue had to be the sheer size of the house compared to her previous home. Sometimes she struggled to believe she was the sole daytime inhabitant. At least she had her dogs.

As she covered the desk with a drop cloth, her thoughts veered to Steve Johnson again. She imagined him seated behind the same desk, plotting his embezzlement scheme. Zoey pondered Steve's motives. Did greed drive him, or desperation? From the little information she'd collected, she figured it was greed. He'd stolen millions and disappeared, leaving his wife behind to grapple with the consequences—betrayal, financial ruin, and not knowing what happened to him. Unless Sarah actually knew where he was. But that didn't make sense. Why would she stay in the house all alone, waiting years for it to sell, if she could have been with her husband enjoying the money together?

Steve's abandonment struck Zoey as deeply disturbing. What sort of person could do that to their spouse? In her mind, his betrayal was worse than his theft.

Lost in thought, Zoey smoothed blue painter's tape over the moldings and chair rail, then opened the first can of paint. Nothing else had the power to transform like a fresh coat of paint, though it smelled terrible, and the chemical fumes would inevitably give her a headache. She tried to open a window, but it was stuck shut and wouldn't budge. The next one opened with a splintering crack of the bottom frame.

Zoey added *office windows* to the list of items that needed fixing and then got to work. Gliding the roller over the walls, she focused on ideas for the cozy mystery she wanted to write. *Lovebirds.* The novel was supposed to take place in an idyllic town with a charming birding store. Her quirky main characters would meet and bond over their shared interest in birds. She could picture the setting, but she still hadn't decided on the main mystery element. Embezzlement and spousal abandonment definitely did not fit the novel she envisioned, yet Steve Johnson's criminal exploits kept creeping into her mind like an insistent whisper that wouldn't leave her alone.

She was almost finished with the walls when the ping of her phone made her jump. Most likely it was just a message from Chris, since she'd been so careful about only giving her new number to a select few people.

She set her roller on the paint tray and went to the fireplace, slipping her phone from the mantle. Sure enough, a note from her husband illuminated the screen.

Hey, babe. I'm slammed here. I'm going to get home a lot later than I hoped. Miss you.

Chris was working long hours since their move. Yet, despite his busy schedule, and the stress that came with a demanding new job, he was still thinking about her. Zoey knew she was lucky. Unlike Sarah Johnson.

Zoey replied, *Thanks for letting me know. All is good here. XOXO*

While the paint dried, Zoey assembled her new chair and placed it behind her desk. One by one, she unpacked her collection of cozy mysteries and bird guides and put them on the shelves. She added a copy of *What to Expect When You're Expecting*, and her newest book, *Birds of Virginia*, a gift she'd recently purchased for herself.

Setting up her new office took the entire day, and it was dark when she finally pulled the painter's tape off the walls, her head achy from the fumes as she'd expected. Her phone pinged again. Anticipating another message from Chris, she smiled inside as she grabbed her phone.

But it wasn't Chris, and when she read the note, an involuntary gasp escaped her lips.

Hello, Zoey. Did you miss me? I must say, I was surprised to see you'd packed up and left town without a goodbye. But don't worry, I know every detail of your new life in the countryside with your dogs.

Zoey's heart plummeted. Her hands trembled as she clutched the phone and read the words again and again. Finally, she took a screenshot of the text, deleted it, and blocked the number.

Her gaze flicked to the windows, half-expecting to find someone peering through the glass. Instead, she saw her reflection—a slight figure, hunched forward, appearing as exposed and vulnerable as she felt.

The dogs' sudden barking made her flinch. Amidst their noise, she heard the soft rumble of Chris's Subaru coming down the driveway. Still shaken from the message, Zoey rushed to finish getting the tape off the walls, balled up, and into the trash.

The tap of Chris's shoes across the hard woods announced his approach. "Sorry I'm so late. Smells like you've been painting."

Zoey hurried to greet him. "Close your eyes. I have a surprise." She guided him into the back room. "Okay, open them."

Chris's eyes widened. "Wow, looks great, Zoey. You did all this in one day!"

"I did. It's going to be my writing retreat."

"I love it. Did anything else happen today, or were you working on this room the entire time?"

This was her opportunity to tell Chris about the message. He would want to know. He deserved to know, but there was little he could do about it. Zoey had already decided not to burden him. Not yet. He had enough on his plate with his job and the work their house required.

"Nope," she said. "Nothing else. Just this."

Chris tapped her nose, drew her closer, and said, "There's some paint on your face. It's cute on you."

Zoey wrapped her arms around her husband's neck, clinging to him as he lifted her off the floor and playfully spun her around.

She was glad she hadn't spoiled the moment for Chris by telling him about the message, though it was too late for her. A spreading doom had eclipsed any sense of joy or accomplishment she should have felt. She tried to appreciate the freshly painted room, but it just wasn't happening. The walls, reeking of chemicals mixed with an underlying mustiness that refused to be erased, now seemed to mock her attempts to create a peaceful refuge.

7

Victoria

Now

The seconds ticked away in the Hamiltons' driveway. Victoria's plans to stay home and basically do nothing seemed to be unraveling, but she waited patiently for Chris to explain the cryptic statement about his wife—*I can't find her.*

Outside the SUV's window, Chris ran his hand through his hair. Finally, he stuffed his hands into his pockets and turned to face Victoria. "You're the FBI agent, right?"

"Yes."

"When our realtor showed us this place, she mentioned you lived down the street," he said, chewing on his bottom lip. "Now I'm really glad you're here."

"Is there something we can do for you?" Victoria asked politely, though it was clear Chris wanted her help, as opposed to Ned's.

"Well...I think so." Chris shifted his weight from one foot to the other. The corners of his mouth twitched. "I'm worried about Zoey. I'm not sure where she is right now."

"When did you last see her?" Victoria asked, thinking Zoey might have gone for a sunrise morning walk with the dogs and didn't return.

"Yesterday morning. Before I went to work. She texted me last night, saying she was spending the night at a friend's house. But she never told me who the friend was. And she still isn't back. She's not answering her phone or responding to texts." Chris swallowed hard. "I'm worried something's happened."

Victoria's FBI training kicked in, and she began mentally cataloging the details. "Does Zoey have a history of going off by herself or not checking in?"

Chris shook his head. "No, it's not like her at all. We communicate with each other every day, even when we're really busy. That's why I'm worried something's wrong."

"But you mentioned she told you not to overreact?" Victoria asked, confused.

"She did, in another message she sent me last night, before she stopped responding."

"Do you have a tendency to blow things out of proportion?" Victoria lightened her tone for the question, hoping not to anger him.

"What? No. Nothing like this has ever happened before, so I don't think I'm overreacting."

Victoria took a few seconds to process the information. "Have you tried tracking her phone?"

"Yes. It's off. The last location was near the pond at the end of our street, but she wasn't there when I checked this morning. And we had that storm yesterday." Chris raked a hand through his hair again, his distress evident.

"Did you contact any of her friends?" Victoria asked, though the question seemed too obvious to pose.

"That's the thing. I don't know who to contact. To be honest, I didn't think she had any close friends here. It's...with us being new to the area, and Zoey not working, I mean, she's been here," he pointed to the house, "...getting everything settled...she hasn't had a lot of opportunities to meet people yet. When you showed up and introduced yourself, I figured you were the friend she was with."

Chris seemed to search Victoria's face, as if he were desperate for her to change her story and admit she'd been with Zoey.

"Sorry. It wasn't me," Victoria said.

"Well, it has to be someone in the neighborhood, because Zoey didn't take her car. Her Toyota is in the garage. I don't think someone picked her up because she had our dogs with her."

"Did she say the dogs were with her?" Victoria asked. "Or could they have gotten out of the house on their own?"

Chris looked confused again. "They can only get out if someone opens the door for them, and all the doors were locked when I got home. Besides, their leashes and collars were gone, too. Now that you found the dogs, I'm worried Zoey might have left her friend's house early this morning, and something happened on her walk home. She could have gotten lost on a trail or..."

"It's a safe neighborhood. No crime," Ned said, looking to Victoria for agreement.

Victoria didn't respond. Danger could show up in the most unexpected of areas, and an accident or medical emergency could happen anywhere.

"I don't want to jump to conclusions. Zoey wouldn't want me to blow this out of proportion and embarrass her, or myself, if she's at someone's house. I mean, like I said, she specifically told me not to overreact. So, I guess I'm just trying to figure out what's going on for my own sake. But if she doesn't show up soon, I'm going to call the police. I should, right?"

"Yes," Victoria told him.

She empathized with his hesitancy to involve the police, a reluctance she often saw. Its origin was often rooted in denial. Calling the police made this a big deal. The instant Chris elevated the issue to law enforcement, Zoey's absence shifted from a misunderstanding with a reasonable explanation—she was nearby, at a neighbor's house, unaware her phone battery had died—to an admission something was terribly wrong. No one wanted to face that reality. Maybe, if he got lucky, Chris wouldn't have to. Sometimes it really was all just a misunderstanding. In addition, Zoey had specifically told him not to overreact. Victoria had to admit that seemed a little strange, but perhaps, despite what Chris had told her or what he believed, he had a history of exaggerating situations.

Chris remained by the SUV's open window, looking around as if Zoey might walk down the driveway at any moment. "I'm not familiar with all the trails. I haven't had time to explore yet. She could be out there on a path I'm not aware of. I could have missed her."

"Okay, Chris, here's what we're going to do," Victoria said. "Ned and I will go back to the pond area and take another look around. In the meantime, stay here in case Zoey returns."

"Thanks, I really appreciate the help."

"Don't mention it," Ned answered. "That's what neighbors are for."

Chris and Ned exchanged contact information.

"Please send us a current photo of Zoey, so we know who we're looking for," Victoria said.

"Sure. Yeah. That would help, wouldn't it? She might be upset because I'm making a big deal of this, but I'd rather be safe than sorry." Chris forced a small smile, but only looked worried as he made a mock salute gesture and stepped away from the SUV.

Ned put the vehicle in gear and headed down the Hamiltons' driveway. Victoria's instincts signaled trouble ahead. Knowing so little about her new neighbors, she wasn't sure if she would regret her next steps.

8

Zoey

Then

Normally, Zoey woke and headed straight to the bathroom. Not this morning. A lightheaded, dizzy sensation kept her sitting on the side of the bed for a moment, her bare feet suspended a few inches off the floor. A wave of nausea rose from her stomach. In response, a thrill coursed through her body. The not-quite-right feeling inside her could be the aftermath of the Thai takeout Chris had brought home last night. Yet, it could also be that she was pregnant.

The strange sensation passed in a minute or two, but the tingle of hope remained. Zoey rested her hand over her abdomen and imagined the tiniest seed of a child growing inside her. Yes, she was excited, but she couldn't get ahead of herself. Determined to stay grounded, rather than leap to conclusions, she promised to wait a few more days before taking a pregnancy test.

If a child was coming, all the more reason to get to work on her novel, she thought as she prepared a healthy breakfast. After eating, she drilled holes above the window frames and hung new curtains in the family room, then filled the bird feeders, a daily task now that birds had discovered the food.

Later, seated in her office, which still smelled like chemicals, she opened the top drawer of her desk to drop her pens inside. The drawer appeared empty until she glimpsed something white tucked in the back corner. A paper clinging to a nail or screw. She tugged, and the corner tore. Instead of tossing the paper in the trash bin, she took a closer look.

Someone had written and underlined *Magnolia Estates* at the top. Beneath the title were dates, each accompanied by a sum of money. The amounts grew exponentially from a few thousand to millions, with the final number at eight million dollars. Zoey's mind raced with questions. Was this Steve's handwriting? Did the amounts represent the money he had stolen? Had he started with small withdrawals to see if anyone would notice before he went for the big bucks? Zoey held the paper between her fingers, wondering if the police would find it useful, or if they already had all the evidence they needed.

The doorbell rang, startling Zoey so much she dropped the paper and shot upright. Her dogs sprang to life, barking as they raced toward the front of the house.

Feeling strangely complicit with Steve's criminal endeavors, which made no sense to her, Zoey slipped the paper back inside the desk and closed the drawer before getting up. There had been dozens of deliveries, each accompanied by the ring of her doorbell. She'd hurried to the door in eager anticipation each time, and not once had she been afraid. But that was before the threatening text message arrived, when she still believed no one from the past could find her.

Heading toward the front of the house, she told herself there was no reason to feel so worried. She cracked the door open with caution, again positioning her leg across the gap to keep her excited dogs from darting outside.

A man in his late thirties or early forties stood on her top step. He wasn't carrying a package, and he hadn't left anything on her porch. There was something slightly off-putting about the way he leaned against a column and stared at her as though he was assessing more than just the house. Maybe it was his dark, menacing eyes.

Glancing past him, she spotted his truck parked in the driveway. A magnetic sign on the door displayed an advertisement for *Tri-County Handyman*.

"Oh, hi. You're early. Come on in. I'm Zoey."

"Jake," he said, as he entered the house.

Unlike the other prospects Zoey had called, Jake had actually called her back and set up an appointment to come over. She'd gone online and checked his business page. It displayed pictures of Jake engaged in various jobs. To the best of her recollection, the images didn't look like the man with her now, though the same thing could be said about her. At the moment, she barely resembled the polished headshot she used on her social media profiles, back when she still had them.

Zoey considered asking Jake for ID, but decided it was unnecessary. She'd seen the magnet on his car.

"Did you just move here?" Jake asked, stopping in the foyer by her side. Only a few inches separated them. There was no reason for him to stand so close.

Zoey stepped back, pretending to notice something through the window. "I moved here just over a week ago. I've got a long list of repairs and projects."

She didn't like being alone in the new house with a stranger. At least not this one. Something about him made her uncomfortable. But the excitement of getting the renovations underway made her push aside her unease.

Jake followed Zoey to her office. She located the list of repairs from a neat stack of papers on her desk, next to the daunting home inspection report and index cards with notes for her novel.

"You work from home?" Jake asked.

Zoey's voice faltered as she answered, "Um, yes."

"Big house for just one person, isn't it?"

She involuntarily tensed. "No, it's not just me. My husband lives here too," she said, trying to balance politeness with her growing discomfort. "He works from home sometimes. He's in the office today, but not normally."

That wasn't true. Chris's job required him to work in the D.C. office Monday through Friday, but the lie flowed easily. A lie of self-defense. Zoey wished Chris was with her now. He had wanted to be there to meet with the handyman but was already behind with his work responsibilities and had too many in-person meetings.

Zoey scanned her list. The sheer number of items was overwhelming. Where to even begin?

"Don't do plumbing," Jake said.

Zoey zeroed in on one of the least pressing tasks, but one that carried personal importance. "The fireplaces are wood-burning, and we want to convert them to gas." The idea of burning wood inside her house scared her.

A haunting image from her youth resurfaced—the scarred torso of her third-grade classmate, Claire Watson. On Christmas Eve, Claire's nightgown had caught fire from a glowing ember. Zoey could still hear Claire's shrill voice describing her burning flesh and the subsequent pain. And when Claire lifted her top...well, Zoey would never forget the grotesque, mottled skin.

Gas logs offered a cleaner, safer ambiance. With the simple push of a button, the fire disappeared. No embers left behind. No soot to clean.

After Jake inspected the fireplace, he moved closer again, invading her personal space and making the large room suddenly feel small.

Zoey crossed her arms over her body. There was no way she could stand having this man in her house unless Chris could be there, too. Zoey didn't care if Jake was the most skilled contractor in Virginia or if he could start the renovations tomorrow. He made her too uncomfortable.

"All the windows are stuck. That's a new discovery I just added to our ever-growing list, but most of the work is on the exterior," she said, avoiding his eyes by staring at the paper in her hand.

"Let me have your list," Jake said.

Zoey handed it to him. She was already retracing their steps, eager to usher him out the door.

They were halfway there, Jake walking behind her, when he asked, "What about the basement? How is it looking?"

"Um, I don't understand." A slight chill ran through Zoey's body. He was too close again. She could sense him, though she didn't want to turn around and see him. She only wanted him gone.

"Your man cave in the basement. How does it look?"

"The basement is unfinished. There is no man cave down there."

"The previous owner wanted a basement remodel. A man cave, he called it. I came out here and gave him an estimate. He never got back to me. It really pisses me off when that happens. You know, I come all the way out here to give these estimates and don't charge a thing. I expect common decency in return."

Zoey thought it strange Jake hadn't mentioned his previous visit to the house until now. With her hand on the front door, she asked, "When was that? When did you give the estimate?"

"Five years ago. In October. I keep records and I checked before I came here today."

Zoey opened the creaking door. "Oh. Well, it's a shame they never got around to having it finished. Would be nice. My husband would have really appreciated a man cave in the house."

"Every home on this street has a basement. You can tell from the way the lots slope down. I'm sure they're all done up real nice. If you want, I can do for you what I was going to do for the previous owners. I can work on that door of yours, too, when I'm here. Get rid of that creak." A grunting sound came from deep inside Jake's chest as he looked around the foyer again. "I'll check out the exterior work and get back to you with an estimate soon. I have two other jobs lined up before I could start here. Not sure how long they'll take yet."

Zoey forced a grateful tone. "Okay, thank you." She hoped the other jobs would take forever.

Jake trudged out and Zoey was quick to close the door behind him and turn the bolt. She remained by the window, watching him stop on the stairs and take a few pictures of the porch with his phone. She kept an eye on him as he clomped around outside, consulting her list and taking more pictures. Finally, he got in his truck and drove off. Even as he turned onto Mountain Meadows Road, her discomfort persisted.

9

Zoey

Then

Dinner had been ready for hours. The meal was nothing extravagant, just a simple salad and roasted chicken breasts seasoned with garlic and rosemary the way she and Chris liked.

The front door opened with its usual creak. Zoey was even more aware of it now, thanks to Jake the handyman.

Chris's footsteps echoed through the hallway. "Sorry I'm so late again. I could not get out of there. Something smells delicious. I hope you didn't wait for me for dinner."

"Of course I did. I wanted to."

Zoey noted the exhaustion on her husband's face, the lines that were a little more pronounced than usual and the bags under his eyes, though he remained remarkably handsome.

"How was work?" she asked.

Chris released a tired huff, his shoulders slumping. "Just, you know, I'm still deep in learning curve mode. The pressure's on, and it's like they're expecting more from me than I can deliver right now. I'm struggling to keep my head above water. Half the time they're speaking their own language there, with all their acronyms. I got confused today, and it didn't go unnoticed."

Zoey frowned in sympathy. "I'm sorry, honey, but I'm also sure that will change for you the more you get settled. What about your colleagues? Do they seem nice?"

"They're fine," he said, though she picked up on the hint of reservation in his voice.

As he rubbed the back of his neck, Zoey wondered what his female coworkers thought of him. Chris's rugged handsomeness still left her almost as awestruck as the day they met three years ago.

Chris's employer had assigned him to collaborate on a marketing campaign with Zoey's firm. His striking good looks drew everyone's attention. Including Zoey's. Her friend Kim was one of those people who exaggerated everything for effect or out of boredom. Her marketing pitches were overly effusive—"the absolute best," and "if this is what you want, there is no one better to do it,"—and needed toning down. But in describing Chris, she was dead on when she fanned herself with a notebook, whispering, "Oh, my God. He could not be hotter."

Zoey had agreed. During Chris's first presentation, she missed half of what he said because she was so distracted. But as they spent hours working together, and she learned to concentrate in his presence, she discovered there was more to Chris than just his appearance. He was kind, patient, and clever—a pleasure to be around.

In a private moment during one of their late-night work sessions, Zoey shared that she'd always wanted to write a book, but she needed an immediate and steady paycheck, so she turned to creating marketing campaigns instead.

"You know, I work for a tech firm now, and it's great—I mean, it really is," Chris began, with his usual thoughtful expression. "But if you had asked me when I was a kid, I would've told you I wanted to be an astronaut.

Exploring the unknown, space, the stars, the planets, all of that fascinated me."

The endearing glimpse into Chris's childhood dreams made Zoey smile.

"But it's the people we work with who make a job good or bad or great, I think." His sincere gaze met Zoey's. "The right people can make even the longest hours and the toughest challenges enjoyable."

At his words, a warmth spread through her body.

"And you," Chris said, nudging the conversation back to Zoey. "You're really talented. It's clear from the way you write, even if it's 'just marketing campaigns.'" He made air quotes to let her know he was using her phrasing, not his. "You have a way with words."

Zoey blushed, appreciative of his encouragement. "Thanks, Chris. I'll write a book someday. For now, though…I'm pretty happy here. You're right that it's the people who make the difference." She held his gaze for a beat longer than necessary before looking back down at her papers. Another wave of heat crept over her face, and she didn't doubt she was blushing.

Chris was great to work with, but Zoey thought their connection ran deeper. Thoughts of him followed her home from every meeting, and an electric current buzzed between them when they were together. Yet, for the first few months, their relationship had to remain strictly professional because Chris represented one of her firm's largest accounts.

Shifting back to the present, Zoey's eyes dropped to the gold wedding band on her husband's ring finger. She hoped his new coworkers in Virginia, especially the women who would find his looks and charm irresistible, would see the ring as a boundary not to be crossed, regardless of the temptation.

Zoey focused on her husband now, searching his eyes for another reason he looked so drained. "Is there anything else bothering you? Do you think you made the right decision taking the job?"

"Oh, definitely. One hundred percent," he answered, leaning on the countertop. "I didn't mean to complain. It's going to be great. More opportunities. More income. We got this house, didn't we? And a fresh start. There's no one here to bother us."

The truth lodged in Zoey's throat. She didn't have the heart to tell him he was wrong.

"The food looks great," Chris said, taking a seat at the table. "I never got a chance to eat lunch." He dug into the meal, groaning in pleasure with each bite. His appreciation made Zoey wish she'd prepared something better and more of it.

"Get any writing done?" he asked between mouthfuls.

"Not today. There was just too much going on."

"What was...oh, I almost forgot. Did the remodeling guy come?"

Zoey pressed her lips together and nodded. "Yes. Tri-County Handyman. A guy named Jake. I don't want him to come back."

Chris straightened in his chair, his demeanor shifting from relaxed to alert and protective. "What did he do?"

"I just got a creepy vibe from him. He made me uncomfortable to the point that I sort of hope I never have to see him again. And he'd been here before, to our house."

"When? And for what?"

"He gave the Johnsons an estimate for remodeling their basement, but they never used him. Here's the strange thing. Jake said he gave them the estimate five years ago in October. Steve, the husband, disappeared just a few weeks after that in November."

"How do you know when he disappeared?"

"I Googled it. I was curious. Don't you think it's odd? Why would Steve ask someone for an estimate on remodeling the basement if he was planning to skip town? And it wasn't his wife who wanted the work done. Jake gave every indication the estimate was for Steve."

Chris shrugged. "I can't answer those questions. But look, if you don't want to hire this guy, then we won't. Wait a few days, then thank him, and tell him you found someone else, or his rates are too high. Just don't leave him hanging."

"I won't. But it's not like we have anyone else. Everyone I've called is booked for ages. Too busy to even give us estimates."

"Don't worry, we'll find someone else. What about the name I got you from the guy at work?"

"He hasn't gotten back to me yet."

"I'm sure he will. So, besides the handyman, anything else happen today?"

A part of Zoey was itching to tell Chris she'd woken up feeling a bit off, and she suspected it could be morning sickness. Uncertainty and the fear of disappointment held her back. She was already keeping secrets from him, which she didn't like, but she needed to wait until she knew for sure she was pregnant. Fingers crossed, things might be different this time.

10

Victoria

Now

In search of Zoey, Ned pulled out of the Hamiltons' driveway, turned left, and headed to where they'd found the dogs earlier that morning.

"If I were in Chris's shoes, and you hadn't come home, and I didn't know where you were, I'd have dialed the police already, no hesitation," he said. "Makes me wonder if Zoey has a habit of doing things like this, even though he said she doesn't."

"Yeah, she might."

"We should have asked to see the texts she sent him. You might be able to tell a lot about the situation from those."

Victoria nodded, already peering out the window for signs of her missing neighbor.

Ned took his hand off the wheel and gestured to the glove compartment. "Hey, I've got some protein bars in there. Can you grab me one?"

Victoria popped the glove box and took out two protein bars. She tore open one package and handed it to Ned before opening her own. It wasn't the breakfast she'd had in mind. When she worked long hours and traveled, she often resorted to protein bars or convenience store snacks for sustenance. She'd hoped her vacation "diet" would be different, and they'd have delicious foods that didn't come straight from a package, but her stomach was protesting too much to hold out for something better.

"What you said about no crime in the neighborhood isn't exactly true," she said. "Someone else disappeared from that same house."

Ned took his eyes off the empty road to gape at her. "Really? When?"

"Before I moved here. He was an attorney who embezzled millions from a real estate investment project he was involved with. Then he took off. Left his wife behind."

"Is he in jail?"

Victoria crumpled the packaging from her bar and stuffed it into the cup holder. "No. He was never caught."

"So he got away with it," Ned said, turning off the main road toward the common area.

"So far. A person can hide pretty well with millions of dollars if they're careful and smart about it, but greedy people usually slip up."

Ned's phone chimed. Chris had sent a photo of his wife. It was a recent shot that captured Zoey with her arms outstretched against the backdrop of her new home. Her smile was huge below expressive brown eyes and high cheekbones. A glowing, medium-toned complexion suggested she was bi-racial. She wore a casual outfit of a t-shirt and cut-off shorts.

Zoey seemed cheerful, but a single photograph had its limitations. It captured only one instant, frozen in time.

Victoria studied the photo a bit longer before biting into her protein bar. Ned had already finished his. She offered him another.

"I'm good for now. Let's help make sure Zoey is okay, and then I'm going to make us the breakfast I promised."

Victoria hoped that was what would happen. But with Chris's worried expression still ingrained in her mind, she wasn't so sure.

Ned eased his 4Runner into the arc of a gravel circle and parked parallel to the grassy edge of the common area. They got out, and Victoria surveyed their surroundings. Beyond a patchwork of trees, she could make out the pond, snatches of the walking path around it, and part of the gazebo's green roof.

"What should we be looking for?" Ned asked. "Besides Zoey, obviously."

"Anything out of the ordinary. Disturbed ground, keys, scraps of fabric, the dogs' leashes, signs of a struggle. Anything that might not belong or may point to a direction she might have taken."

"I didn't notice anything earlier, did you?"

"No. But I was zoning out on our run. This time I'm going to focus. If you find something, just mark the area and let me know." Victoria got two rolls of bright orange trail marker tape from a bag in the back of the SUV and handed one to Ned.

She gestured toward a tree with a large white square painted on the trunk. "I'll start there and loop back. Holler if you turn up anything."

"I will." Ned pointed toward a trail marked by a yellow triangle. "I'll take that one. We're going to lose cell service once we head up the mountain, so shout extra loud if you need me."

As they went their separate ways, Victoria remembered when she first moved to Mountain Meadows. The sheer number of paths and trails around the neighborhood delighted her. The options seemed endless, which could also lead to confusion. A fallen tree might alter or obscure a path, making it entirely possible Zoey had become disoriented in the woods. The recent storm had only compounded the risk, with freshly fallen branches littering the trails. She could be injured, unable to hear them or unable to respond.

Victoria walked slowly, scanning the ground for irregularities. Ned's occasional shouts of "Zoey!" traveled through the air, mixed with the crunch of fallen leaves and the snap of twigs under her feet. Crows cawed in the distance as a squirrel scurried up a nearby tree trunk.

A small patch of white among the browns and greens caught Victoria's eye. She was wary at first. The trails were home to several snake species, including the highly venomous copperheads she had encountered on multiple occasions. But this wasn't a snake.

Separating the leaves and squatting down, she got a closer look at the object. A tiny, mud-caked button. Twice, it slipped through her fingers before she grasped it securely. Picking things up was one of the few tasks that still troubled her since losing several fingertips to frostbite a few years ago. Once the button was firmly in her hand, she determined it wasn't from Zoey; the caked dirt suggested it had been there for some time.

"I didn't see anything, did you?" Ned asked when they reunited by the pond.

"No signs of Zoey. Perhaps that's a good thing."

Ned and Victoria descended the stone steps leading toward the gazebo, navigating around a recently fallen branch. At the gabled entrance, Ned took a dramatic step back, extended his hand with a flourish, and gave a theatrical bow. "After you, my lady."

Victoria couldn't help but smile, playing along with his charming antics. She accepted his gesture with mock formality. "Well, thank you, my gallant..." She tried to come up with something funny, but that simply wasn't her strength. It was also why she appreciated Ned's silly side.

Holding hands and laughing, they crossed the threshold to step inside.

Splashes of color caught their attention. Two leashes—one with flowers, the other plaid—hung over a bench in the back of the structure.

Victoria and Ned exchanged a concerned look.

From the gazebo, Victoria looked around again, her gaze lingering on the pond. For a few heartbeats, she contemplated the possibility Zoey might have somehow ended up in the water. The area surrounding the pond offered no hazards—no treacherous ledge, no slick incline, and Victoria dismissed the morbid thought as improbable. She didn't want to believe Zoey had disappeared under the water's dark surface.

———

Chris stood at the end of his driveway, gazing down the road, his phone pressed against his ear as Ned and Victoria approached.

Ned rolled down the car window in time to catch the deep frown on Chris's face and to hear him say, "I swear, if you did something..."

His words and angry tone surprised Victoria.

"You better be telling the truth," Chris said, before cutting off the call.

"Who were you talking to?" Victoria asked.

"That was just someone we knew in California. Doesn't matter. She doesn't know where Zoey is. Did you find anything?" he asked, looking hopeful.

"We didn't see Zoey, but we found these leashes in the gazebo." Victoria lifted them to the window for Chris to see.

His expression darkened. "Those are ours."

"I was just wondering," Victoria said, "...can Zoey swim?"

Chris gave her a sidelong look before answering. "Yes. She grew up in Los Angeles near the beach. She was a lifeguard in high school."

Victoria was relieved to hear that.

"I better start calling women in the neighborhood to find out who Zoey was with yesterday," Chris said. "Do you know the other women who live here, Victoria?"

Victoria offered an apologetic look as she shook her head. For the second time that morning, she had to admit she didn't know her neighbors. "Sorry, Chris, I don't. I travel a lot for work so I..." She gave up trying to explain because her excuse sounded lame, and went with, "I can help you find their phone numbers."

"Most people won't answer a number they don't recognize," Ned said. "But it's Saturday. There's only what? Six or seven other houses on the street besides us? We'll go with you to knock on some doors, in case anyone has seen Zoey."

Victoria nodded her agreement. She wasn't surprised Ned had offered his support again.

"I really appreciate all your help," Chris said. "She had to be with someone on this road."

"And she never mentioned hanging out with anyone in particular?" Ned asked.

Chris wrinkled his brow. "She's had a few exchanges with the person in charge around here, but I wouldn't say they were friendly."

Victoria exchanged a puzzled glance with Ned. "We don't know who that is."

"I met her once. Her name's Grace," Chris said.

That would be Grace Fairchild. Grace and Victoria had crossed paths in their youth, growing up in McLean, Virginia, but never quite connected. Grace was a few years older. Victoria's world had revolved around horses and the stables; Grace's interests, whatever they were, lay elsewhere.

Grace had a reputation for being well-informed, which was a nice way of saying she had a habit of minding other people's business. She was like that growing up, and perhaps even more so now. If anyone knew something about the goings-on in the neighborhood, it would be Grace.

11

Grace

Now

As Grace sifted through the stack of mail, unaware of what occurred that very moment at her nearest neighbors' house, a brightly colored flyer demanded her attention. *15-Year College Reunion: Save the Date!* The words leaped right off the page, stirring a flurry of emotion within her.

Grace had all but forgotten about her alma mater in recent years. She'd been so busy with other things. She was pregnant for the second time at their fifth reunion, and had no desire to attend, feeling more like a whale than a social butterfly. As for the tenth, she couldn't recall hearing anything about it, though she could only assume it had come and gone without her.

Her college memories awakened a melancholic yearning. Freshman year had been her first true taste of freedom from her controlling father, former Governor George Stanford, and her demanding mother.

Growing up, every aspect of Grace's existence was subjected to their critiques—her speech, her clothes, her posture, her choice of friends. Flawlessness was not just expected, it was enforced as the only acceptable standard. The relentless pursuit of perfection had defined her existence for as long as she could remember. Away from her parents, Grace could finally breathe. For those fleeting years, she was simply allowed to live.

During her sophomore year, Grace had fallen hard for Sean Piddle, a hockey player with the body of a god. Unfortunately for their relationship, she had no intention of ever becoming Mrs. Grace Piddle. She simply couldn't bear the sound of that name. She'd had to break it off with him before things got too serious. After Sean, she paid close attention to such important details.

Grace and her husband Craig met during their senior year under rather unromantic circumstances—a raucous frat party thrown by a mutual friend. Perched on a stained and threadbare couch, their red plastic cups in hand, Grace and Craig spent the evening commenting on the surrounding partygoers, establishing their connection in a haze of alcohol. Grace remembered feeling a profound connection to Craig. He was handsome then, and his last name, Fairchild, unlike Piddle, held a certain prestigious allure. She could envision taking it as her own someday.

Since getting married and having their first child right after college, Grace and Craig had forged a path that defied the initial expectations of Grace's skeptical father and the judgmental whispers of her family's social circle. Craig's success as a real estate developer had silenced any doubts about his ability to provide for a family.

A few years ago, he'd considered running for governor or U.S. senator. For no apparent reason, he'd changed his mind. Maybe she could convince him it would be a wonderful opportunity for their family. The start of a dynasty. Grace wouldn't mind living in the Virginia governor's executive mansion for a few years, as her own mother had done recently.

Setting the reunion flyer aside with a satisfied smile, Grace began preparing. She opened her calendar and scheduled appointments for Botox, laser treatments, and highlights to ensure she looked her absolute best for the event. After all, it was a chance to reconnect with old acquaintances and flaunt her success. She would make sure everyone there admired and appreciated her.

In the meantime, she had issues to deal with at home in Mountain Meadows. With a determined toss of her perfectly styled hair, Grace turned her attention back to the Hamiltons, intent on re-establishing her reign as the unofficial queen of the cul-de-sac.

12

Zoey

Then

Zoey spread out a drop cloth on the splintered planks of the back porch and assembled two bird houses and one feeder. She chose bright colored paints to attract birds and butterflies. Dipping her brush into the sky-blue paint, she set to work, coating the small roof, bringing the miniature house to life with each stroke.

Painting the bird houses provided a way to procrastinate working on her novel. The familiar act provided a fleeting sense of accomplishment and also alleviated some of her homesickness. Still, she didn't want to let anyone down, especially herself. She had to make progress on *Lovebirds*. The novel was her chance to create something wonderful and share her passion for bird watching with the world, and yet, it was starting to feel like a burden. Weighed down by the expectations she'd placed upon herself, she made a solemn promise to resume her writing efforts when she finished painting.

She drank a cup of decaf coffee while her projects dried, then carried them to the front yard and found ideal spots for each. Stepping back, she admired her work. She loved the way the garden was transforming into a whimsical haven. Though she'd cleared the ground of debris, she wouldn't pull the dead plants until spring. The dried flowers would provide seeds and coverage for birds.

A sleek black Range Rover glided down the street, headed toward the back of the neighborhood. Zoey raised a hand in greeting, but the driver didn't seem to see her.

Shrugging off the brief interaction, she returned to the house and sat down to write at Steve Johnson's desk—she still thought of it that way rather than as her own.

Zoey stared at the nearly blank screen before her, the cursor blinking. She had deleted the entire first page of her novel, dissatisfied with her opening lines. No matter how many times she tried to set the scene, it just felt...wrong. Her focus drifted, and she envisioned Steve Johnson hunched over in the same manner, his eyes narrowed in concentration just like hers, as he plotted his real-life crimes.

Had he ever sat there, plagued by the same self-doubt she was experiencing? Could that be what made him completely abandon his life, his spouse, and his home, giving up everything to become a fugitive? And what about Sarah? She must have been so lonely and depressed after her husband left. What Zoey felt now paled in comparison to what Sarah must have gone through. To what she might still be going through.

Zoey had never met Steve or Sarah Johnson, and yet she couldn't stop thinking about them, especially when she was in the office sitting at their desk. Maybe buying a place with an unusual history wasn't such a good idea. Yet she loved the house and was determined to make it a home.

Frowning, Zoey refocused her attention on the fictional world she was trying to create—a world she could control.

Usually, Zoey took pride in her ability to set goals and conquer them. She had graduated college with honors while working almost full time in food service. At her last job, she had risen from junior marketing analyst to team leader faster than anyone.

She thought when she quit her full-time job, she'd get so much more done without interruptions from colleagues, phone calls, and meetings, but that wasn't happening.

When her phone pinged, she ignored it, determined not to get distracted when she was finally close to getting some actual writing done. It pinged again and curiosity got the better of her, though it was likely Chris saying he would get home later than expected again. "Later than expected" had become the new normal.

When Zoey flipped the phone over, the words on the screen sent a chill down her spine.

I can't forget about you just because you left California, Zoey. I'll be there soon to remind you you're going to pay for what you've done.

The vicious message hit Zoey like a punch in the gut, the words jumbling together into a trail of fear. She took a screenshot, deleted the text, and blocked the number, her heart pounding in her ears.

The urge to call Chris was nearly overwhelming. But again, she resisted.

As always, the threatening messages had arrived a few days apart. It was like a cruel game designed to keep her on edge and to chip away at her sense of security. Each day without a message gave her a false sense of safety that shattered when the next message arrived. This latest one had darkened her mood like an impending thunderstorm, making it impossible to focus on her novel.

Still seated at her desk, the enormous office felt like a suffocating cage. The too quiet house seemed to close in around her. She had to get out of there, away from the taunting silence. She sent Chris a quick message to tell him she was going for a walk. Grabbing the dogs' leashes and her binoculars, she headed for the trails, intentionally leaving her phone behind. The threatening messages couldn't follow her now. She'd find peace outdoors with her dogs.

But as Zoey stepped outside, the menacing words echoed in her mind: *I'll be there soon...You're going to pay for what you've done.*

13

Victoria

Now

As Victoria, Ned, and Chris walked across the Hamiltons' yard, the white bricks of the Fairchilds' residence came into view through the foliage. Those bricks had been red until recently.

The roar of an engine drew their attention. A large truck rumbled past on its way out of the neighborhood. The truck bed was loaded with chainsaws and wood chippers. The logo on the side advertised emergency tree removal services.

"They sure got out here early," Ned said.

Victoria nodded and turned to Chris. "Does Zoey have family in the area?"

"No. Her only other family is her father. He's in California, and they're not that close. I called him though, on the off chance they'd been in touch recently."

"Could I look at the messages Zoey sent you? If you don't mind." Victoria knew she'd just asked to see the personal correspondence between a husband and his wife, but if she was going to help Chris, even in an unofficial capacity, she needed to view their last string of communications.

Chris hesitated for a moment before retrieving his phone. Holding it up, he used facial recognition to unlock the device, then tapped through to the messaging app. It took him longer than Victoria expected to pull up the conversation.

When he finally handed her the phone, the reason it had taken so long became clear. Chris had captured screenshots of the message thread rather than showing her the full interaction. The images he shared only displayed what he wanted her to see. Victoria wondered why he would limit the context. Was there something embarrassing or deeply personal in his previous messages? Or something more ominous?

The group stopped walking as Victoria examined the screenshots. Each image captured a string of blue text bubbles filling the right side, representing Chris's messages. Only two white bubbles appeared on the left—Zoey's sparse replies. Victoria started reading from the top, eyes trailing over the first text Chris had sent the previous day at five pm.

Chris: *Sorry, it's such a late one. I'm planning to leave in an hour unless there's a last-minute emergency.*

Zoey: *I'm with a friend. Don't worry.*

Chris: *Who is your friend?*

Chris: *Hey, Zoey. I'm home now. Looks like you have the dogs with you. I'm going to grill chicken and make pasta. When are you coming back?*

Chris: *Hey? Getting worried about not hearing from you. Who is your friend? Call me.*

Zoey: *I'm in one of my moods. Feeling a bit overwhelmed and need some me-time. Don't trouble yourself waiting for me. And please don't overreact. I'm going to stay the night here.*

Chris: *Where is here? Who are you with???? Why are you in a mood? Please call me back.*

Chris: *Where are you?*

Chris: *I'm really worried. Please call back asap.*

Chris: *Did I do something wrong? Are you still mad about the other night?*

Chris: *Zoey??? You have to tell me where you are.*

Chris: *Where are you? Why aren't you answering?*

The messages from Chris continued, escalating with concern and desperation, but there were no further responses from his wife. Victoria read the mostly one-sided exchange again, focusing on the few messages from Zoey.

The first seemed vague and somewhat dismissive. *I'm with a friend. Don't worry about me.*

Why hadn't she mentioned the friend's name? Even after Chris asked, Zoey didn't answer. That seemed strange and triggered a red flag in Victoria's mind.

The second message from Zoey offered more insight into her personality and state of mind.

I'm in one of my moods. Feeling a bit overwhelmed and need some me-time. Don't trouble yourself waiting for me. And please don't overreact. I'm going to stay the night here.

There was a lot to analyze in that message. Victoria detected an undertone of exasperation and perhaps entitlement. She tried to withhold judgment on her neighbor. Zoey hadn't expected strangers to read her private messages. Yet in Victoria's experience, it was in moments of perceived privacy that true character often surfaced.

"I don't mean to pry, but what does she mean by 'one of my moods'?" Victoria asked, handing Chris's phone back.

"I honestly don't understand what she's talking about," Chris answered.

"Does she have moods where she does unpredictable things?" Victoria asked as they resumed their walk toward the Fairchilds' house.

"No. Not since I've known her."

"How long have you known her?" Victoria asked.

"Almost three years. We've been married for a little over a year. Zoey's very goal oriented. When she gets her mind set on something, it's like there's no stopping her. But I wouldn't call that a mood. It's just her personality."

"Any reason she might want to stay away from you?" Victoria asked. Even with a gentle tone, her question was invasive. Rude even, considering this wasn't an interrogation. Chris might not want to answer, and he might not tell her the truth, but Victoria still had to ask. He could have a bad temper and a history of blowing things out of proportion. If Zoey feared Chris and was trying to escape him, Victoria wasn't about to help track her down. And yet, from the tone of the messages, it didn't sound like Zoey was in an abusive marriage. It seemed that if anyone had an upper hand in the relationship, that person was Zoey.

"We're fine," Chris answered, though he hesitated before continuing. "Things have been a little stressful lately, because of the move and all the changes that go with it. We're both still adjusting, and we've got...I guess what I'd call normal relationship challenges. I've been working too many hours."

"And the thing that happened the other night? You referred to it in the messages. The thing that might have made her mad?" Victoria asked.

Chris bit into his lower lip before answering. "We had an argument the day before yesterday when I got home from work. But it wasn't...I've never hurt Zoey or forced her to do anything, I promise you. I have no explanation for what is going on right now, but I think something is wrong."

No matter what the couple's fight had been about, or how bad it might have been, the dogs were the reason Victoria agreed something wasn't right. Her quick glimpse into the Hamiltons' home told her Zoey loved those dogs. They were healthy, groomed, and well trained. Finding them unleashed and alone signaled a problem.

As the trio approached the flagstone path winding through the Fairchilds' yard to their front door, Victoria hoped Grace might have answers.

14

Zoey

Then

Zoey trudged along the trail, her pace dictated by Finch and Wren's frequent stops to sniff and mark their territory. As they emerged from the tree line, the common area stretched out before them. The hedges stood in uniform perfection, no wayward branch daring to protrude beyond the others, and late summer flowers dotted the manicured beds with color.

A large sign proclaimed the area as the *Private Property of Mountain Meadows*, a warning to anyone who might not belong there.

When she and Chris had chosen this neighborhood, the trails, the lush green spaces, and the pond were major selling points. Zoey had spent the past week walking the dogs along these paths and had yet to see another soul. At first, she had appreciated the solitude. But as she surveyed the deserted common area now, that same sense of isolation made her feel frightened.

There was no one around. No one to greet her or offer a casual wave. Yet Zoey couldn't shake the unsettling sensation of being watched. The hedges were tall and thick enough to conceal a silent presence. She fought the urge to look over her shoulder, unwilling to validate her suspicions.

When they neared the pond, Wren and Finch strained against their leashes, desperate to play in the water.

Zoey hesitated before unleashing them. This would be her first time letting them swim. There was no one else around to object. Yet something about the murky water unsettled her. Despite her wariness, she unclipped their collars. Finch and Wren raced toward the dark pond and launched themselves into the water.

Zoey settled onto a bench inside the gazebo to watch her dogs. Before the move to Virginia, this was what she imagined life would be like as a resident of the Mountain Meadows neighborhood. Yet now that she was here "living her dream" and feeling incredibly lonely, she doubted her decision to leave her former life behind. She had to remind herself the change was her choice, her path to the large home and yard so perfect for a family, and something they couldn't have afforded in Los Angeles. She also had complete freedom—*this* is what she wanted. Once they had children, she'd no longer be alone during the day. She'd be busier than ever.

As her dogs played, she envisioned her future children, a boy and a girl, in neon orange life jackets paddling little canoes or kayaks across the pond with the dogs swimming beside them. Zoey realized she now viewed so many things through the lens of prospective motherhood.

Birdsong coming from a nearby tree prompted her to raise her binoculars to her face. Above her, a Northern Mockingbird hopped gracefully from limb to limb.

A loud splash made Zoey lower her binoculars.

In the blink of an eye, Finch sprang from the pond like a projectile and barreled down the path away from Zoey.

"Finch!" Zoey shouted. Her mouth fell open as his motivation for leaving the pond became clear.

A woman wearing pristine white pants and a rose-colored blouse emerged from the walking path. She froze as Finch bounded toward her.

"Finch, stop!" A sickening wave of dread hit Zoey, and she leaped to her feet.

Fueled by an unbridled desire to spread his joy, Finch ignored her and kept running.

The woman shrieked.

"Finch! No! Come!" Zoey shouted in the loudest, most commanding voice she could muster.

Immense relief washed over her as Finch obeyed and trotted back to her with his tail still wagging.

"Good boy. Good boy," Zoey murmured, crouching to attach his collar and leash.

Wren trotted over to join them, and Zoey quickly fastened her leash. With the dogs secure, Zoey redirected her attention to the woman in the white pants, pants with an actual crease—a peculiar choice for a walk outdoors. Her flawless makeup failed to conceal her anger as she strode toward them.

"I'm really sorry about that," Zoey said, still grateful nothing truly awful had occurred.

The woman's fury persisted. She narrowed her eyes and said, "Your dogs should not be off leash if you can't control them. And this is part of a private neighborhood. It's not a public park."

Zoey held her ground and kept her chin up as her defensive instincts kicked in. Despite the less-than-ideal beginning, this encounter marked her first interaction with a neighbor, and she was determined to steer it in a more positive direction. Forcing a smile, she said, "Again, I'm really sorry about my dog. And we live here, in this neighborhood. I just moved about a week ago. I'm Zoey. Zoey Hamilton."

The woman looked taken aback. Between her dark lashes, her gray eyes were unblinking. "Oh. You're the one with all the bird feeders."

"Yes. I paint those and sell them online."

"I see. Well, I'm Grace Fairchild. The neighborhood president. I trust you enjoyed your welcome basket."

"Oh, that was you? Thank you. It was really something. I love it. So does my husband. It was amazing," Zoey said, though under Grace's disapproving gaze, Zoey felt anything but welcomed.

She had to glance down to remember what she was wearing. Cut-off jean shorts, a faded *I'd Rather Be Birding* t-shirt splattered with paint, and tattered sneakers. The same outfit she'd worn the day before, though Grace wouldn't know that. Sweaty and disheveled, her hair frizzed in every direction was not the polished first impression she wanted to make on her neighbors. Especially not this neighbor in her designer clothes looking like she'd just come from having her hair blown out at a salon. But surely Grace would understand that Zoey was in the throes of unpacking and settling in.

"What kind of work does your husband do?" Grace asked.

"He works with tech start-ups."

"Tech start-ups?" Grace asked, as if the words had left an unpleasant taste in her mouth. "And what about yourself? Do you work outside the home? Or do you devote all your time to...painting those bird feeders?"

"Well, until recently, I was a Vice President of marketing for an advertising firm in Southern California." For years, the role had defined her. Though it wasn't always fun and caused its share of stress, it had always given her a deep sense of belonging and purpose. "For now, while I have the luxury of time, I'm doing something I've always wanted to do. I'm writing a novel."

"A novel? How nice. It's just the two of you, then? No children?"

Zoey held back from saying, *Not yet, but I think I'm expecting.*

Another woman appeared at the end of the trail. She wore yoga pants and a baggy top over her slim frame. A ponytail held her strawberry blonde hair back. "Hello!" she called with a wave.

Grace beckoned the woman over. "Zoey, this is Faith Humphrey. She lives across the street from me. And Faith, this is our new neighbor, Zoey Hamilton."

Faith and Grace. An interesting combination of names. Zoey wondered if someone named Charity or Hope might show up to complete the trio.

Wren chose that instant to shake her entire body, sending water droplets spraying over everyone.

"Sorry again," Zoey stammered, stepping farther from the women and pulling the dogs with her.

"Were they in the pond?" Grace asked, emphasizing the last three words as if the mere thought of it disgusted her. "That water must be filthy."

"They're labs and most labs love water. These two certainly do," Zoey explained. "They grew up swimming in the ocean almost every day in California. When we were looking to move, one of our top criteria was having a body of water nearby. This pond is perfect. I'll hose them off when I get home."

"Yes, you'd better," Grace said with a frown. "Faith and I have a school fundraising event to discuss, so we have to be on our way."

Faith grinned at Zoey. "Looks like I need to get going. This is a working walk, but it's nice to meet you. Looking forward to getting to know each other."

"Same," Zoey answered.

Faith jogged off to catch up with Grace, who had left without looking back.

As their figures disappeared on the trail, Zoey stood alone with her dogs. Her sense of isolation grew heavier and settled around her like a shroud.

15

Grace

Then

It was late afternoon, and the children were busy with after-school activities. Grace stood behind the rare granite of her kitchen island, and Faith sat across from her, sipping sparkling lemon water. Despite the leather seat with the sheepskin back, a luxurious custom creation, Faith shifted her weight as if she couldn't get comfortable. Her gaze wandered around the newly remodeled kitchen. "This room looks incredible. So different from the last time I was here."

"It better look different," Grace answered, searching for any hint of envy in her neighbor's eyes. Grace counted on her designer to stay ahead of current trends and give her an incredible, unique look until her next remodel. "My mother approves, thank goodness. I hadn't done much with the space in...." Grace lifted her eyes toward the ceiling as she calculated. "...almost six years. It was long overdue."

"I don't know about that," Faith murmured, looking skeptical.

With a conspiratorial raise of her brows, Grace asked, "So tell me, what did you think of our new neighbor?"

"Zoey seems nice."

"I brought her a fantastic welcome basket. From the neighborhood, of course."

"Oh. That was thoughtful of you."

"It was. After all, it's been ages since we've had a new neighbor, and it seemed like the right thing to do. It must be difficult for her, coming from such a different background. However, I don't think she has the slightest idea who I am," Grace said, eyeing the canapés and artisanal cheese platter she'd set on the counter.

"What are you talking about? She's from California. Why should she know who any of us are?"

"Well, because...never mind. It's no matter," Grace said. "Zoey told me she's writing a novel."

Faith raised her glass to her lips. "A novel? Interesting. What sort of novel?"

Grace shrugged. "I didn't ask. I still can't get over her clothes. Let's just hope that wasn't a fair representation of how she normally looks when she leaves her house."

Faith looked right past Grace and out the rear window. It was something Faith did often, suddenly averting her gaze rather than responding, and it never failed to annoy Grace.

"I suppose every neighborhood has its share of...you know...outliers. One family that doesn't quite belong. When I was growing up, we had the Vargas family." Grace lowered her voice as if someone might overhear. "They had a daughter my age who went to the local public school. My mother forbade us from playing with her or setting foot on her property."

Faith didn't seem to be listening, so Grace sighed. "That awful garden needs a complete overhaul. It was a sight before Zoey arrived, so it's not entirely her fault. It's all because of what Steve did. Taking off on Sarah and leaving her with nothing. All their assets frozen. Sarah had barely a dime. Such a shame. She really let that house go."

Faith spun around, and a flash of something ignited behind her eyes. "Sarah had more important things to deal with than updating her house."

"I'm well aware, darling," Grace said. "Of course she did. And just between us, Craig and I were charitable enough to give her some financial help. It seemed like the proper thing to do. Though, to be frank, it was more a gift than a loan, since I highly doubt we'll ever see a penny returned to us." Grace waved her hand to the side. "Of course, one always wonders if Sarah had any inkling of what her husband planned before he did it."

"She said she didn't," Faith answered.

"And everyone always tells the truth, don't they?" Grace laughed. "Sarah's decision to wait for her husband to come back instead of selling their house immediately was utterly misguided. Clinging to such futile hopes—delusional, if you ask me. I'll tell you one thing, if Steve ever dares to return, he'll find himself behind bars without a friend to his name."

"It's heartbreaking what happened to Sarah," Faith said. "And I always liked Steve. He seemed like such a nice man."

Grace rolled her eyes. "Oh, Faith, you have a habit of seeing the good in everyone, don't you? But let's be honest here, Steve Johnson was the furthest thing from a decent man. He's nothing but a greedy, spineless little thief. He's probably sipping cocktails on a Caribbean beach, living it up while we're here suffering the aftermath of his decisions."

"We're hardly suffering, Grace."

"Life in prison would be a luxury he doesn't deserve. Stealing from all those investors seems worse than murder." Grace closed her eyes, needing to calm down. Every time she allowed Steve's actions to infiltrate her thoughts, her blood pressure surged. Anger bubbled inside her, and she couldn't help wishing the worst on him. Vivid images of retribution flickered through her mind, leaving her appalled and yet gleefully invigorated. She'd never share those dark fantasies with another soul.

Along with the compulsion to appear above reproach, Grace had inherited a vengeful streak from her family, who settled scores with ruthless precision. Her father had orchestrated the downfall of several political rivals who dared to insult him. Grace's younger brother, a shrewd businessman, had left competitors in professional ruin, ensuring they'd never recover. Grace was proud to uphold her family traditions. No offense toward her went unanswered.

However, out of consideration for Steve's wife, Craig had persuaded Grace to drop the matter. It was generous of Craig, she supposed, and she appreciated that about him. With Steve missing, her options for revenge were limited, anyway. She could only destroy his reputation further, and this she did every chance she got. If Steve ever returned to Virginia, he would rue the day he crossed the Fairchilds.

Grace took a few deep breaths and said, "Craig and I decided it was best to erase Steve from our minds and move on. Unfortunately, I have to pass his house every day, and it's a stark reminder of everything he did. I just hope Zoey gets that house and the gardens in order. She also needs to get rid of those tacky contraptions on the giant poles."

Faith sighed. "Those are birdhouses."

"Whatever they are. Apparently, Zoey paints and sells them, though I can't imagine who would ever want to buy one. But one is more than enough. And if I catch those dogs off leash again..."

Faith crossed one leg over the other in an interesting display of her flexibility. "I think you're overreacting, and I don't understand why the birdhouses bother you so much. Why are you so focused on Zoey?"

Grace narrowed her eyes in surprise. "Now why on earth would you ask me that?"

"Well, I suppose because you can't seem to stop talking about her. And the welcome committee? It's a nice idea. I would have liked to help with it, but since when does the neighborhood have one?"

"Since now," Grace snapped. "What sort of people would we be if we didn't make a point of welcoming our new neighbors?"

16

Zoey

Then

S truggling to concentrate on the novel she wanted to write, Zoey kept reliving what had happened at the pond the previous day. The images flashed through her mind in a relentless loop—Finch bounding out of the pond, sopping wet and jumping onto Grace, depositing muddy footprints all over her white pants and pink blouse. It hadn't happened, Zoey reminded herself. Finch hadn't even touched Grace. So why were the memories haunting Zoey like a colossal train wreck she was helpless to stop?

The most vivid image was Grace's horrified expression. Her wide eyes and scowl had etched themselves into Zoey's memory. Was her disapproval merely a reaction to Finch running loose? Or had Zoey's appearance, her unruly hair, lack of makeup, and paint-splattered clothes played a role?

Zoey pushed herself up from her desk and went to the kitchen to refill her coffee. Changing to decaf hadn't been easy. She needed the caffeine. But if there was a baby growing inside her, she would do nothing to jeopardize its health.

In California, she'd shared her coffee breaks with Kim, a close friend and colleague who had been Zoey's lifeline many times. Zoey missed her now.

As she sipped the decaf brew alone, she checked her email and was surprised to find one from Jake with an estimate for the work on the house. The cost of each item was less than she'd expected, which only made not wanting to hire him more frustrating.

Zoey's fingers rested on her keyboard as she contemplated how to respond. She wasn't comfortable hiring Jake. Needing time to weigh her other options, options she had yet to find, she settled for a diplomatic: *Thank you. I'll discuss this with my husband and get back to you soon.*

As soon as she set her phone down, a text arrived.

Zoey felt a rush of worry. She'd acted so eager for someone to handle her projects and renovations, and now, despite Jake's very reasonable estimates, she'd told him she needed to think about it. Had he noticed? Was he angry?

After taking a deep breath to prepare for his response, she picked up her phone and read the new message.

Your pathetic marriage won't have a happy ending, Zoey. I'm going to make sure of it.

Her body went stiff as her hands formed fists, a visceral reaction. She'd expected an unpleasant response from Jake, but this was worse. As always, Zoey took a screenshot, blocked the number, and deleted the message. She gripped her phone tighter, tempted to hurl it at the fireplace. She'd done that before. All it got her was a trip to the U Break We Fix store and a bill for replacing her screen.

Zoey looked around the empty room, wanting someone to tell her what to do next. She needed a friend, and she didn't have one in Virginia. However, it was just past noon on the west coast. Kim always took a lunch break. The timing might work out.

Settling back into her chair, Zoey called her friend.

"Zoey! How's Virginia treating you? Do you miss us?"

Just hearing Kim's voice, buzzing with her big personality, lifted Zoey's spirits.

"Every day," Zoey admitted. "More than you know. But I don't miss the traffic. How's the team holding up without me? My replacement settling in okay?"

"Great. Like she was born for it. We nailed the Parker-Swanson pitch. You went above and beyond transitioning her. She already knows more than me."

"Oh, stop it. You are amazing and irreplaceable," Zoey said, her words genuine as she drained the rest of her lukewarm coffee.

Kim's laughter filled the line. "I know. Just fishing for compliments. Wanted to make sure you didn't forget me while you're out there all alone in your dilapidated mansion. Met any new friends yet? Any southern belles?"

A horn blared on Kim's end of the call, painting a vivid picture of Kim's surroundings and a typical day in downtown LA.

"No, only because I've been pretty caught up with the dilapidated mansion, as you so aptly called it. It's more consuming than I thought. We're having trouble finding anyone available to get started on the work. I've barely left the house, to be honest."

"What about *Lovebirds*? Don't tell me you're hoarding chapters from me. You worried about my brutal honesty?" Kim teased, nudging Zoey about the novel they'd discussed several times.

"It's... simmering. The first chapters still need more work." That was an understatement. She and Kim had always enjoyed critiquing each other's writing and helping to strengthen it. Zoey couldn't wait to share her novel with Kim. The problem was getting to a point where she had actual chapters to share.

Kim's sigh came through loud and clear. "Just promise me it won't turn into a novel that never sees the light of day because it doesn't get past the great idea stage. The first draft doesn't have to be perfect, remember?"

Zoey huffed. "You don't have to worry about that. It won't be." She shifted gears, her voice taking on a serious tone. "Hey, you didn't, by chance, give my new number to anyone, did you?"

"I have not shared your contact info with another soul, just like you asked. Why, what's up? Oh, no. Shoot. Tell me I'm wrong. You're getting calls and texts again, aren't you?"

Before Zoey could reply, unsettling sounds came from the living room. Dreaded sounds, ones she had been fortunate enough not to hear in a long time. Retching and gagging.

Distracted, Zoey said, "Kim, I'm sorry, I have to run. Something not good is happening with one of my dogs. I'll call you later."

"Okay. Say hi to Chris, and send me the pages, Zoey. Love you."

"Love you, too." Zoey tossed her phone onto the couch and rushed toward the living room. She gasped at the sight of Finch standing in the center of the new carpet, head hung low, retching.

"Oh, no, baby. Not there, please, not there." She grasped his plaid collar and tried to pull him away, but it was too late. His mouth opened wider than she'd thought possible, and a nauseating brownish-green fluid with lumps splattered onto the carpet.

Wren whimpered near the front door, signaling her urgent need to go outside.

"Hold on, Wren," Zoey pleaded. "I've got to deal with this mess first."

Zoey led Finch off the carpet and onto the wood floor, determined not to release him until he finished getting sick. It took a while, and Wren's cries continued.

Once Finch had emptied himself, Zoey concocted a solution of dish soap and water, grabbed an old towel, and tackled the stained carpet on her hands and knees. The vomit on the hardwood floor would have to wait. Fortunately, Wren quieted her cries as Zoey scrubbed.

Finished cleaning, Zoey wiped her forehead with the back of her hand and surveyed the carpet. She could still see a stain. Clutching a trash bag, she made her way outside, passing Wren in the foyer. Wren wasn't her usual cheery self. She hung her head and looked ashamed. Something brown speckled the dog's back legs. That's when the horrible, pungent odor hit Zoey. Clutching the trash, she hurried to the front door and exclaimed, "Oh, no—no—no."

Diarrhea covered the new interior doormat and smeared the bottom of the door and the surrounding walls.

Zoey stood staring with her mouth open, too shocked to do anything else.

17

Zoey

Then

Desperate to help her sick dogs, Zoey entered the veterinary clinic's waiting area. A small terrier lunged from the corner, straining at the end of its leash to yap at them. Finch and Wren, usually the life of any canine gathering, rallied just long enough to wag their tails.

After taking a clipboard stacked with forms from the woman behind the reception desk, Zoey sat on the edge of a chair.

The terrier continued yapping, but Zoey's dogs remained listless on the tiled floor, too unwell to respond. Their uncharacteristic behavior and prolonged illness had Zoey so concerned she had trouble recalling her phone number and her new address. Was it 6630 or 6613? She checked her phone to make sure she got them right. She wished Chris was with them.

Zoey glanced up to find the terrier's owner staring at her with concern. Zoey wondered for a second if she was still wearing her pajamas, but no, she'd changed into sweats.

A veterinary technician in scrubs with paw prints entered the waiting room and said, "Zoey Hamilton."

Zoey followed her to an exam room.

"We're glad you brought them in," the vet tech said. "Tell me what's been going on."

"They've been sick since yesterday," Zoey explained.

As she recounted their ongoing symptoms, the vet tech looked at Zoey with such kindness and empathy that Zoey instinctively straightened her posture to seem less overwhelmed by the situation.

"Dr. Simpson will be with you soon," the vet tech said, leaving Zoey alone again to shift uncomfortably in the hard chair, wring her hands together, and worry about her poor dogs.

To pass the time, she checked her messages and saw one from Jake the handyman.

You want me to get started on your place next, I'll just need a 50% deposit.

Before she could respond to Jake, Dr. Simpson knocked on the door.

He was a kind-faced man in his sixties with gray hair, a gray beard, and a pleasant smile. "New patients?"

"Yes. We just moved here. I drove from Los Angeles with them less than two weeks ago."

"Well, welcome to Virginia. Let's figure out what's going on with these two. When did it start?" he asked, crouching down to examine Finch.

"Yesterday. In the early afternoon. And it's been nonstop since then." Zoey's gaze flitted between her two dogs and the vet. Wren and Finch whined softly, tugging at the threads of Zoey's already frayed nerves. She worried they might have to go outside and relieve themselves again.

"Have they been into anything unusual recently? A change in their diet or exposure to any new substances?"

Zoey imagined her dogs coming across something toxic, like rat poison. No. That was impossible. Finch and Wren hadn't been out of her sight.

Zoey's weary exhale carried the weight of the past few weeks. "I had to change their dog food because the kind I used to give them, I can't find it here. But this seems like a lot more than the result of switching food."

"Moving can be as stressful for animals as it is for humans," the vet said, again with an obvious measure of sympathy Zoey appreciated, and yet one that made her feel weak. "I'm sure you're feeling a little out of sorts, too, aren't you?"

"I am," Zoey answered. "Definitely." The acknowledgement brought a sharp sting of tears she was quick to blink away. A bone-weary tiredness had taken hold of her body. Could pregnancy make her feel like that? Maybe a little, though more likely, the move had been more taxing than she anticipated. Her sleep had been restless, haunted by lists of things yet to be done and her search to find someone to do them. Having no friends or family nearby wasn't helping. And then there were the threatening texts, unpleasant history repeating itself, making it seem like she hadn't really escaped from that part of her life at all. So, yes, everything felt a little alien in this new place, including the dog food on the shelves. She had underestimated the impact of so many changes.

"Let's examine them to make sure it's just the stress of the move or the diet change we're seeing here," the vet said. "Or is there anything else you can think of that they might have gotten into?"

"We don't have a fence yet, so all their time outside has been on a leash. Oh, they also swam in a pond in my neighborhood. They love to swim. They used to go in the ocean whenever we had the opportunity in LA." Until that moment, she'd assumed they'd eaten something poisonous or contracted a terrible virus. But in a sudden surge of realization, she felt sure the pond water was to blame. "Could something in the pond have caused this?"

She remembered news headlines from the past—people and pets dying from toxic chemical spills or brain-eating amoeba after swimming in contaminated water.

Dr. Simpson moved his gloved hand over Finch's abdomen. "That's a real possibility. In cases like these, I like to take a few steps. First, I'd like to run some tests to rule out any infections or parasites. We'll take a stool sample from both dogs to check for anything unusual. Meanwhile, consider getting the water from the pond tested. And until we understand what we're dealing with, it would be best if you kept them away from your pond."

Zoey nodded. "Yes, of course."

"I'll prescribe some anti-nausea and anti-diarrheal medicine to help with their symptoms and start them on a course of antibiotics. Those should help until we have more information."

Zoey appreciated Dr. Simpson's guidance. Her dogs seemed to be in capable hands with him. She would do whatever it took to keep them happy and healthy. For now, they were her only babies.

"You need to take it easy, too," he added. "Moving is a big deal. Give yourself, and them, some time to adjust."

———

When Zoey returned from the vet, a plate of cookies sat on the top step of her front porch. Oatmeal chocolate chip, wrapped in clear cellophane with a bow made of straw. They were clearly homemade—the surfaces not quite smooth and the perimeters slightly irregular—and they made her mouth water. A note in the center of the plate said: *Welcome to the neighborhood! -The Humphreys (Mark, Faith, and Lexi) 6640 Mountain Meadows Road.*

Was this another neighborly gesture, or was there something else behind it? Zoey wasn't sure why she was feeling so cynical, but she was. Perhaps because she wanted to avoid what her dogs had just endured. She couldn't help wondering if someone had tampered with the food.

Feeling paranoid, she unwrapped the package and bit into her first cookie. Was there a strange taste? An odd texture? She waited, her paranoia on overload, then decided she was being irrational. The cookie was delicious. Between taking care of her sick dogs, the cleaning, and the trip to the vet, Zoey hadn't eaten all day. Still, before taking another bite, she waited a few more seconds, paying attention to her breathing and heart rate and half expecting something terrible to happen. A minute passed. She was still okay. Feeling foolish about her hesitance, she devoured two more cookies. Not the ideal pregnancy diet, but they tasted fabulous.

The house still smelled awful, like the worst kind of sickness. She went from window to window in the family room, searching for the ones she could get unstuck and push open to let in fresh air. While the dogs rested, she undertook another round of mopping and scrubbing.

Much later, exhausted, she slumped in a chair behind her computer for a crash course in contaminated water. She was certain that's what had caused her dogs' illnesses. The timing was too precise to ignore. Both dogs had gone into the water and both dogs were sick the next day.

Picking at the hem of her t-shirt, she suddenly worried about her own health. She'd cleaned dog feces and vomit, breathed in bleach and disinfectant fumes. What if she'd unknowingly endangered the baby growing inside her?

Desperately wishing she could have a do-over of the last two days, Zoey hurried to the bathroom to scrub her hands once more.

"Smells like a bleach factory in here," Chris said, setting his laptop bag on the kitchen floor and placing their takeout dinner on the counter.

Zoey managed a weary smile. "Yeah, well, it's been one of those days." She eyed the paper bag, hoping Chris had bought something healthier than the usual cheeseburgers. Her body craved nourishment.

He bent down to greet the dogs, scratching them behind the ears. "How are they holding up? The meds kicking in?"

"Seems like it. They've had a bit to eat and haven't thrown up since."

"And the vet? Did he have an idea what hit them so hard?"

"We think it's the pond. Algae or bacteria. I'm not letting them near that water again until I'm sure it's safe. There's a lab not far from here that handles testing. I'm going to grab a sample tonight. If the pond is the problem, we can get it treated."

Chris washed his hands at the kitchen sink, his brow furrowed in thought. "But it's not our pond."

"I know. But I can't just wait around for someone else to deal with it. That could take months. If the water isn't a problem, then the dogs can swim again. And if the water is the culprit, I want it fixed. She stood and rummaged through cabinets.

"What are you looking for?" Chris shut off the water, but it kept dripping.

"Something to collect the pond water in. A container? A jar?" Frustration made her grab a drawer and fling it open, then another. "We have some. I just can't remember where I put them."

After jiggling the leaky faucet a few more times, Chris abandoned it and helped Zoey search. Soon after, with a triumphant gesture, he held up an old relish jar he'd retrieved from the depths of a cupboard. "Did we really bring this with us from home?"

"I guess so. Never know when we might need an empty jar—or two or three or six, right?" Her laugh masked the twinge of disappointment she felt. He'd just referred to their place in California as "home." It shouldn't have surprised her. She was the one inside the new house from morning to night, alone. If Mountain Meadows still felt foreign to her, why would it feel any different to Chris, who was hardly ever there? She gazed over her shoulder at one of their nearly empty rooms. The furniture they'd brought from California was too small for the giant spaces and looked out of place. This was their house, but it still didn't feel like home. Zoey wondered if it ever would.

Chris glanced at the takeout bag on the counter. "How about we eat before it's cold? I'll grab the water sample later."

"Sure. Let's eat. I'm starving. Thanks for picking up dinner. But I'll go to the pond after. I need to stretch my legs. Just keep an eye on the dogs for me while I'm gone, okay?"

When things weren't going her way, adopting a proactive mindset helped her regain a sense of control and empowerment. It was her way of steering through challenges, one deliberate step at a time. Today, the water sample. Tomorrow, she'd attempt to tick off another item or two from the ever-expanding to-do list or the inspection report, find a contractor, and make some progress on her book.

She silently wished nothing else would go wrong, but an undercurrent of doom now seemed to creep through the very walls of her house and the neighborhood around her.

18

Grace

Then

The temperature was a crisp fifty-something degrees as Grace and Faith strolled down Mountain Ridge Road. Fall leaves scented the air, reminding Grace of the new candles she'd placed in the guest rooms. A trip to the orchard was in order. Grace dictated a note to her nanny. "Please stop at Briggs for a gallon of fresh cider and spiced donuts before you pick up my children." The children were teens now but didn't have their driver's licenses yet. The nanny had little to do except drive them around and clean up after them.

Putting her phone away, Grace softened her voice to cushion the blow she was about to deliver to Faith. "Before we get to the business of the gala, I have to tell you something." She paused, making sure she had Faith's full attention. "I saw Mark at the club last week."

"Oh. That's nice," Faith said.

"I must say, Faith, he seems to be really taking care of himself. Looks like he's started a new fitness routine and shed a few pounds."

"He did," Faith said. "I'm sure he'd appreciate you noticing. I'll tell him."

"Well, actually, I already told him. I asked him for his secret."

"Hmm. What did he say?"

"He told me he cut down on drinks and desserts at his business meetings." Grace made sure her tone remained serious. "It's just odd, you know? A middle-aged man suddenly working on his appearance without a clear reason. Don't you think?"

"I don't think it's odd at all. Most everyone wants to look and feel good if they can. Both of Mark's parents are taking medicine for high blood pressure now. He's hoping he can avoid that with some lifestyle changes."

"Oh. You really think that's all there is to his change in attitude? His sudden inspiration?"

"Yes. I do. And it's not all that sudden."

Grace sighed. "I'm only looking out for your well-being. I don't want you to get blindsided. My heart would just break if that happened to you."

Faith let out a soft snort. "Well, thank you, Grace. I appreciate your concern. But you don't need to worry about my marriage."

"What kind of friend and neighbor would I be if I wasn't concerned? Everyone needs to worry about their marriage, Faith. Speaking of concerns..." Grace rolled her eyes as they approached the Hamiltons' house. "If anything, their yard has only gotten worse."

The neglected garden was a tangle of brown sticks and decaying gray plants dotted with colorful birdhouses. Beyond the garden, leaves littered the grass, forming thick clumps beneath the trees. Grace had a dinner party planned for later in the week. She could only hope the sun would be down when her guests arrived, so they wouldn't notice the unsightliness as they drove to her house. Not that it was her mess, but still, it wouldn't reflect well on the neighborhood.

The issue required a strong message from the Homeowners Association. There should be no need for such reminders. However, thanks to the Hamiltons, it seemed necessary.

Faith pointed toward one of the bright-colored bird things. "Look, a House Wren."

"What are you talking about? How do you—Oh!" Grace jumped, her hand flying to her heart. A man in jeans and a flannel shirt had suddenly appeared from behind an overgrown bush.

Thinking he might have overheard her, Grace thought back over what she'd just said, if there were any words she regretted. Nothing came to her. Then she noticed the leaf blower the man carried, and she shrugged off any remaining concern.

To her surprise, the man raised his hand and gave a friendly wave. Even more strange, he made eye contact with Grace and started walking a diagonal path across the lawn, heading straight toward her.

Grace would have preferred to continue walking down the road, but this was her chance to voice some of her concerns to a person who might address them. Besides, Faith had already stopped, giving the man one of her sweet smiles.

The man took easy strides toward them. As he grew closer, Grace realized he was exceptionally fit and attractive. She wanted to look away, to stop staring at him, but couldn't. He seemed to be hard in all the places where Grace's husband had softened in the years since they married.

"Hey." The man greeted them with a bright smile that formed tiny crow's feet at the corner of his eyes. He wasn't as young as she'd first thought. "Do you live on this road?" he asked, his voice deep and confident.

"Yes, we do. Hi—" Faith said.

Grace overpowered her and said, "While you're here, I'd like to have a few words with you about this yard."

"Just wanted to say hello. I'm Chris," the man told them.

Grace knew Zoey's husband's name was Chris. But nothing aside from the name fit with the notion that this man might be Zoey's husband.

"Did the new owners hire you?" Grace asked.

"I guess you could say that. Though they aren't paying me very well." Chris laughed as he leaned to one side to set the leaf blower on the ground. With his shirtsleeves rolled up, his forearms hinted at the lean, packed muscles underneath his clothes. "I just moved in a few weeks ago."

His appearance was startlingly different from what Grace expected. Couples typically had some degree of matching attractiveness. Zoey wasn't unattractive. She had smooth skin and a cute figure, but she didn't seem to pay attention to those extra details that mattered. Chris was in a different league than his wife. He was incredibly handsome and masculine. The man couldn't be more comfortable in his own skin. And looking like he did, who could blame him? It simply did not make sense that this undeniably gorgeous man was Zoey's husband.

Beyond that, why was he outside dressed like a lumberjack and blowing leaves? Didn't the Hamiltons have a yard service? Their yard was huge. It would take him forever to manage its care himself. And, more importantly, regardless of the yard size, the residents of Mountain Meadows simply did not do their own yardwork. It was unheard of. They hired people to mow, edge, trim the bushes, and maintain the flower beds.

Faith chimed in with, "Hi. I'm Faith Humphrey. My husband and I live in the Tudor with the beige stucco and stones down the road. I met Zoey a few days ago. She was out walking with your beautiful dogs."

"Ah...Faith of the amazing oatmeal cookies," Chris said, his eyes sparkling. "We really enjoyed those. Thanks!"

Grace finally got her wits about her and said, "I'm Grace Fairchild. My husband and I live in the next house on this side of the road. The one with the white bricks. You can barely see it through the trees this time of year, but it's there. Are you sure you want to take all of this on?" She gestured over his property. "If you're having trouble finding a yard service, I can send you the information for the one we use. They're completely dependable."

"Thanks. I might consider them if it gets to be more than I can handle. Right now, I don't mind doing it. I'm trying to rise to the challenge. Love this fall weather, too. It's a great day to be outside."

Grace couldn't quite gauge whether he was joking or serious. She couldn't conceive of her own husband doing something as mundane as leaf-blowing. His time was far too valuable for such menial labor.

Faith gestured to the front garden. "You and Zoey have created a really neat bird sanctuary out here."

Chris chuckled. "That's not me. That's all Zoey. She tracks the birds every day in her journal and reports them online."

Grace hid her disdain and asked, "So, Chris, what brings you to our quiet little neighborhood?"

"New job. Fresh start."

Again, Grace wondered if there was more to their story, if perhaps they were trying to escape a scandal. After all, she'd found so little about Zoey and Chris online. She conjured scenarios: secret affairs, financial misdeeds, or a dark history that would slowly but surely catch up with them. "What sort of neighborhood did you move from?" she asked, wanting to get to the bottom of the secrecy she perceived.

Chris chuckled. "Well, there was no HOA. We had a small house, tiny by this neighborhood's standards. But we lived a few blocks from the beach. There was always a nice breeze. It was just crowded, you know? Very different from here. No leaves. This is all new to me." He shifted his gaze to the leaf blower. "Just picked this baby up at the store yesterday. Powerful little machine."

"I see." Grace lifted her head toward the sky, elongating her spine, and gave him what she believed was a stunning smile. "Well, since you're still finding your way around the area, if there's anything we can help you with, please let me know. I'll give you the number for our yard service." She let her eyes roam over the exterior of the white colonial. "I also personally know some excellent designers and remodeling companies. They do have a minimum, of course, but I'm sure you have more than enough work here to meet it without a problem."

"Oh. Okay. I'll mention it to Zoey," Chris said. "We have been looking for someone to do some work around here. Things I can't do."

"Good. Good," Grace said, so relieved to hear him say aloud that they intended to make the necessary improvements. The sooner the better. "And if you're looking for a vacation home, my husband can help you. He's involved with some wonderful new developments not far from here."

"I think we're good with homes for now," Chris answered, eyes sparkling again as if Grace had been kidding.

"Is Zoey around?" Faith asked. "We'd love for her to walk with us."

Speak for yourself, Grace thought. "Another time, perhaps. We have to discuss the school gala, and I wouldn't want to bore Zoey with those details."

"She's not here anyway," Chris said. "She went shopping for groceries."

"Next time, then," Faith said. "And I'd like to have you and Zoey over for dinner at my house soon. I'll get in touch with Zoey about it."

Grace assumed she and Craig were also part of the dinner invite, though it was strange Faith hadn't mentioned them. Once she and Faith had said their goodbyes and were far enough away from the Hamilton's house, the leaf blower blasting away behind them, Grace sniffed. "Well, I certainly didn't see that new neighbor situation coming."

Faith frowned. "What do you mean?"

Rather than explain, Grace let the implication linger.

Faith's frown deepened. "What's your issue with Zoey?"

"Issue?" Grace feigned innocence with a shrug. "I don't have any issue, per se. I simply wish she would present herself and her home in a more polished manner. For her own sake and the sake of our community."

Faith's eyes rolled skyward. "Oh, give it a rest. She just moved in. Cut her some slack while she gets settled."

"She's had plenty of time to get things in proper order. There's no excuse for appearing unkempt and disheveled in public. My parents would shoot me if I ever left the house looking like she did."

Grace closed her eyes for an instant to regain her composure. After all these years, her parents' expectations still made her stressed. She needed to shift her focus to the fundraiser details, decisions involving the caterer and the florist. There was the matter of renting upgraded chairs rather than using the plain ones the venue offered. Instead, her thoughts drifted to Chris's handsome features, perfectly proportioned body, and the way the fabric of his t-shirt stretched taut over his muscles. He was quite a surprise, and an appealing new addition to the neighborhood.

19

Zoey

Then

Z oey navigated the narrow and twisting road from the nearest grocery store back to Mountain Meadows, her eyes constantly flickering to the GPS screen so she wouldn't miss a turn. Unfamiliar sights blurred past outside her window. The woods and countryside were nice, but she missed the beach and driving down Pacific Coast Highway alongside a gorgeous ocean view.

With every passing mile, a sad, lonely feeling grew heavier, weighing her down like a heavy blanket.

To her left, a giant road sign indicated the direction of the airport. Zoey's grip tightened involuntarily on the steering wheel. The temptation to buy a one-way ticket, pack a suitcase, and leave Virginia was stronger than she cared to admit.

For a moment, she allowed herself to indulge in the fantasy, picturing herself back in the comforting routine of her old life in California. She imagined living in a new or newish condo where everything functioned as it should, with no traces of the previous owners. She could return to her old job and have daily lunch dates with Kim as they worked on the marketing presentations Zoey excelled at putting together. Her dogs could swim in the ocean without becoming deathly ill. None of it was far-fetched. All of it was doable.

Zoey's heart thumped against her ribs as the airport sign shrank in the rearview mirror. Chris had already invested too much time and energy in his new job. She couldn't ask him to abandon it all and move back to California, not after she'd been the one giddy with excitement over their fresh start in the country.

As soon as she turned into their neighborhood, the now familiar sense of unease deepened. She drove past her neighbors' enormous, manicured lawns and pulled into her driveway. After gathering her grocery bags, she hurried into the house.

When she checked her phone, a message from Jake awaited her.

Did you get my message about the deposit? I need to know if you want to move forward.

Zoey had forgotten to respond to his last message and still wasn't sure what to tell him now. She didn't want him in her house making her uncomfortable. She was uncomfortable enough there already.

Zoey leaned against the counter, allowing the fantasy of escaping back to California to wash over her again. Once more, she pushed the daydreams aside. She couldn't run away. She had to toughen up until she felt settled. Taking deep, calming breaths, she opened her eyes, determined to make the best of her new life, even if the very walls around her seemed to whisper that she didn't belong.

20

Grace

Then

Grace scanned the crowd, searching for familiar faces among the parents and faculty. Spotting Faith, she sauntered through the tables on her high heels and slipped into the empty seat beside her neighbor.

"Hello, Faith, mind if I join you?" Grace asked, her eyes drifting over Faith's choice of clothing—a long sweater over yoga pants—totally inappropriate for the setting.

"Be my guest," Faith answered.

Grace continued to look around from her seat, noting who was and who was not present for the parent-teacher conferences. Emily Bloom sat by herself at a table nearby, looking surprisingly put together for someone with four or five children. Grace wasn't sure how many children Emily had, only that it was too many.

"You know how Zoey doesn't have children?" Grace asked Faith. "She only has those dogs. Now that I think of it, it sounds just like someone else in our neighborhood, doesn't it?"

Faith frowned. "Are you talking about Victoria Heslin?"

"Yes. Victoria. Who else in our neighborhood has an entire herd of dogs? I can't even begin to imagine what the inside of her house looks like with all the hair and dirt they must track in. Did you hear she's engaged now? To a veterinarian. I haven't seen a single write-up about it in any of the usual places. Very odd. Maybe she'll get rid of the dogs and trade them in for children. If that's her plan, she'd best hurry because time isn't exactly on her side."

Grace took a sip of the electrolyte water she carried with her, then pressed her lips into a tight smile. Victoria may be strange, but at least she had taste, an established family line, and old money.

"Can you imagine how wonderful it would be to have all your time to yourself?" Grace asked, barely registering she was speaking aloud. "To have only yourself to worry about. Only your own self to care for. Imagine how luxurious that would be, at least for a few days."

Faith smirked and said, "You really can't imagine? Hmm."

Grace echoed the *hmm* sound in her mind, a subtle mocking of Faith's demeanor. On the surface, Faith's life seemed picture-perfect. Her husband, kind and doting, her daughter, poised and polite. But everyone knew the age-old saying: *ignorance is bliss.* In Grace's opinion, it existed specifically for people like Faith.

She was too naive, too trusting, to see the cracks in the façade, whereas Grace's instincts were honed by years of navigating treacherous social landscapes. Husbands shouldn't be trusted, including her own. Better to be suspicious and vigilant than blindsided.

"How is Mark?" Grace asked, testing the waters to see if she could create ripples.

"He's well. Just working long hours as usual. He's traveling this week."

"Traveling again?" Grace arched an eyebrow to ensure her skepticism wasn't lost in the subtleties of her tone. Perhaps ignorance was the secret to Faith's mostly peaceful demeanor. Yet Grace couldn't fathom leading such a life. She thrived on maintaining constant control.

Grace's husband made plenty of money, so much in fact, that she didn't understand where it all came from. Nor did she need to. All that mattered was they had more than enough. Yet Craig still had time to socialize and play golf and meet up for lunches and dinners at the club several times a week. In contrast, Faith's husband Mark was always "working." Grace suspected Mark's "travels" involved another woman, one who wasn't as nice and naïve as Faith.

Despite Grace's hints that Mark might be up to no good, Faith remained oblivious. Almost as if she were purposely ignoring the information Grace presented.

Watching Faith smile at another parent, a familiar sense of irritation stirred within Grace. Not for the first time, she questioned why she tolerated Faith's presence at all. Sure, Faith possessed a certain beauty, an essential element Grace needed to surround herself with. Faith had delicate features, porcelain skin, and a lovely, toned figure from teaching yoga classes. Yet she never had anything interesting or juicy to share. Her conversations were devoid of the salacious gossip Grace craved.

Perhaps, Grace mused, Zoey Hamilton, even with her tacky t-shirts and cut-off shorts, might prove a more intriguing prospect. Grace could easily help Zoey improve upon her wardrobe and get her house in shape. For a fleeting moment, Grace entertained the notion of getting to know Zoey. A dinner party would mean more time in the presence of Chris Hamilton, who was nothing short of drop-dead gorgeous. But Grace quickly dismissed the idea as ridiculous. No matter Chris's appeal, the Hamiltons were not Grace's sort of people.

With a barely perceptible sigh, Grace plastered on her most benevolent smile, preparing to once again plunge into the dull waters of polite conversation with Faith. Instead, Grace spotted something new—an unremarkable ring on Faith's right hand. Grace hadn't noticed it previously, and she always noticed other women's jewelry.

"Is that a new ring?" Grace asked.

Faith lifted her hand, giving it a little side-to-side sway. "Yes."

"From Mark?"

Faith nodded.

Grace clasped her hands on the table, leaning toward Faith. "It's always smart to wonder why your husband is giving you an unexpected gift."

Faith burst into laughter. "The gift was hardly unexpected. It was a birthday present. From Mark *and* my daughter. He took Lexi shopping and let her pick it out." Faith continued to smile as she shook her head. "Not everyone has a hidden agenda, Grace."

"Believe what you will," Grace replied. "I'm only trying to help. I hope you would do the same for me someday, if needed."

21

Grace

Now

This is certainly unexpected, Grace thought after unlocking her front door. Between the pots of freshly planted yellow mums, still drooping from yesterday's fierce storm, three unanticipated visitors stood on her doorstep—Chris Hamilton, Victoria Heslin, and an unfamiliar, handsome man. Everyone had worried expressions instead of the cheerful ones she'd expect for a social call. They looked the way Grace would feel if she showed up for an important event and discovered someone else wearing the exact same outfit. Yet, none of the visitors had dressed for a significant outing. The group's attire was more suited to cleaning out a messy garage than stepping out in public.

Chris wore rumpled clothing that seemed hastily chosen from his hamper. Victoria and the stranger beside her seemed to have come straight from a sweaty outdoor workout. It appeared none of the three had made time for a shower that morning. Nevertheless, Grace greeted them with a smile.

"Well, hello, and what a surprise. To what do I owe this...?" she asked, wanting to finish her sentence with the word *intrusion*, but letting them fill in the blank instead. Still smiling, her gaze settled on the handsome stranger.

He introduced himself as Ned Patterson, Victoria's fiancé, who now lived with her, confirming the rumors. He had a lean and athletic build and a strong jawline. It irked Grace that *both* Chris and Ned were better looking and in better shape than her own husband.

Though they all lived on the same road, Grace rarely saw Victoria in person. Occasionally, she'd catch a fleeting sight of her running or walking her dogs. She did, however, see Victoria in magazines and on the news. Grace hated to admit it, but Victoria always looked fantastic in her own chic, barely trying way.

Grace scrutinized Victoria's hand to check out the size of her engagement ring. There was no glittering diamond there. No trace of jewelry of any sort. Only her grotesque hands. Several fingers ended at the knuckle, the ones she'd lost to frostbite after a plane crash that had dominated the news. Grace felt a strong pang of distaste, thinking Victoria ought to wear gloves or at least keep her fingers hidden away inside pockets.

Grace raised her own hand, a deliberate movement meant to catch Victoria's attention. There was a time and a place for sophisticated understatement, but modesty did not exist when it came to one's engagement ring. Craig understood that now. Grace had made sure of it. The engagement ring she flaunted these days was twice the size of her original one. Craig had redeemed himself splendidly.

Victoria's eyes didn't waver from Grace's face, and it appeared her dazzling ring went unnoticed.

"Have you seen my wife? Zoey?" Chris asked, bypassing any pleasantries as he peered past Grace and right into her home. He sported glasses he wasn't wearing when they met, lending him a smoldering intellectual look.

Ignoring his question, Grace opened the door wider. "Please come in and make yourselves comfortable in the sunroom. I'll get some drinks. Sweet tea, perhaps?"

They stepped off the porch and into the foyer wearing their sneakers, likely carrying traces of mud and other filth between the treads. At this moment, those remnants were finding a new home on Grace's polished wood floors, and she couldn't do a thing about it until the cleaning crew came back on Monday. Her ingrained good manners forced her to keep smiling.

"No, thank you. Drinks aren't necessary," Chris said, still standing in the foyer.

"Nonsense. All of you look like you could use some refreshment. Were you hiking together? Must have been a long one."

"I'm just here to ask if you've seen Zoey," Chris said.

"Well, yes, certainly I've seen her before," Grace answered.

"I mean recently," Chris explained. "Zoey was with a friend yesterday, but she didn't say who."

"Oh, and you thought she might be with me?" Grace forced a smile. "I'm sorry. Zoey and I were not together."

From where he stood in the foyer, Chris scanned Grace's house as if Zoey might be hiding in the library or a guest room. Grace didn't mind. Now that she understood why they were there, she felt a twinge of exhilaration, sensing herself at the epicenter of an unfolding drama. "Have you contacted the police yet?" she asked.

"Not yet. I'm pretty sure she's with someone in the neighborhood, or at least she was," Chris answered.

"Oh, I see. Well, you know how it is when you visit someone and enjoy yourself so much, you simply lose track of time." Grace folded her arms across her chest. "And the two of you are helping him, I presume," she said, directing her statement to Ned and Victoria. "Are you sure I can't get you something to drink while you're here? It's early, I know, but a Bloody Mary might be nice. Or perhaps you would prefer something stronger, Chris, considering…"

"No." Without adding a thank you, Chris shook his head. "Is there anyone else here who might have seen her?"

"I'm the only one home," Grace offered. "My husband is golfing. My children are at a lacrosse tournament."

"What about last night?" Chris asked. "Did you see her then?"

"I'm afraid not. I was gone all day. An afternoon appointment, then met my husband at the club. He came straight from a long day meeting with clients." Grace wasn't sure why she was offering so much information, yet she continued. "We had dinner, then drinks, and didn't get back until around ten. We were with two other couples—the Parsons and the Whitneys. You might know them, Victoria." Nearly everyone who was anyone was familiar with both well-established families.

Victoria nodded.

"You know," Grace told Chris, "I recall an eerily similar situation with the former occupant of your house. It was years ago, of course. My children were in bed. It was long after dark, and then out of the blue, Sarah Johnson showed up here just like you have, asking if I'd seen her husband. He too, was missing." Grace placed her hand over the soft skin at the base of her throat, again putting her diamond ring on full display. "You know how that turned out, don't you? Now, of course, I'm not saying Zoey has done anything criminal, but it's certainly a coincidence."

"What the—? Zoey hasn't done anything wrong." Chris scowled at Grace. It didn't make him any less handsome, only fiercer. Apparently, she'd hit a nerve with him.

"If you weren't with Zoey and haven't seen her, that's all I need to know," Chris said, turning for the door.

Grace didn't want them to leave. She wanted to be right in the middle of this interesting, potentially scandalous development. "Have you checked with Connor Rhodes yet?" she asked, with all the feigned innocence she could muster. "Perhaps he and Zoey hit it off and developed a friendship ...or something." The mere thought of what she was stirring up delighted her, until she realized the implications of having them talk to Connor. Who knew what else he might reveal if questioned? Grace couldn't risk it. Flustered, she was quick to backpedal. "Actually, never mind my suggestion. He's almost never around. I doubt he'll be of any help to you."

"Thanks," Chris grunted, not sounding genuine at all.

Grace remained courteous. "Of course, anytime."

Ned offered a half smile in parting as the threesome left her house and headed down the wide stone steps together. Grace was disappointed to see them go. Their visit was over much too soon, and she wouldn't be privy to whatever happened next. "I hope you find her," she called after them. "And don't get too worked up about the situation. Perhaps Zoey was just in a mood and needed some time to herself."

The men were too far away to hear, but Victoria pivoted at the bottom of the stone stairs. Her piercing blue eyes seemed to penetrate Grace's soul.

"What did you just say?" Victoria asked.

An unsettling pause followed before Grace recovered and clarified her statements. "Well, you haven't been with your fiancé very long, have you? You're not married yet. Eventually, you'll understand. Sometimes we just need a little me-time. Time to ourselves, away from our husbands. A brief break from everything."

Grace held her tight smile and stood up straighter while Victoria studied her with an expressionless gaze. Grace couldn't tell what was going on in Victoria's mind.

"Are you covering for Zoey?" Victoria finally asked.

"Why would I do that? Zoey and I have barely spoken. I know nothing about her situation. I can't imagine what sort of problems she and her husband are having in their marriage, or what she may be running away from."

"What makes you think she ran away?"

Grace shrugged. "I don't know if she ran away, but she didn't exactly fit in here. I don't think she had any friends."

"How do you know that?"

"She might have mentioned something in passing out on the trails. I told her about you and your dogs, by the way, since you have that in common. Sounds like she didn't reach out to you. In any case, I can assure you, she hasn't confided in me regarding her whereabouts."

"Okay," Victoria said, her eyes still locked with Grace's.

"Don't be such a stranger in the future, Victoria. We're neighbors, after all."

"Yes, we are." Without another word, Victoria turned around. Jogging to catch up, she closed the distance between her and the two men.

Grace stayed by the door, her smile fixed in place, her eyes trailing her neighbors as they neared the end of her long flagstone path. A critical glance at her own yard revealed fading flowers and grass that should be a deeper shade of green. Those were symptoms of the changing season, but also, the gardener simply needed to do better.

When the trio reached the road, they walked three abreast, heading toward Faith's house.

Grace pressed the door closed and locked the bolt. She entered her formal dining room, walked past the massive slab of live-edge walnut that served as the table and went to the window overlooking the side yard.

Clutching the sill, she stood to the side, out of sight, in case anyone looked back. From there, Grace watched her neighbors approach Faith's house. She wondered what Faith would divulge, and more importantly, she prayed Connor Rhodes wasn't home. He held secrets Grace couldn't afford to have anyone else know. Secrets that could jeopardize everything.

22

Victoria

Now

C hris pressed the doorbell to the Humphreys' three-story Tudor house while Victoria and Ned stood behind him on the porch.

A privacy fence enclosed the backyard and the pool Victoria had once spotted through an open gate. Storm-tossed leaves dotted the flower beds and the fresh mulch surrounding every plant.

While they waited, a black Range Rover cruised down the road and pulled into the driveway across the street.

Victoria was still thinking about Grace's peculiar parting words. She had almost mirrored the unusual phrase from Zoey's message to Chris about "having a mood." Coincidence? It might mean nothing, but it could mean Grace knew Zoey better than she had let on.

The Humphreys' door swung inward. Faith's eyes lit up just before her expression wavered, then settled into a hesitant smile. "Oh, hello."

Chris cleared his throat and introduced himself. "We met a few weeks ago. I live down the street. I was working on my lawn."

"Of course." Faith's smile warmed. "I remember you."

"I'm Ned Patterson. Victoria and I live in the first house on the road."

"Pleasure, Ned. And Victoria, it's nice to see you again," Faith said.

Victoria wasn't sure if their paths had ever crossed. Her memory rarely failed her, especially with faces. Faith was likely being polite since they should have met by now after living on the same street for years.

Before the visitors had a chance to explain why they were there, a door at the back of the foyer swung open. A man emerged from below, ascending the last steps of a basement staircase. He wore khaki-colored pants and a checked button-down shirt. Pausing at the top of the stairs, his eyes flickered over the unexpected guests before he stepped fully into the foyer, pulling the door firmly shut behind him.

Faith turned to fully acknowledge the newcomer's presence.

"Hey. What's going on?" the man asked, moving to join them at the front door. His tone was friendly, but his eyes remained guarded. A muscle in his jaw quivered—a sign of tension.

A fresh round of introductions ensued, this time including Faith's husband, Mark Humphrey. He stood a few inches taller than Faith, with thick brown hair and a shadow of stubble on his jaw. He appeared to be about ten years older than his wife.

"Everything okay here?" Mark placed his hand on his wife's shoulder.

"I'm looking for my wife. Zoey. Was she here? Or is she here?" Chris asked.

"Zoey? No, she wasn't with me." Faith's concern was immediate. Slight creases appeared between her eyebrows. "I'm not sure when I last saw Zoey, though I put a note in your mailbox yesterday. I asked her about coming to dinner."

"Were you here last night?" Victoria asked Mark.

"Me? No. I just got home from a three-day trip to Chicago. I haven't seen anyone except my wife and daughter since I got back to town. Sorry," Mark said, looking directly at Chris. "You must be really worried if you're out looking for her."

"I am worried," Chris answered. "We just stopped at Grace's house. She hasn't seen Zoey either. Can you think of anyone else in our neighborhood who Zoey might be friendly with? Anyone else she might know?"

Faith's gaze drifted across the street, where the peaks of an arched roof appeared above the tree line. "There are the Normans across the way. Zoey might have struck up a friendship with Linda. Except, the Normans recently had their first grandchild, and they've been with their daughter in Colorado for over a week."

Mark spoke next. "Next to the Normans are the Mullers. They have an apartment in D.C. We hardly ever see them. Which just leaves Connor Rhodes."

"Is he married?" Chris asked. "Would he have a wife or girlfriend around Zoey's age who lives there?"

"Not that I'm aware of," Mark said. "Single guy. Huge house. Never made sense to me. And he's not around often either."

Faith waited until her husband finished speaking to add, "I see Connor at the yoga studio sometimes."

"He has a black Range Rover, right?" Ned asked. "I'm pretty sure he's home now. Just drove in."

A loud crash resonated from the depths of the Humphreys' house, drawing puzzled looks from everyone.

"What was that?" Chris asked.

Faith and Mark shared a quick, unreadable glance.

"I think it was Murdock, our cat," Mark said with a half-hearted chuckle. "He's a little terror, knocking things over and getting into everything."

"Yes, he's always exploring places he shouldn't," Faith said. "You should see him during the holidays. We've learned the hard way not to decorate with anything breakable."

Mark held up a finger as if he'd suddenly had an idea. "Is the vacuum running?" he asked his wife.

Faith smiled. "Yes. That's what it is. He loves chasing the little robot vacuum around."

The crash had sounded quite heavy, not like something a cat might cause. Yet, as if on cue, a large gray cat with green eyes sauntered into the foyer. Its gaze swept the group with feline indifference.

An abrupt switch of subjects could throw someone off, deny them the chance to fabricate an answer. Seizing the moment of distraction, Victoria asked, "Do you know if Grace and Zoey spend much time together?" She wanted to hear if Faith's answer would differ from what Grace had told them.

"Grace?" Faith looked down at her cat as she answered. "No, I don't think so. Why? I thought you just came from speaking to Grace."

"We did," Victoria said.

Faith placed her hands together in front of her chest. "Grace can be difficult sometimes. That's just how she is. She has her own ideas about a lot of things. She's convinced my husband is cheating on me, for example."

Mark laughed. "I assure you, I'm not."

Faith smiled at her husband before resuming a more serious expression. "I hope Zoey is all right."

"We do, too," Victoria answered.

Chris looked out the door and across the road toward the nearest house. Connor Rhodes, who none of them knew well, was their last hope of finding Zoey with a "friend" inside the neighborhood.

23

Victoria

Now

The trio quickened their pace as they marched toward Connor Rhodes' home. With its sharp, contemporary lines, the tall custom residence stood out in stark contrast to the more traditional architecture lining Mountain Meadows Road. Not that outward appearances mattered much. Victoria had seen unspeakable horrors unfold behind the facades of the nicest homes. Evil could fester anywhere.

Thinking about things she'd experienced in the course of her investigations made her stomach turn. Or was it just grumbling from hunger? The protein bar she'd eaten earlier wasn't enough to satisfy her after their run.

"Mark and Faith seem like nice people." Ned's words did little to break the tension that came from the dwindling chances of finding Zoey with a neighbor.

"Yeah, they do," Chris murmured, his thoughts understandably preoccupied. "Neither of you have ever met Connor before?"

"We haven't. Ned hasn't lived here very long, or I'm sure he would have by now," Victoria answered.

Victoria hadn't missed Grace's strange behavior earlier when Connor's name came up. Grace had suggested they speak with him, then quickly changed her mind. It sounded like Grace and Connor might have some unpleasant history together.

"About how old is Connor?" Chris asked.

"I'd say he's in his late thirties, just from what I've seen of him driving by a few times," Ned said.

Ned hung back a few strides and whispered to Victoria. "He's assuming her friend is a woman. What if, you know, she was lonely and...?"

"Shh." Victoria silenced him, raising her eyebrows and holding them up so Ned got the hint. He wasn't the best at keeping his voice down. He thought he was quieter than he actually was. Luckily, Chris didn't give any sign he'd heard.

Victoria had been entertaining the same notion about Zoey's relationship with her so-called "friend." Had Chris considered the possibility his wife had willingly spent the night with another man? Did the Hamiltons have a history of infidelity in their marriage? In Victoria's current role as a supportive neighbor, she hesitated to broach the subject with Chris. However, if Zoey was inside Connor's home, if she'd spent the night there, it didn't bode well for the Hamiltons. Victoria braced herself for what could be a difficult and awkward awakening for Chris.

From the side of Connor's porch, neat piles of building materials in the back of the property drew Victoria's attention. Two tarps, sagging under pools of rainwater, covered mounds of something. The piles implied an abandoned project, perhaps a greenhouse or a guest cottage. If the Hamiltons' bird feeders bothered the HOA, Victoria wondered what they had to say about the building materials. Nothing, she supposed, since Connor's backyard wasn't visible from the street. Instead, intricate layers of landscaping—rock formations, exotic evergreen bushes, and slender willowy trees—captured the attention of anyone passing by.

Chris pressed the doorbell on a huge iron door. A loud, distinctive chime echoed from within the house, but there was no other response.

Victoria stepped forward and rang the doorbell a second time. The door swung open, revealing a tall man with a shaven head dressed in workout gear and open-toed sports sandals. He peered at them through frameless glasses. "Whatever it is you're selling, I don't want any," he said. The twinkle in his eyes and a trace of a smile softened his words.

"Connor Rhodes, right? I'm Chris. Just moved in down the road recently. Victoria and Ned are helping me out this morning. We were hoping you might have seen Zoey. My wife."

Maybe it was a lot to process, because Connor continued to stare at them, time enough for the wind to blow a few leaves across the porch and wedge one in the corner of the open doorframe.

Connor's brow furrowed before it smoothed again, and he focused on Victoria. "Victoria Heslin," he said. "Sorry about my greeting there. I was kidding. Sort of. The last time my neighbors roped me into something, it didn't work out well for any of us. But that was a long time ago. Different neighbors. I won't hold it against any of you. Come in."

Victoria wanted to ask Connor what had happened, sensing it might shed light on Grace's reluctance to involve him. Yet whatever transpired between Connor and the other neighbors seemed relegated to the past. It shouldn't be the focus of this visit. The more urgent matter of Zoey's whereabouts took precedence.

Connor ushered them into a large living area so stark and bare the effect was almost startling. The inside was immaculate. Not a speck of dust or pet hair to be found on the floor or the few pieces of contemporary furniture. Nor were there any personal items, aside from a large, framed photo of Connor with another man around his age. The atmosphere was so sterile, almost Zen-like, it made Victoria wonder if Connor was the person who had complained about unnecessary yard décor, prompting the HOA email they had all received.

"I just got back from a yoga class. I have a state-of-the-art gym in my basement and access to some amazing online classes, but I really like this one particular teacher in town. Anyway, I'm about to make a pot of green tea. May I offer you some as well?" Connor asked.

"Appreciate that, but we're here about my wife, Zoey. Have you seen her?"

"She's missing?" Connor rubbed his thumb back and forth over his knuckles. He avoided making direct eye contact, his gaze flickering around the room before settling back on Chris.

"She told me she was with a friend, and she didn't take her car, so I thought she was with someone in the neighborhood," Chris answered.

"She wasn't with me. I don't know her. I hardly know anyone on this street." A small muscle or tendon rippled along the edge of Connor's jaw. "I'm acquainted with Grace and her husband, and Faith, because she's a yoga instructor, and...I can't remember her husband's name."

"His name is Mark," Ned said. "We're all in the same boat here. I just met them today. We need to get a little better acquainted. Makes it easier to rally when something goes wrong."

"The thing is, some of us chose this neighborhood precisely because of the privacy it offers," Connor answered.

Victoria silently agreed with him, and yet, it made her study him even more closely.

"Is your wife...is she well?" Connor asked Chris. "Or are there medical or mental health issues?"

Chris wrung his hands together. "No. Zoey is fine. Healthy. She doesn't take any medications. She's just missing. And now, I have no idea where she is or who she's with. She's just... gone."

"You didn't see her when you drove home last night, or this morning on your way to your yoga class?" Victoria asked.

"I didn't see anyone else last night or this morning," Connor said, the words coming out a bit too quickly. "Any chance she might have been homesick, missed wherever you came from, and you know...left?"

"She'd never do that to me." Something raw and urgent flickered in Chris's eyes, as if he'd just mentally crossed from concern to desperation.

Connor's story about rarely being in the neighborhood matched what Victoria knew of him. When he was there, he kept to himself, maybe even actively avoided the neighbors. Victoria didn't see anything wrong with that, considering she tried to do the same. Perhaps he was an introvert like her. But someone else might consider it suspicious. Connor's behavior made it unlikely he and Zoey had struck up a relationship of any sort, but there were other, more sinister possibilities.

24

Grace

Then

Grace arranged fresh flowers in an exquisite new vase that shimmered under the overhead lighting. She lit the candles on the fireplace mantel, taking a moment to observe the way they flickered, playing off the rare stones behind them just as her designer said they would.

Settling behind her desk, she began her daily ritual of sifting through her messages with an air of detached efficiency. She deleted most without reading them until one made her stop. She narrowed her eyes at the one from Zoey Hamilton.

The temptation to dismiss it as unworthy of her time and continue her digital purge was strong, yet curiosity—or if she were being honest with herself, the desire to find fault—prevailed. She clicked to open the message.

To: Grace Fairchild

Subject: The pond water.

This is Zoey Hamilton, your new neighbor. I hope this message finds you well. Unfortunately, my dogs got sick after playing in the pond last week, the same day I met you. I got the water tested. The attached results indicate the presence of toxic algae blooms and cryptosporidium. Immediate treatment is necessary, or the contamination will only get worse.

Please let me know the name of the company handling landscaping and neighborhood concerns for the Mountain Meadows community. I am more

*than willing to communicate directly with them about the necessary actions
and to oversee the process.*

Thank you,

Zoey

Grace huffed and swiveled toward the bookshelves lining one wall of her office. They held an exquisite collection of carefully chosen hardback novels, each one curated by her interior designer to complement the room's aesthetics. If only she could choose her neighbors similarly. Who did Zoey Hamilton think she was, overstepping her bounds and issuing demands? How presumptuous for a newcomer to dictate the process for something that concerned the entire neighborhood, with zero regard for the established protocols that had served Mountain Meadows well for years. And who did that remind her of? Steve Johnson. He'd had no respect for common decency. Interesting how he and Zoey might have that in common.

Grace pushed her Eames chair away from her desk and strode out of her office, scooping the robot vacuum off the floor on her way out. Her nerves couldn't tolerate the incessant whirring and thumping against furniture. So much for the product's claims of being silent, she thought, thrusting the device into its charging stall.

The equally nerve-grating sounds of a football game streamed from the family room, where Craig slumped on the couch watching television. Grace noted the slight roundness of his belly and had to look away.

In the kitchen, she went straight to the stainless-steel refrigerator and withdrew a bottle of imported beer. With a smooth motion, she removed the top using a bottle opener concealed beneath the granite island. After pouring it into a frosted glass, she jammed a wedge of lime on the rim and marched into the family room. She handed Craig the beer, and he took it, barely looking away from the screen.

Grace's exasperated sigh echoed through the vaulted-ceiling room. She waited for her husband to turn around so she could vent with a proper audience. When he failed to acknowledge her, she said, "That woman will be the death of me."

Still no reaction from Craig, but Grace continued. "I mean, who does she think she is?"

"Huh? Who?" Craig finally asked.

"Our new neighbor. The one who moved into the Johnson's house."

"What did she do?" Craig still hadn't looked away from the game, aside from the brief instant related to the beer handoff.

"She's complaining to me about the pond."

"Tell her to call the HOA. That's what they're paid for. You're not supposed to have to do anything. You do too much volunteer work as it is."

"Yes, I know," Grace said, though he was missing the point. She simply wanted her husband's attention, not his advice. Yet, Craig was correct about the HOA. Grace had no obligation to deal with neighborhood matters. Her self-appointed role as a liaison between the community and the Homeowners Association was voluntary. All Grace had to do was pass the HOA's contact number on to Zoey. Grace's ongoing reluctance to do so eluded her. Maybe it was a matter of trust—she simply didn't trust Zoey Hamilton.

The game cut to a commercial break, and finally, Craig turned to look at Grace. "What's wrong with the pond?"

Grace huffed. "She wants it cleaned for her dogs."

Craig's eyes widened. "Really? I didn't think anyone in the neighborhood ever used the pond. But it can't be too much trouble to throw some chemicals in there, can it?"

"I'm not sure what's involved or if it makes sense for the community. That's why I need to stay on top of the matter."

Craig's brow furrowed. "Okay, then," he said. "You know best. Stay involved if you think you should."

"Yes. I really don't think I have a choice. I don't trust her."

Grace grappled with her conflicted emotions, torn between the part of her that wanted to maintain control at all costs, and the part that wanted to forget Zoey Hamilton existed.

Zoey represented something different. Her presence disrupted the familiar dynamics of the neighborhood. Thus, it fell to Grace to keep a close eye on her.

Yet Grace had to acknowledge the issue already ran deeper. Somewhere along the line, perhaps unknowingly, she had made a silent commitment to making life difficult for her new neighbor. Grace wanted Zoey to suffer.

25

Zoey

Then

As late summer gave way to fall, a chill crept into the air, hinting at the changing seasons. Any day now, the broad-winged hawks would begin their migration, drifting southward along the mountain range. Yet the thought failed to improve Zoey's mood.

Bundled in a windbreaker and sweats, with binoculars around her neck, she headed down a wooded path with her dogs. About halfway to the common area, she heard movement, a swishing of clothing, and footsteps ahead. Rounding a bend, a flash of white appeared through the foliage. Zoey's footsteps faltered as Grace came into view.

Zoey was hit with an instinctive urge to spin around and hurry off in the opposite direction. She kept moving forward because she needed to speak with Grace, to follow up on the unanswered emails she'd sent about the contaminated pond water.

"Hello, Zoey," Grace practically cooed, though Zoey thought she detected condescension in her neighbor's voice.

Zoey maneuvered her dogs off the trail and into a patch of leaves and brush. *Be the light you want to see in others,* she told herself, putting a smile on over gritted teeth. "Hello, Grace. I'm glad I ran into you."

Grace made a show of looking around for a spot to step off the trail and keep her distance, though Zoey had already moved her dogs off the path.

"Sit," Zoey commanded and felt a small surge of pride when her dogs promptly obeyed. Zoey returned her attention to Grace. "Did you have a chance to read the message I sent you? About the pond?"

Arms crossed over her body, Grace wrinkled her upturned nose. "A message?"

"I emailed. I also left you a voicemail."

Grace laughed. "I didn't think anyone left voicemails anymore. I certainly don't check mine. What is it I can help you with?"

Zoey was determined not to let Grace get to her. "I had the water tested. It's contaminated. I sent you the report and asked what needed to be done to get it treated. Can you get me a contact number for the company that does the maintenance for the neighborhood? I'd like to talk to them about the problem."

"No, no. That's not how things work around here. We have covenants and by-laws to adhere to. I'll take care of it. Don't you worry."

"Thank you," Zoey said, though now she wasn't sure if Grace meant she would find the contact person or get the pond treated. Either way, at least Grace was now in the loop, aware of the situation. Zoey was grateful she'd had the water tested already. Thanks to her efforts, the neighborhood association already possessed solid data on the problem and could skip the testing step.

Zoey was about to keep walking when Grace said, "I hope you'll start feeling like you fit in better here. It must be so hard not to have the same connections and history the rest of us share."

Zoey didn't know what to make of Grace's sympathy. "I haven't met many people around here," she admitted.

"Faith and I were talking about you the other day and came up with something. Have you met Victoria Heslin? She lives in the first house, the gated one. You can hardly see it from the road."

Zoey shook her head. Victoria's name rang familiar. The realtor had dropped it in passing, calling her a famous FBI Agent. Zoey had intended to do an internet search that same day, but amidst the chaos of the move and settling into the new house, the idea had slipped through the cracks.

"Victoria has dogs, too," Grace said. "Greyhounds. A lot of them. She doesn't have children either. You two might hit it off."

"Oh, okay, thanks."

Grace sighed. "I hope you don't mind me saying, but you look positively worn out. And Lord knows how much work you still have ahead of you with that house. I assume you're planning it all out now. And your poor husband struggling to tackle the yard work on his own, I can't even imagine. But we are all so excited to see the changes. Truly, we can't wait for the transformation. Best of luck with it all."

"Thanks," Zoey said, again. She never knew what to expect out of Grace. Maybe she wasn't as bad as Zoey was making her out to be.

"And Zoey, do try to look after yourself while it's all happening. I can recommend some wonderful spa services for you, ones I use myself. Not everyone shares their beauty secrets, but I'm happy to do so because I can see just how much you could benefit." With that, Grace turned and resumed walking down the trail.

"I can see just how much you could benefit," Zoey muttered under her breath in Grace's pretentious tone.

Zoey continued her walk, but the beauty of her surroundings had faded into the background. Each encounter with Grace had left her with a sense of inadequacy, a feeling she didn't measure up. The bitter sentiment clung to her despite her efforts to shake it off. Normally, she wasn't insecure. But since moving to Mountain Meadows, she just hadn't felt like herself.

Familiar with most of the neighborhood trails now, Zoey chose one that brought her back to the main road. She walked along the pavement, passing Victoria's estate. Two greyhounds trotted along the perimeter of the fence, noses skimming the ground.

Perhaps she and Victoria could be friends.

At home, Zoey settled into the Johnsons' wingback chair, wondering if Steve Johnson had ever experienced the same profound emptiness she currently felt. Funny how she'd lived in this house for a few weeks now, and seemed more aware of Steve's presence than she had when she first moved in.

She searched the internet on her phone for information on Victoria Heslin. The agent's experiences overflowed with drama, far beyond anything Zoey had imagined.

Tragedy had marked Victoria's early life when her mother died during the agent's college years. According to news articles, an abduction gone terribly wrong resulted in the mother's death. It was the reason Victoria had joined the FBI. She'd channeled her trauma into the pursuit of justice so others wouldn't suffer what her own family had endured.

Zoey's chest ached with a dull, familiar pain as she contemplated the loss she and Victoria shared. Snippets of that time—the police officers at their door, an image of their family car obliterated into an almost unrecognizable shape, and the enormous weight of emotional pain—were etched into her memory. The sharp sting of grief hit her again and again at random times: her mother would never come home again, would never see Zoey graduate high school or college, she'd never meet Chris or her future grandchildren. Zoey's loss took the form of empty spaces at every celebration where her mother should have been. Right now, feeling lonely and homesick in her new home, the ache to talk to her mother seemed especially strong.

Did Victoria feel the same longing for just one more moment, one more conversation? Everyone's grief and suffering were unique. Yet a strange comfort came from knowing and speaking with others who had walked a similar path. It offered a connection. One Zoey needed more than ever.

Zoey got up to make a mug of tea, then returned to her chair to dig further into Victoria's life. Each discovery left Zoey more impressed. The agent had worked numerous high-profile cases that had not only reached the news but dominated headlines: solved murders, thwarted abductions, and standoffs with a cartel. She'd even survived the catastrophic crash of Skyline Flight 745. To think that this courageous woman lived just up the street on Mountain Meadows Road!

Zoey hoped she'd soon have an opportunity to get to know Victoria.

26

Victoria

Now

Victoria and Ned finally sat down to the breakfast they'd both been looking forward to, though later than anticipated due to their encounter with Chris. Their hunger overwhelmed any desire for conversation; they devoured their meals in comfortable silence, exchanging only occasional appreciative glances. After they finished, Ned moved around the kitchen, compiling a grocery list as Victoria loaded their empty plates into the dishwasher.

"Now we know some of our neighbors," he said. "But I'd rather have met them under different circumstances."

Victoria agreed.

"Chris seems like a decent guy," Ned said, staring into the open refrigerator. "I can't imagine what he's going through right now. The thought of not knowing where you are...Everything else in my life would be on hold. Nothing would matter except finding you."

"Same goes for you. Though I think you'd manage just fine without me," she teased, trying to lighten the mood.

Ned spun around and pulled her into an embrace that ended with a passionate kiss. "No, I wouldn't be fine without you. No chance. You are irreplaceable. I love you, Victoria."

"I love you, too."

"The thing about Zoey, she's either in trouble, or she's intentionally ignoring Chris and he's clueless about it. So, I'm not sure who to feel sorry for right now," Ned said. "If you ever need some space or whatever it was Zoey mentioned, I'll deal with it, but just don't shut me out, alright?"

"I promise I won't. And I'm sure there's more to this situation with Zoey than we know."

When Ned left for the grocery store, Victoria sat down at her desk to think about the information she had.

They didn't know for sure if Zoey was truly missing, rather than needing time to herself, which is what her texts implied. But Victoria couldn't ignore the significance of the Hamiltons' dogs running loose, their leashes left behind at the gazebo. Still, she was torn between the instinct to get more involved and a reluctance to plunge into affairs so close to her doorstep.

The fact that another resident of Mountain Meadows had once "disappeared" bothered her. She wanted more information on Steve Johnson's case, and she knew just who to ask. Her friend and colleague, Payton Jennings, in the FBI's financial accounting department. She handled cases of financial fraud.

Victoria sent a message inquiring about Steve Johnson's criminal charges and his FBI files.

The dots dancing across Victoria's message screen came immediately. Payton responded with, *Hey, are you spying on me???*

Confused by Payton's odd response, Victoria abandoned their text stream and called her friend.

"Why did you just ask me about the Steve Johnson case?" Payton asked right away.

"Because Steve Johnson used to live near me. He embezzled money—allegedly, I should say. He wasn't tried and convicted. Steve has been missing since the money disappeared. After some recent events in my neighborhood, I guess I was curious. I'm on vacation, thought this would be a good time to look into it while I have the time."

"You're not going to believe this, but I got asked to look through some cold cases and that's actually one I chose. It's on my desk right now."

"Why that case?"

"Honestly, because the file was pretty slim. There just isn't much in it. That concerned me. If you like, I'll send you a copy of what we've got. I'd love to have your thoughts. Always grateful for your insight."

"Yes, please send it to me."

"Can I say I'm surprised you're on vacation?"

Victoria laughed. "I got a letter from HR. It was a use-it-or-lose-it situation, and I actually had some pressure to use it."

"And you thought digging up an old case was a good way to spend your downtime?" Payton chuckled.

"The recent event I mentioned...A woman on my street might be missing. She lives in the same house where Steve Johnson used to live. I guess it just feels like a good time to learn more about what's occurred here."

"Oh. Okay. Hmm. Well, share your thoughts after you read the case notes. And I hope the missing woman from your neighborhood is okay."

"Yeah, me too. Thanks."

The FBI's files on Steve Johnson would soon land in Victoria's inbox. Yet the more pressing matter of Zoey's whereabouts remained. A few hours had passed since Ned and Victoria had left Chris. Enough time for the situation to have changed, for better or worse.

Victoria texted Chris to find out.

He answered: *Still haven't heard from her. I called the police.*

Victoria was glad to hear it. *Keep me updated on what happens after you speak with them and let me know if I can help in any way.*

Chris responded: *I will. Thanks. I'm glad I met you this morning. I'll keep you updated.*

As Payton had pointed out, Victoria was supposed to be on vacation. Getting involved in her neighbors' business was not part of that. However, she felt a powerful pull to intervene because someone was missing and Zoey was, after all, a neighbor. However, that was also the primary reason Victoria shouldn't get involved. Digging into her neighbors' lives and unearthing their secrets could get ugly.

After a prolonged stare at her laptop's background screen—her greyhound pack, each of them facing the camera, ears up, a shot she'd never be able to replicate—she made her decision and logged in.

She wasn't a particularly good neighbor, as Ned had established that morning, his humor only partially masking the truth. Victoria excelled at many things, but niceties like socializing and selecting housewarming gifts weren't her forte. Her talents lay elsewhere. She had an innate sense for following trails of evidence, piecing together fragments until the full truth emerged, regardless of the risks.

In past cases, her dogged persistence had served her well, yet also carried a steep price. More than once, she'd come dangerously close to losing her life. Though she might have flinched, she was proud to say she'd never backed down.

Helping to find Zoey offered Victoria an opportunity to make a positive impact on the community she called home. It was her chance to be a "good" neighbor. At least for now, she could maintain a discreet distance and monitor the situation.

Considering Steve Johnson's case file was on its way to her, and Zoey Hamilton was missing, Victoria's plans to do nothing but relax on her vacation were about to change.

27

Victoria

Now

With Zoey's disappearance at the forefront of her thoughts, Victoria honed in on the person who troubled her the most when they'd gone door-to-door that morning: Grace Fairchild.

When asked if she was covering for Zoey, Grace had looked Victoria dead in the eye and stated, "No." Her gaze remained unwavering, her voice steady—no discernible tell or cracks that might betray dishonesty.

Victoria didn't enjoy distrusting her neighbors, but something about her interaction with Grace nagged her. Beneath Grace's veneer of polite cooperation, there was an undercurrent of evasiveness. Victoria suspected Grace might be withholding information, perhaps even protecting Zoey for some unknown reason. If Victoria could prove Grace was otherwise occupied the entire day when Zoey claimed to be with a friend, that would help dispel Victoria's suspicions.

Victoria had noticed the fresh glow on Grace's face, along with the slight peeling of skin along her chin—signs of a recent facial and peel treatment. There were many spas in the vicinity, but only one was considered the premier establishment, the most exclusive of them all.

From her home office, Victoria dialed Charest Medical Spa. "Hello, this is Grace Fairchild," she began, altering her voice when someone answered the appointment line. "I need to verify the exact time of my last appointment for my personal records. Could you please confirm that for me?"

The spa receptionist was efficient, quickly pulling up the details. "I see your facial appointment was yesterday. It was scheduled for two PM with Vicky. Was everything okay? Or was there a problem?" she asked, sounding deeply concerned.

"Everything was fine. Thank you so much for your help." Victoria hung up quickly and turned her attention to Grace's claim of having dinner with her husband at the club. Longview Country Club was one of the most established and selective clubs in Virginia. Pretending to be one of her father's friends, a long-time member, Victoria called Longview.

"Hello, this is Helen Strauss. I hope you're doing well. I have a bit of an unusual request. It seems someone left something behind after dinner last night, and I'd like to return it. She was with the Parsons and the Whitneys, but I'm afraid I didn't catch the name of the third couple. Can you help me with that? It was a dinner reservation. Around six. I can't remember exactly. It might have been Craig Fairchild and his wife, but I'm not sure."

After a brief pause, the club employee confirmed the details. "You were correct. That was Grace Fairchild and her husband with the other couples you mentioned. They had a seven o'clock reservation. I was working last night and remember seeing them together. Whatever you need to give Mrs. Fairchild, we can handle it for you."

Victoria thanked the employee and quickly disconnected the call. She reviewed what she had learned: Grace's facial appointment was at two PM, and her dinner reservation was at seven PM, leaving several unaccounted-for hours in between. A timeframe that aligned with the messages Zoey had sent her husband.

While it didn't mean Grace knew where Zoey went, she certainly could have been with Zoey yesterday afternoon. And if Grace was closer to Zoey than she had let on—because how many people used the distinct phrase *in a mood*—why was she now lying about it?

28

Zoey

Then

On Saturday afternoon, the dull gray sky beyond the window mirrored Zoey's somber mood. Rather than write, she bought a few more items online to fill up the rooms that still seemed so big and empty.

Now that she didn't have a job, the main contrast between weekdays and weekends was reduced to the mere presence or absence of her husband. Chris still had work to take care of for his job on Saturdays and Sundays, but at least he was working from home, rather than miles away at his office.

Zoey rose from her desk and went to check on Chris in the dining room, where he'd set up his computer and monitors. Chris had strewn a notebook and papers across the table, but he wasn't there.

A faint sound drew her to the kitchen. She found Chris crouched on the floor, flashlight in hand, peering under the sink.

He craned his neck to look up at her. "Hey. I'm taking a break to try to fix this leak."

"Oh. Can I help?"

"Nah, it's a one-person job. Not much room under here."

Zoey made a cup of coffee and returned to her office. Sinking into her chair, she checked her inbox to see if anyone had gotten back to her about the repair projects. There, she found an email with the subject: *Update on Mountain Meadows Pond.*

The email read:

Mountain Meadows Community,

Due to recent concerns and demands regarding the neighborhood pond, the HOA has treated the pond for bacteria and algae. Those of you who are eagerly waiting to go in it, please wait another week for the treatment to take effect.

Finally, someone had taken care of the water issue. However, there was more.

Out of consideration for your neighbors and the overall value of our properties, please refrain from using or limit lawn decorations in your yard when they are visible from the main road. Thank you for your cooperation.

Could it be...was she referring to—? No. Zoey shook her head, dismissing the thought as paranoia.

The note was signed from the neighborhood HOA, but one component of the Gmail address was *Mrs. Fairchild*, making it obvious who had sent the message. Zoey thought Grace was targeting her unfairly. But why? Maybe Grace had a perfect life and was so bored, she got off on meddling with others. Perhaps her superior attitude was ingrained to the extent she didn't know any other way to be.

Wren nudged Zoey's leg, prompting her to remember the note contained good news. The pond underwent treatment. In another week or so, her dogs could swim again.

Zoey leaned sideways to pat Wren. Her hand froze in mid-air, lingering over her dog's head. She'd just felt something she didn't want to acknowledge—a dampness in her underwear. She pushed her chair away from the desk, praying she was mistaken. It wasn't that; it was something else, there was another explanation—just not that one.

Gripped by a terrible sense of foreboding, she left her office, moving almost in slow motion, putting off what she did not want to find. She passed Chris and went into the bathroom. Closing the door, she stood with her back against it. She was reluctant to confirm her fears, yet she couldn't avoid the truth forever. With a slow exhale, she turned to face the mirror. Her reflection revealed a mix of fear and sorrow, her lips drawn into a tense, worried line.

Swallowing hard, she tore her gaze away, unable to bear the sight of her own troubled expression any longer. She lowered her pants and her underwear and confirmed the unwelcome arrival of her period.

The bathroom walls seemed to close in on her like some claustrophobic nightmare. She stared into the mirror again. A lump formed in her throat, and a sudden welling of tears blurred her reflection. She closed her eyes, but the oppressive feeling refused to relent.

She couldn't allow herself to fall apart over this. No matter how disheartening, it shouldn't have come as a surprise, especially not now. As the veterinarian had told her, the move, despite being something she wanted, was a stressful experience. Her well-being had paid the toll. Next month would be different. Once everything settled down, her body would cooperate, and she'd finally get pregnant. Yet the growing sense of hopelessness within her refused to be calmed by empty reassurances.

They'd already been trying for what felt like an eternity, starting with their honeymoon. A month before their wedding, she'd ceremoniously dumped the remainder of her birth control pills in the trash to usher in the future she and Chris both wanted. How was she still not pregnant? The irony of vigilantly using protection for so many years, as if pregnancy was a forgone conclusion without measures to stop it from happening, was not lost on her. It all seemed like a cruel twist of fate.

Zoey forced herself to take a deep breath. "Think positive. You have so much to be grateful for," she said aloud, her voice wavering as she held back tears.

She tried to reframe the delay as an opportunity. If she could finish *Lovebirds* before the baby arrived, she could channel all her energy into being a mother. She had nine more months to do it now. Yet the thought rang hollow, drowned out by frustration and despair.

"Zoey? I'm going to the hardware store. We need a different type of wrench to fix the faucet," Chris said from outside the bathroom door.

Zoey struggled to pull herself together.

Minutes later, he knocked and asked, "Zoey, are you still in the bathroom?"

"Yes," she answered, trying to sound normal.

"Uh, is everything okay? You've been in there a long time."

Zoey stifled a sob.

Chris pushed the unlocked door partway open. He found her standing at the sink with tears streaming down her cheeks.

"What's wrong? What just happened?"

One more thing she didn't want to tell him, though she should. She whispered, "It's...I thought I might be pregnant, but I just got my period."

"Oh, Zoey." He wrapped his arms around her, warming her body with his strength. "It's okay. It's okay," he murmured.

Leaning against him, she appreciated his support, but nothing felt okay. It felt like everything important to her was there for the taking, and yet just out of reach. The more she grasped for her goals, the more they eluded her.

"You didn't tell me," Chris whispered. "How far along did you think you were?"

She sniffed a few times and swallowed. She hadn't lost their baby because she'd never been pregnant. The only thing she'd truly lost was the opportunity. One more month had slipped away without bringing her any closer to her dreams.

"I thought I was a few weeks along, but I wasn't. There must be something wrong with me. I should have gotten pregnant by now. It shouldn't take so long."

Chris tilted her chin up, ensuring she met his gaze. "There's nothing wrong with you, Zoey. But maybe one of us needs a little help in the baby-making department. Look, it's like when the dogs got sick, you went to the vet, figured out the issue with the pond, got it tested, and you fixed the problem. We'll do the same. Get tested and find a solution together. Lots of people go through this."

She appreciated his patience and understanding, since he wanted a family as much as she did. Yet doubts still plagued her. "What if it's me and it can't be fixed?"

"Then we'll come up with an alternative plan. Okay? Not everything is easy, but worse things could happen, Zoey. We'll get through this. Just like we have with everything else."

"I know," she murmured.

"Together."

She sniffed again. "Together."

As they held each other, she let his words sink in. He was right. She just had to pull out of her funk and move forward.

They would get through this.

The world wasn't out to get her.

No one was trying to steal her happiness.

Well, that wasn't exactly true.

29

Victoria

Now

On Sunday, the day after they met Chris and learned Zoey was missing, Victoria and Ned were up early again. The sun was still rising when Victoria went outside, squinting against the glare. Ned was coming in from the backyard. She met him in the center of the patio and leaned into him, resting her head against his slow and steady heartbeat.

They stayed that way, absorbing the peaceful moment, until Ned stirred, pulling back just enough to meet Victoria's gaze.

"Have you heard anything from Chris?" he asked.

She shook her head.

"Think it's too early to call him?"

Victoria had been thinking the same thing. "If Zoey isn't back, I doubt he's sleeping."

Ned retrieved his phone and placed the call. A few seconds later, the line crackled to life.

Chris's voice came through the speaker, "I still haven't heard from her. I don't know what to think. I'm really...afraid."

Victoria and Ned exchanged worried looks.

"What are the police doing?" Victoria asked, hoping they'd made some progress.

"It's one detective, as far as I know. Sullivan. Detective Sullivan."

"I've worked with him before. A few years ago." A beat passed before Victoria added, "He did good work then." Her thoughts flew back to her previous case with Detective Sullivan. They were part of a team tracking down a spree killer known as The Numbers Killer. Back then, Sullivan was a highly functioning alcoholic. For his sake, and that of the community, Victoria hoped he'd gotten into a program and those days were behind him.

"Could you give the detective a call and see what he's thinking? Would you mind doing that for me?" Chris asked.

"I don't mind. I can do that. I'll tell you if I hear anything. Try to stay calm. Let Sullivan know if you think of anything else that might help him help you."

Victoria's extensive experience with missing person cases taught her the longer Zoey was missing, the less likely there would be a happy ending.

Perhaps Zoey had suffered a head injury and was now grappling with amnesia, rendering her unable to recall her home address. Yet, why the radio silence on her phone?

Maybe she had reached a breaking point in her marriage and her new life and had impulsively boarded a flight back to Los Angeles, covering her absence with lies.

Those possibilities were the most optimistic scenarios Victoria could conjure now, and she hoped one of them explained Zoey's disappearance. But worst-case scenarios were not mere by-products of her imagination. She'd seen them materialize into heartbreaking realities.

Memories of past investigations flickered through her mind. The frantic calls from worried families, the endless hours following up on leads and searching for clues, and then the elation of finding a victim before it was too late. Victoria wanted that sort of ending for the Hamiltons.

As she went into the house to get her work phone, she hoped her history with Detective Sullivan would allow for a straightforward exchange.

"Sullivan, it's Victoria Heslin from the FBI. How are you?" she asked as she returned to the patio.

"Good, Heslin. It's been a while. A long while." Sullivan's gruff voice crackled through the line. "What can I do for one of the FBI's finest?"

"I hear you're working a case in my neighborhood."

There was an incredulous puff and a brief pause before he asked, "Mountain Meadows? That's where you live?"

"Yes. Mountain Meadows Road."

"Sheesh. Nice digs, Heslin. I was there yesterday doing a door-to-door. Only two houses were empty. One family out-of-town visiting a new grandbaby. The other's gotta be yours. The first house with the fortress of a fence around it."

"That's right. I'm on vacation this week. Missed your visit, but I'm glad to connect now."

"Your house isn't listed under your name. You live with your family or something? Is it your parents' house?"

"No. It's not listed under my name for privacy reasons."

"Got it. So, you're friendly with Chris Hamilton and his wife? Any insights there?"

"I've never actually met his wife. My fiancé and I met Chris yesterday and helped him search the neighborhood because he was worried about Zoey." Victoria glanced over at Ned, who was listening intently.

"Your fiancé? Congratulations. Would that be Dante Rivera, by any chance?"

"What? No." A rush of heat came to her face at the mention of her colleague and the way the detective had assumed she was with him romantically. "My fiancé is Ned Patterson."

"Oh. Why does his name sound familiar? Oh, wait. He was in the plane crash with you, wasn't he?"

"Yes, he was," Victoria said, growing a little impatient with the detective's personal questions.

"Did you meet on the plane?"

"No. Ned was and still is my veterinarian. We were traveling together. Anyway, we found the Hamiltons' dogs loose in the neighborhood yesterday morning." Victoria could hear the scratching of Sullivan's pen against a notepad as she spoke.

"And that's how you connected with Chris Hamilton and learned about his wife's disappearance?"

"Yes. Chris said he hadn't seen Zoey since he left for work on Friday."

The scribbling of Sullivan's pen echoed through the phone. "Hmm. The thing is, someone reported seeing a woman who matches Zoey's description get into the passenger side of a blue Subaru Crosstrek on your street at two pm the day she disappeared."

"Really? Do you have more details on that lead?"

Sullivan grunted. "That's all I've got. Anonymous tip that got called in. Chris definitely owns a blue Subaru. Are there any others in your neighborhood? I'm asking, but I already ran the addresses through the DMV registry and I'm not seeing one."

Victoria mentally reviewed the vehicles she'd seen coming and going on her street. None were blue Subarus except the one she'd seen at Chris's house yesterday morning. While not an unusual vehicle, a California license plate combined with the bike rack would make it stand out as his. "I can't say I've seen any others," she told Sullivan. "The caller didn't mention a license plate or other distinguishing features?"

Sullivan paused, the sound of rustling papers coming across the line. "Nah, just the make, model, and color of the vehicle."

"And they called it in rather than coming forward directly? Because, yesterday, we canvassed the neighborhood with Chris and no one we spoke with claimed to have seen Zoey." Of course, there were other possibilities besides those who lived there. Cleaning crews, yard maintenance, package delivery drivers. Food deliveries. The mail carrier. But how would any of them have learned Zoey was missing?

"The anonymous tip makes me a little wary, to be honest, but it's the best lead I have at the moment," Sullivan said.

Victoria nodded, though Sullivan couldn't see her. "I'd be happy to lend a hand in the investigation, if you think it would be helpful."

"All right, Heslin, I appreciate your call. I'm gonna head over to the Hamiltons' place, see if I can get Chris to explain the blue Subaru. But first I have to grab breakfast. Can you recommend any decent places around there?"

"Yes. The Gap Deli. In fact, I'll meet you there in fifteen minutes and I'll buy."

When the conversation ended, Ned was staring at Victoria with an expectant look. "I heard what you said. The detective suspects Chris, doesn't he?"

Victoria rested her phone on her leg and stared out at the rolling mountain hills. "Sullivan is just following up with the only leads he has so far. Someone claims they saw Zoey get into Chris's car the day she disappeared."

Ned frowned. "Chris said he hadn't seen Zoey since the previous morning."

"I know."

"Sounds like someone is either mistaken or..." Ned trailed off, leaving the implication unsaid.

"Someone is lying," Victoria finished for him, her jaw tightening. Whether the liar was Chris or someone trying to frame him, she didn't know.

A familiar surge of determination coursed through her veins. She locked eyes with Ned, and said, "I intend to find out."

30

Zoey

Then

The glow of the television flickered across the darkened bedroom as Zoey and Chris rested next to each other in bed, their feet entwined beneath the covers. Zoey frowned, her attention fixed on the screen. "Huh? I must have missed something, and it seems important," she said, turning to her husband. "Did you get that last bit?"

Silence greeted her question.

Propping herself up on one elbow, Zoey studied Chris's face in the dim light. His eyes were closed, features relaxed. "Hey," she whispered, "you still with me?"

Chris's eyes snapped open, momentarily disoriented. "Yeah, yeah. I'm awake."

A knowing smile played at Zoey's lips. "Could've fooled me."

"Just resting my eyes for a second," he mumbled, already drifting off again. "But I should probably call it a night. Back-to-back meetings tomorrow. You can keep watching if you want. I'll catch up later."

Zoey reached for the remote. "Nah, it's no fun without you. I'll turn it off. Besides, I'm beat too."

Zoey wasn't actually tired, despite the bottle of red wine she'd finished on her own. Now that she wasn't pregnant—why not? She'd slept in late that morning, as she had every day for the past week. Chris had left the house for work long before she got out of bed. It was hard to believe, but in a way, she missed those moments just after the sun came up at their little house in Redondo Beach, when they had both rushed to get ready, flying out the door together to beat traffic.

She hadn't even fallen asleep yet, and already she was looking forward to tomorrow evening, when Chris would come home.

If only they had family who could come and visit. But there was only Zoey's father, and since her mother's death, he didn't want to go anywhere.

Zoey spent a few more seconds watching her husband sleep in the glow of the television. As the screen dimmed, a corresponding shadow fell over his face. "I love you," she whispered.

"...you too," he mumbled and rolled onto his front.

Zoey glided her hand over the duvet until she found the remote hidden beneath. She stopped the program and powered down the television, immersing the bedroom in complete darkness. Settling into her pillows, she contemplated the next day's agenda—filling the feeders, walking the dogs, attempting to write, finding someone to fix the leaky faucets and peeling paint and rotted wood—until she dozed off.

The jarring ring of her phone disrupted her sleep and echoed through the quiet room.

"Isn't it after midnight?" Chris grumbled.

It was. Any call after midnight couldn't be good. Zoey's initial worry flashed to her father in El Segundo, California. Had something happened to him?

"Who is it?" Chris asked.

"I don't know yet."

Zoey glanced at her phone on the nightstand. She didn't recognize the number, only the familiar Los Angeles area code. It wasn't her father. "Probably just a spam call."

Zoey let the phone ring until the persistent ringing ceased. Feeling uneasy, she closed her eyes again. Her rest was short-lived as her phone vibrated with a new message notification. Zoey unlocked the screen.

Sweet dreams, Zoey. I'm the nightmare you can't escape. I'll be watching.

Bile rose in Zoey's throat, and she flinched when Chris placed his hand on her arm.

"Everything okay?" he asked.

She didn't want to tell him. She needed to believe the communications would stop. They couldn't go on forever, especially if Zoey didn't respond. Yet her hesitation seemed to trigger Chris's concern.

"What's going on?" he asked, sitting up to glimpse her phone over her shoulder. He read the message and cursed. "It's Susan?"

"Who else could it be?"

"She found your new number," he said, stating the obvious.

"Yes. I don't know how. She does not want to give up. It's like tormenting me has become her life's purpose."

"I'm so sorry," Chris said.

He pulled Zoey into his arms, kissed the top of her head, and stroked her hair as he held her.

"It sounds like she knows where we live," Zoey said.

"No. She's just making that up to scare you."

"Well, it's working." Zoey looked up at him, her eyes searching for reassurance. "You don't think she'd ever..."

"What, babe?"

"It really seems like she wants me dead."

Chris cupped her face, forcing her to meet his gaze. "Please don't even say that. She's not well, and she's doing this because of her own insecurities, but she'd never actually harm you."

"I guess if I'm no longer around to torment, her little game has to end." Zoey let out a bitter laugh. "Not sure that's very comforting."

Chris held her closer, and Zoey felt the tension radiating from his warm body. It wasn't his fault. Zoey knew what she was getting into when she married him. Once Susan found out they were engaged, she had lost it.

"At least a week has passed since the last message. I thought she might have gotten a life and given up, but that's not the case."

Chris's muscles tensed. "This wasn't the first message? She's already contacted you since we moved here?"

"Yes. A few times," Zoey said, feeling Chris's heart pound under her cheek.

"Where are the other messages?"

"I deleted them, but I have screenshots. They all came from different numbers. I haven't responded to any. I just block them. Either she keeps buying burners, or she's batting her eyelashes and asking random people if she can borrow their phones."

Chris moved to his side of the bed and grabbed his phone off the nightstand.

"What are you doing?" Zoey asked.

"I'm calling her." Chris dialed and put his phone to his ear.

Zoey had a second to register how quickly he'd placed the call. Apparently, he still had her number on his phone. "Susan. It's Chris. Don't start this again. Enough."

Zoey strained to hear Susan's response but couldn't.

Chris's tone was firm, but not angry. "You and I never had a good future together. You didn't want children, and I did. Zoey has nothing to do with our relationship ending. She is my wife. She's been my wife for a year now. That's not going to change. We're happy. I want you to be happy, too."

Zoey wrapped her arms around her legs and listened to her husband's side of the conversation.

"You have a career," Chris said. "Friends. Family. You're a beautiful woman. You're better than this, Susan. Please make an appointment to talk to someone. You need help."

Seconds of silence stretched out in the dark room. Chris's comment about Susan's beauty echoed in Zoey's mind. The fact was undeniably true, but she wished he hadn't said it aloud.

Chris stood up. "I don't want this on your record, but I can't have you harassing my wife. We have everything you've sent. You don't want it out there. One more text and I will call the police. So, please, for your own sake, stop. Do not contact Zoey ever again."

Without waiting for a response, he ended the call and set his phone back down on the nightstand.

"I wish you had told me sooner," he said, getting back into bed. "But for now, just try to forget about it."

Zoey nodded. "I will."

But she couldn't.

31

Zoey

Then

Unable to sleep, Zoey flashed back to when the red-haired demon, Susan, had entered her life. It was at the conclusion of the marketing project with Chris.

During the project, Zoey had done her best to let Chris know she was unattached without actually telling him. She slipped subtle phrases like "cooking for one," and "another night out with my girlfriends," into their conversations.

Zoey hoped the project's end would mean a new beginning for them. If Chris had picked up on her hints, they could take their relationship to another level. Their project team's celebratory dinner was the perfect place to find out.

Zoey had spotted Chris at the bar, an open seat next to him. This was her chance.

"Fancy meeting you here. Is this seat taken?" she asked.

He turned, smiling at her in a way that made her weak in the knees. "It is now," he said. "Have a seat."

The loud music and conversations provided an excuse for her to lean in close to him just to be heard.

"Can I get you a drink? Not that I'm buying, my boss is paying, but it's the thought that counts, right?" Chris asked.

"Sure. I'll have a glass of white wine."

Chris flagged the bartender and placed the order, then turned to Zoey. "Are you already on another project?"

"I have a few days off and then I start on a new pitch." She dipped her head, then looked up at him. "I'm going to miss our brainstorming sessions."

"Yes. Me, too," he said, wrapping his hand around his beer.

Zoey didn't remember the conversation that followed after her wine came, only that it was relaxed and comfortable and yet the connection between them was charged with an attraction she'd never experienced before. She remembered, however, the exact moment she saw a sudden shift in Chris's entire demeanor. One second, he was laughing, and the next, he was stiff and surprised. Zoey followed his gaze to the gorgeous, fair-skinned redhead strutting toward them. A form-fitting sheath dress hugged her fabulous figure. She looked like a movie star or a model, but the most memorable thing about the woman was her angry, piercing glare. It didn't take Zoey long to realize the glare was targeted at her.

Chris stood. He had recovered from his initial surprise and smiled awkwardly. "Susan? Is everything okay?"

"No. It's not okay. You told me you were at a work dinner."

"I am." He gestured to the table with others from the project team, then to Zoey. "This is Zoey. She's with the marketing firm we hired."

"Really?" Susan's voice dripped with disdain. She sized Zoey up as if deciding where best to stab a dagger. "This is how you discuss marketing?"

Chris's complexion reddened to the hue of an intense sunburn. "Susan," he uttered, sounding mortified.

"We have to talk. Let's go. Before I make a scene in front of all your *coworkers*," Susan snapped, putting emphasis on coworkers as if Zoey was anything but.

People were already staring. Susan attracted attention simply by breathing, and only more so with her purposeful stride and snarling expression. Everyone in the restaurant could tell something jaw-dropping was about to unfold.

Kim observed from the other end of the bar, eyebrows raised, one hand covering her mouth to shield the smirk her eyes gave away.

Zoey had done nothing wrong, yet a flush of heat climbed to her cheeks. Chris had never mentioned a significant other. Zoey was sure of it. She didn't understand who the beautiful woman was exactly, but she had clearly staked her claim on Chris.

Zoey had waited months for the project to end, daydreaming about a romantic relationship, only to have it end in such an unexpected way. The humiliation she felt left her at a loss for words. Finally, she managed to say, "Goodbye, Chris. Um, thanks for all your insight on the project. It was nice working with you," in her most professional-sounding voice. She tucked her purse under her arm and turned away before he could say more. Even as she fled to the ladies' room, she half expected him to follow with an explanation, but he didn't.

Later, drowning her disappointment in a pint of ice cream on her couch, she replayed the events from their meetings and in the bar over and over. She'd believed they'd hit it off, and he'd felt the same about her. Getting that so incredibly wrong was heartbreaking.

Zoey couldn't resist comparing herself to Susan, which only fueled feelings of inadequacy. Susan was one-in-a-million beautiful. And yet, Zoey couldn't seem to forget about Chris.

One month later, he called.

"I want to apologize for what happened when we were out with the project team. Can I take you to dinner and explain?"

She wanted that so much, but unfortunately, she could easily conjure an image of the gorgeous woman who shot daggers with her eyes. "Are you involved with anyone else?"

"No. I promise you. The woman who showed up in the restaurant was my ex. She was having a hard time accepting she and I were done. She gets it now."

That's all Zoey needed to hear. She didn't want to hear anything else about the mental state of his ex-girlfriend. All that mattered was the relationship was behind him.

The evening with Chris was wonderful. Zoey was right about their dynamic.

A few months after their first official date, when Zoey and Chris had already declared their undying love for each other, Zoey received her first message from Susan. It was the first glaring sign she hadn't moved on, and the road ahead with Chris might be troubled.

You may have Chris fooled, but I know exactly what kind of person you are. You stole my life. Now it's my turn to take everything from you.

Now, almost two years later and after a cross-country move, Susan still hadn't given up.

"Zoey?" Chris asked, interrupting her recollection, and proving he couldn't sleep now either.

"Yes?" she answered, rolling onto her side and draping her arm across his bare chest.

"I'll never let anything happen to you."

32

Victoria

Now

Detective Sullivan was waiting at the casual restaurant when Victoria arrived. He looked tired and his dress shirt and slacks weren't the best fit, but absent were the red nose and broken capillaries that once made his drinking problem evident. He no longer reeked of the mouthwash, mints, and cologne he had used to disguise the scent of alcohol. She was glad to see he was doing well and hoped he stayed that way.

They ordered breakfast at the counter and took their food to a small corner table with a chessboard painted over the top. Sullivan set a notebook down beside his plate.

"We worked the Numbers Killer case together, didn't we, Heslin?" Sullivan's gravelly voice held respect. "Seems like a lifetime ago."

Victoria nodded, recalling the intensity of the investigation. "Yes, and yet, that's one of those cases that will stay with us forever, won't it?"

The detective emitted a humorless chuckle. "It will. By the way, that's quite a property you've got. How long have you lived there?" he asked before digging into his egg and ham sandwich.

"Four years." Affording the property on her FBI salary, even combined with Ned's income, would have been difficult without the trust fund she'd received from her grandfather. The yard was perfect for her animals. Though the house was more than she needed, she'd taken full advantage of its surroundings. She hiked or jogged on the nearby trails whenever she could.

"You're really slumming it when you come into work, aren't you?"

Victoria dumped a small packet of granola over her yogurt. "I love my job, Detective. That's why I do it."

"Yeah, you must." He widened his eyes as if he found her statement hard to believe. "What made you go into law enforcement, anyway?"

"When I was in college, my mother was abducted. I remember the waiting, the not knowing, feeling helpless. I never wanted to feel that way and thought I could help others in similar positions."

"Your mother...was she...is she okay?"

Victoria shook her head. "No. My family received a ransom request. We were prepared to pay. And then something went wrong. My mother never came home. She died."

"Oh. I'm sorry."

"Yeah. Me, too. That led me to join the FBI. I don't regret it. Anyway, let's talk about Zoey Hamilton. You checked the Hamiltons' credit card and ATM transactions?"

"Yep. Zoey and Chris share accounts, so it was easy to do. No activity on her credit or debit cards. No recent withdrawals." Sullivan grunted as he flipped through the pages of his notebook. "I spent the last hour going through her phone logs and texts. All her local calls went to businesses. She's not on social media, so not much to see there."

"She's not on any social media sites?"

"None that I could find."

"Unusual," Victoria said, leaning forward in her chair. "What else have you found?"

Sullivan put his sandwich down. "I spoke with one of Zoey's friends in California. She had some interesting things to tell me. Apparently, Chris's ex, a woman named Susan Cruz, has a history of harassing Zoey. Mostly online. When I checked the Hamiltons' phone records, guess who Chris has been calling recently?"

"Susan?"

"Yep. In the days before Zoey's disappearance."

"What did he have to say about it? What were the calls about?"

Sullivan shrugged. "I don't know yet. That's another thing I'm going to ask him in person once we finish here. That's what I've got so far. It's enough to suggest Chris Hamilton might not be the concerned husband he appears to be." Sullivan hunched over as he went in for another bite of his sandwich.

"What do you make of the text messages Zoey sent him?" Victoria asked.

"If she actually sent them. There's a chance he fabricated those messages to throw us off."

"Chris showed me screenshots of the message string, rather than showing them to me on his app. Made me think there might be other communications he didn't want me to see."

"I saw everything. The Hamiltons had a fight."

"He mentioned a fight. He wasn't trying to hide it from me, though he didn't say what the fight was about. Do you know?"

"They were fighting about his ex. According to Chris, Zoey was angry because Susan was harassing her again, and Chris didn't want to report it to the police. Zoey also believed Chris had recently shared information about their personal life with Susan."

"Hmm."

"We're keeping tabs on him now. We've got a city vehicle stationed on your street, posing as maintenance. They're installing monitors atop the streetlights as we speak. It's a good option for that neighborhood where an unmarked vehicle would stick out. Rest assured, we're watching everyone in Mountain Meadows."

"Guess I'll have to watch my step, then."

As soon as Sullivan finished eating, he wiped his mouth with a napkin and said, "Gotta go."

"I'd like to check in with you to keep updated. And if there's anything I can do to assist, please ask. Our neighborhood connects to miles of trails, and I walk them all the time. I know them well."

"Appreciate the offer, Heslin. I'll keep you posted on any developments, and I might take you up on that help, depending on what I learn today. Enjoy the rest of your vacation, or as much of it as you can, given the circumstances."

33

Zoey

Then

The fertility specialist appointment was two weeks away. Testing first, then hopefully, they'd find the help they needed. The treatments opened the door to the possibility of twins, perhaps even triplets. The thought was a little overwhelming—three babies at once in her petite frame—but maybe worth it. A multiple pregnancy would make up for lost time and ease the feeling she'd fallen behind on her goals and dreams.

In the meantime, Zoey pondered what else she could do to feel like she was moving forward and getting back on track.

Finch jumped up from his bed and looked at her, wagging his tail, his way of suggesting a walk. As always, he was bursting with energy.

Zoey retrieved the HOA email regarding the pond treatment and read it again. She calculated how many days had passed since the treatment. Eight.

"It's time," she told her dogs. "You can finally swim again!"

She sent Chris a message to let him know she was going out. It wasn't something she usually did, but the recent communications from Susan had Zoey feeling more wary than carefree. She leashed the dogs, grabbed her binoculars and two tennis balls, and made her way to the pond.

As the dogs raced into the water to play, a sense of calm washed over her. Some things were worth waiting for, and eventually, everything fell into place. It was going to be okay. All of it. The house would get fixed, she'd make progress on her novel, make friends, and get pregnant. She just had to stay patient, rise through the challenges, and have some faith. A smile graced her face as she tossed the balls and watched Finch and Wren swim after them.

Fifty or more throws later, she'd lost track long ago, her arm was sore, though her dogs remained endlessly enthralled. Zoey scanned the trees for birds, then checked her inbox, discovering an email about a recent delivery to her house. The new fall weather clothes she'd ordered. Sweaters for her. Flannels for Chris. The email included an image of the box on her porch.

She called the dogs from the water and was pleased when they obeyed, albeit after hesitating to make sure she really meant it. When she got home, the package waited as expected. What she didn't expect was a smaller box behind it. The label was typed, addressed to Zoey Hamilton, but there was no return address.

Before Zoey could open the boxes, she had to hose off her dogs, then dry them. When Finch and Wren were clean, Zoey brought the packages inside and placed them on the kitchen counter. The smaller box remained a mystery. It was lightweight and seemed empty. She shook it gently and heard nothing. Curious, yet also cautious, she opened the package.

Inside, nestled within a single sheet of white tissue, she found a photograph of her and Chris on the porch of their home in California. Someone had scratched black X's over Zoey's eyes. It wasn't just the desecration of her face that shocked her. Normally, Zoey photographed well, but in this particular shot, the angle and timing were awful. She was laughing, her mouth open in an odd, unflattering way that made her look disfigured. It was the worst photo she'd ever seen of herself. One she would have instantly deleted had she known it existed.

A handwritten note accompanied the photograph.

I found you and I'm watching. Always watching. Tick tock. Tick tock. Better watch your back.

The text messages and phone calls were bad enough, but the delivery of the unsettling photograph and frightening handwritten note filled Zoey with dread. Susan had found them. She'd sent the awful picture to prove she knew their physical address.

What would Susan do next? The uncertainty was worse than the actual threats. Crossing to the window, Zoey peered out, half-convinced Susan had hand-delivered the package and was now lurking behind the trees separating the Hamiltons' house from the Fairchilds.

Zoey checked the lock on the window, her fingers fumbling on the latch. She moved to the next one, then the door, where she pushed the deadbolt into place, hurrying to secure the house. A strange hush had descended, muffling every sound except her pounding heart. Try as she might to barricade herself within, she couldn't escape the creeping sensation something unwelcome had slipped inside with her.

When the house was locked up, she sunk into the leather chair in her office, curling into herself, fighting the urge to scream. Susan had already wreaked so much havoc on Zoey's life. Thinking back on some of those incidents now made Zoey shudder. Especially what happened two years ago, right after Chris proposed.

Back then, the excitement of Zoey's engagement was still so fresh, she could hardly concentrate on anything else. She'd been in her Los Angeles office, struggling to meet a crucial marketing presentation deadline, when a high-priority interoffice notification popped up on her screen. The subject line—*Notification of Unprofessional Conduct*—piqued her curiosity, which quickly turned to horror.

The email contained accusations directed at her. All of it lies and slander. To make matters worse, the note went out to the entire firm.

She was still reeling when her boss beckoned her to his office. On her way there, Zoey felt the weight of her colleagues' shocked glances.

Her boss had the email pulled up on his screen. "This isn't the first allegation I've received about you recently. Yesterday, someone claimed you were unprofessional and unreliable and demanded I let you go."

"That can't be right. I've never had a complaint before. Who was it? What did they say I did?"

"We're trying to find out who sent the email. I trust you, but this needs to stop. It's distracting. It doesn't look good."

"Yeah, obviously." She was further embarrassed when she realized she was crying.

The following week, just when she'd recovered from the shock of the awful email blast, things got worse.

She was in bed scrolling through her social media account, a mindless and relaxing routine she sometimes enjoyed while waiting for Chris to come home. Right away, she noticed something odd. She had way more notifications than usual. She clicked on a post from a friend's wedding and her blood ran cold.

Can't believe Zoey has the nerve to smile after sleeping with the groom. #slut #whore

The next one, on a post about Zoey's recent promotion: *Guess sleeping your way to the top really pays off, huh?*

On a photo of Zoey at dinner with a few of her girlfriends: *None of you would be friends with Zoey if you knew what she says behind your backs. #fakefriend*

There were more, all from different accounts, people Zoey didn't know and had never heard of. Fake accounts, obviously, but would everyone else pick up on that? Each vile comment assaulted her character and credibility. Zoey didn't have a shady past. She didn't talk behind people's backs. She'd never fooled around with her boss or anyone at work, and certainly not with her friend's husband! Her integrity had always been a source of pride. Why was someone hellbent on destroying her reputation?

Her friends called and messaged her that evening. Kim from work. Friends from college. Zoey's aunt. They shared her outrage about the posts and tried to make her feel better.

"What's wrong?" Chris asked when he came into the bedroom that night and found her crying.

At first, she was too embarrassed to show him, but then she did. "None of it is true," she said.

Chris read in silence, his body tensing with each line. "You don't have to tell me they're not true. I know you, Zoey. Do you have any idea who could do this?"

Zoey shook her head. "I had no enemies," she whispered. "Not until Susan. It has to be her. She must have found out we got engaged."

"She wouldn't..." But Chris didn't even finish his sentence.

"It's her, isn't it?"

Chris looked pained. "We don't know for sure."

That was enough to convince Zoey. "Why is she doing this? Why does she hate me so much?"

Chris pressed his fingers against his forehead. "She doesn't hate you. She's just...she's messed up."

"Is there something you haven't told me?" Zoey had never wanted to ask about his ex, but now it seemed she had no choice.

"Susan wasn't just my girlfriend. We were engaged."

Engaged? Shocked, Zoey got out of bed and moved away from Chris. "You never told me. The night in the restaurant...when she came looking for you, were you engaged then?"

He shook his head. "No. I'd already broken it off with her. I don't want to talk about the reasons, just that there were some critical relationship things we couldn't agree on. It was for the best for both of us, but I think the breakup pushed her over the edge, made all her insecurities worse."

"If she's the one doing this to me, I have to report her. I have to call the police."

Chris looked miserable as he held up his hands. "Please don't. Just don't respond to her, and please don't call the police. Let me talk to her."

"But..." Zoey stared at her fiancé. "Do you...do you still love her?"

"No. Zoey, I promise you. I don't love her, but I used to, or at least I thought I did. And... I care about her." He blew out a loud breath. "I knew she had some psychological issues, and I feel guilty that breaking off our engagement might have brought out the worst in her. I just want her to be okay. I don't want it to be my fault she's not happy."

Zoey nodded slowly, realizing it was possible to admire Chris for his concern and also resent him for it.

Now, almost two years after that night, Zoey sat curled up in Steve Johnson's chair, wondering if she'd made a mistake by not insisting they report Susan's harassment to the authorities. Were there lines Susan had yet to cross? What if her vendetta was far from over and the worst was yet to come? As long as Zoey and Chris were together, would she always be looking over her shoulder, flinching at shadows, and wondering what next?

34

Victoria

Now

The FBI files detailing Steve Johnson's disappearance and the alleged embezzlement had arrived in Victoria's inbox while she was at The Gap Deli with Sullivan. She read through the information when she got home.

A missing person investigation kicked off after the police received a distressed phone call from Steve's wife. Sarah Johnson was visiting her sister in Arizona and grew increasingly worried when Steve stopped responding to her communications. She flew home early, but Steve wasn't there. Sarah never saw him or heard from him again.

The similarities between Steve's situation and Zoey Hamilton's were eerily similar. Both had vanished without a trace, leaving a worried spouse behind hoping and praying their loved one would return with an explanation that would make everything okay and reset their lives back to normal.

Sarah Johnson was still waiting. Victoria couldn't let it take so long to find out what happened to Zoey. She pictured Zoey's huge smile from the photo Chris sent. The thought of her life getting cut so short made Victoria sick.

She got up from her desk to refill her water and give her dogs snacks, then returned to the file.

A week after Steve vanished, the police made their next discoveries. The first—Steve's Volvo parked in a long-term lot at the airport. The second—a hefty sum had disappeared from a troubled development called Magnolia Estates. Steve was the legal counsel for the project.

Obstacles had plagued the upscale community since its inception. Permits were denied. Lawsuits were filed. When the project stalled, the development brought Steve in as legal counsel. A year later, money meant to cover land clearing, site preparation, and builder payments disappeared.

That's when the FBI took over the case. The embezzled funds had vanished into a network of untraceable offshore holding companies. Steve had access to the money, and he was gone.

The FBI's investigation notes were sparse, almost as if parts were missing. Victoria wanted to know more. She shot another message to Payton.

You were right, there isn't a lot in the Steve Johson file. Could you find a list of the other investors in the Magnolia Estates Fund? We should speak to some of them about Steve's role.

Payton responded she would look into it.

Thanks. And keep me posted on anything you discover.

35

Sullivan

Now

Two days had passed since Zoey Hamilton's disappearance. Detective Sullivan had little to show for his efforts so far, but that could change at any moment. As he guided his dusty sedan up the long driveway leading to Agent Victoria's estate, he couldn't resist appraising the incredible property. The gates alone probably cost more than his yearly salary.

He killed the engine and stepped onto a cobblestone courtyard between her garage bays. Compared to his rental, this place was a mansion fit for royalty, and yet, he couldn't begrudge Victoria anything. The woman had been through hell and back several times. He'd brushed up on her case history after their breakfast. Since they'd last worked The Numbers Killer case together, she'd endured harrowing experiences—gunshot wounds, abductions, brushes with death in the most hostile of environments, and she'd also spent a grueling week in an arctic wasteland. Victoria was only in her mid-thirties, and yet she'd survived ordeals that would break most people, and she'd emerged as a legend in law enforcement circles.

His own journey seemed mundane in comparison. Since their work together, he'd endured a silent struggle to claw his way back from hitting rock bottom. Yet he took immense pride in maintaining his hard-won sobriety each day, knowing the alternative was always lurking, just one terrible decision away.

"Detective Sullivan, thanks for stopping by," Victoria said, stepping onto the terrace, as poised and polite as ever. "Any news?"

He scrubbed a hand across his stubbled jaw. "Not yet. We still haven't located Zoey. The husband remains a primary person of interest. He hasn't left the neighborhood these past few days."

"Did you search their house?" Victoria's patient expression betrayed no judgment, only interest.

"Top to bottom. Not a single trace of Zoey, nor signs of a struggle. Almost all her belongings are present—purse, credit cards, luggage. Only her phone and keys are missing. No forced entry, though we confirmed the Hamiltons never changed their locks after moving in."

Victoria shielded her eyes with her hand. "Those leashes I found must be important, then. Whatever happened, it seems to have occurred outside."

"Right," Sullivan said.

"What about the former girlfriend? What did Chris say about the calls with her?"

"He said he only called Susan to tell her to stop harassing Zoey. I analyzed the Hamiltons' phone records and messages. He could be telling the truth. His calls do line up with the timing of recent messages his wife received, though not entirely."

"Did the LAPD bring Susan in for questioning?"

Sullivan sighed. "They can't find her. No record of her traveling, though."

"Are you saying she's also missing?"

"Missing or hiding, which moves her to the top of my list of suspects, though Chris swears Susan has nothing to do with his wife's absence. I find it odd he's so protective of someone with a documented history of harassing his wife. Makes me think he still has feelings for his ex."

"Hmm. Any other leads while you're waiting to find Susan?"

"Chris mentioned a handyman who met Zoey at the Hamiltons' house. She told Chris the guy made her really uncomfortable. He sent Zoey some intense messages about starting the work. I wouldn't say threatening, but I didn't like the vibe. I'm headed to talk to him next."

"Sounds good," Victoria said. "Let me know if there's anything I can do for you."

"Thank you. I have yet to dig up any clear-cut evidence of a crime. It's still possible Zoey took off. While the LAPD helps me locate Susan Cruz, I'm going to keep looking into everyone, particularly in your neighborhood, until we find out what happened."

Sullivan parked his unmarked car on the street near Jake's current work site. Hammers thumped and power tools whined as the detective made his way through construction debris and mud.

His breath caught as he neared the contractor's trailer and spotted a garbage bin with empty beer cans. The scent of stale alcohol wafted out, igniting that itch in his mind. Sullivan's mouth watered. He could taste cold, frothy beer. He remembered the exact location of the nearest bar.

Sullivan tore his gaze away, reciting the serenity prayer. Not today, he promised himself. Popping a piece of gum into his mouth, he entered the trailer and asked the site supervisor for Jake. The supervisor pointed to a gruff-looking contractor taking measurements. Passing the garbage bin for the second time, Sullivan tasted beer again. He pushed the sensation down, as he did several times every day, chomping hard on his gum.

Approaching Jake, Sullivan presented his identification. "I need to ask you a few questions about Zoey Hamilton. She lives in the Mountain Meadows neighborhood. You recently gave her an estimate and sent her some follow up messages."

Jake set his tools aside and wiped his hand on his pants. "Yeah. I know who she is. Looks like she wasted my time. What about her?"

"She's missing."

"Why would that bring you to me?"

"Her husband said you made her uncomfortable. She said she was hesitant to hire you for the job."

"Did she now?" Jake gritted his teeth and met Sullivan's eyes. He took a long time before answering. "I sure didn't mean to offend anyone. That's not good for business. Guess I better work on that."

Sullivan nodded. "Wouldn't hurt. I saw the texts you sent her. Kind of aggressive. Now I'm trying to gather all the facts. Can you tell me where you were last Friday?"

Jake glared. "I was here, working on this project. Got here early and left after dark. You can ask the crew to back me up. They'll tell you."

Sullivan methodically interviewed each crew member. One by one, they corroborated Jake's presence. A bearded carpenter even produced time-stamped photos of Jake and others working throughout the day and drinking together later.

Satisfied, Sullivan snapped his notebook closed with a thump. Jake appeared to have an airtight alibi that ruled him out as a suspect. Sullivan wasn't surprised. His years on the job had taught him the most dangerous of perpetrators *didn't* make people uncomfortable. They didn't give off warning signals that made people recoil. Instead, they concealed dark intentions behind veils of normalcy. A friendly, inoffensive neighbor who waved every morning on his way to work could just as easily be the one secretly spying and fantasizing about unspeakable things.

Sullivan had no choice but to peel back the layers on everyone who recently interacted with Zoey until he found the real culprit.

36

Zoey

Then

Zoey waited until they were in bed before she told Chris about the package and the horrible photograph with the x's over her eyes.

Chris yanked a pillow out from behind his head and punched his fist into the middle. Zoey wasn't sure if he was adjusting the pillow filling or expressing anger.

"She must have mailed it before I last spoke with her," he said.

That might be true, but it didn't make Zoey feel any better about his mentally unstable and vindictive ex having their new address.

"I'll call her and make sure." Chris swung his legs over the side of the bed and got up.

"Now?" Zoey asked.

"Yes. This needs to end," he said before leaving the room.

Alone in their bedroom, Zoey's eyes drooped as she waited for Chris. She must have fallen asleep for a moment because the next thing she knew, she woke to an empty bed. When she didn't find her husband in the bathroom, she went downstairs to look for him. Eyes barely open, she squinted in the darkness, her bare feet growing cold on the wooden floors. The door to the backroom, her office, was closed. Chris's voice came from behind it.

The room hiding all the secrets, she thought. Then *what secrets?* She was half asleep, not making sense.

She could hear Chris, but not what he was saying. He was whispering. Even with Zoey supposedly all the way upstairs in their bed, he didn't want to risk being overheard. Goosebumps prickled Zoey's skin. She wanted to push the door open, but she didn't. She had to trust her husband.

I found you and I'm watching. Always watching. Tick tock. Tick tock. Better watch your back.

Zoey shuddered, suddenly so chilled she needed to get back into bed and under the covers. She turned around and trudged back upstairs.

"Everything okay?" she asked when Chris joined her minutes later. "What did she say?"

"It was like I thought. She mailed the package before our last talk. You won't hear from her again. Trust me. That was the last time. I promise."

Chris sounded confident, and Zoey wanted to believe him, but she didn't.

Hours later, when Zoey woke again, another pat of the sheet beside her confirmed Chris was gone. Morning light filtered in from a small window in the hallway. Zoey stretched and rolled over. She played some daily word games on her phone and checked the news, in no hurry to get out of bed.

When she finally went downstairs, she encountered a distressing yet familiar scene: diarrhea and vomit across the carpets and floors.

At least this time around, Zoey understood the cause behind the chaos. The pond again. Her dogs went in and then they got sick. The water was still contaminated. A quick call to the vet would put Finch and Wren on a path to recovery, so she wasn't as worried as she'd been when this had happened before. She was angrier. She regretted letting them swim again. The water treatment had failed.

Zoey called the vet and explained the situation. After cleaning the house in her pajamas, she threw on yesterday's outfit, then headed out to pick up more medicine. But first, she detoured to the pond.

As she stood at the water's edge collecting another water sample, it felt like she was back to square one and grappling with a problem she might never solve.

Zoey had been wrong in thinking everything would be okay.

37

Victoria

Now

Residents of Mountain Meadows Road gathered around the gazebo by the pond in the afternoon, prepared to search the surrounding trails for Zoey. The Mullers and the Nelsons, who hadn't been there for days, had returned home and come out to help. Joining them were members of the local volunteer fire department, and some of Chris's new colleagues, eager to lend a hand.

Victoria surveyed the group, her gaze moving from person to person, studying the solemn expressions on each individual's face.

One of Chris's coworkers told another, "Looks like those trails go way back into the mountains. She must have gotten lost." His words hung in the air, an attempt to summon reality by sheer force of will. If true, it meant Zoey had been alone in the woods for three days now. Hunger, exposure, wild animals—the threats multiplied with every passing hour she remained missing.

Severe dehydration would set in after three days without food or water, leaving Zoey dangerously depleted. She might have suffered injuries from a fall or an animal attack that had worsened over the past few days. Even if she were alive, her chances of remaining so diminished with every hour.

Two volunteer firefighters were engaged in a whispered conversation nearby. As Victoria walked past, she overheard one say, "Steve Johnson," in a hushed voice.

Mark and Faith Humphrey stood slightly apart from the larger group, arms linked. Beside them was their daughter, Lexi, a long-legged teenager wearing riding britches and a sweatshirt. Lexi kept shooting glances in Victoria's direction, an unmistakable hint of shyness mingled with curiosity.

When their eyes met, Victoria offered a warm smile and approached.

"Hey Lexi, I'm Victoria. I see you came from the barn."

Lexi's cheeks flushed pink. She nodded and tucked a stray lock of hair behind her ear.

Mark gave his daughter's shoulder an encouraging squeeze. "Lexi turns fifteen in just a few days. She's been riding since she was six years old."

Victoria beamed at Lexi. "That's the same age I was when I started riding. It's pretty much all I wanted to do when I was your age. Kept me out of trouble, I realize now."

Grace joined them then, looking like she'd stepped out of a catalog for very expensive hiking gear. She wore boots without a speck of dirt, cargo pants, a fitted jacket, and a scarf around her neck. Craig was with her, wearing golf attire. They'd brought their son Handford along. He was a handsome boy about Lexi's age. When his eyes weren't glued to his phone, they were on Lexi.

"Do you really think we might find Zoey out there?" Grace asked Victoria in a hushed voice. "Or do you think she's somewhere else, and she's going to be very embarrassed when she learns all the fuss she caused because of a little breakdown of sorts?"

Grace's attitude surprised Victoria. How could Grace be so cavalier about a missing woman, unless she knew something the rest of them didn't? "Have you come across new information about her whereabouts? Something you might have remembered?" Victoria asked.

"Me? No. I told you I have no idea where Zoey might have gone." Grace turned to her son. "Have you met Handford?"

"We've never met," Victoria said. "It's nice of you to come."

Handford lifted his eyes from his phone. "I'm skipping lacrosse practice for this because it counts as volunteer hours. We have to do them for my school."

"Handford!" Grace gave her son a pointed look, clearly mortified by his comment. "What you meant to say is you're eager to help find your missing neighbor, if that's even possible, and of course you're concerned for her safety."

"Right. That, too," he said. "I don't even know what she looks like, though."

"We have a picture of her on the table over there. It's great you could help," Victoria told him.

She scanned the small crowd again, searching for one neighbor in particular—Connor Rhodes. He wasn't there, but it was time the rest of them got started.

With Victoria standing beside him, Sullivan gave some basic instructions to the group, outlining what to look for and what precautions to take. He distributed colored tape to mark the trails once they'd checked them.

"Let's do this! Let's bring Zoey home," Craig Fairchild shouted. He clapped his hands with a few loud smacks, as if they were breaking from a football huddle and about to run a play.

The group searched for hours, voices echoing through the woods as they called out Zoey's name. They left colored tabs on the trees to mark their progress and ensure no trail went unchecked. Victoria parted tall dead grasses, looked behind fallen trees, and peered over every ledge and culvert she came across. She found no signs of Zoey.

As the sun dipped below the horizon, the search party members re-grouped at the gazebo as planned.

Two long card tables awaited with white linen tablecloths and a lavish display of heavy appetizers, desserts, and drinks from a nearby restaurant. Grace stood behind the food, encouraging everyone to help themselves. "Thank you for coming out to help us find Zoey," she said. "We're all such a wreck about her absence. We just appreciate your help more than we could ever say."

While most people helped themselves to heaping plates of food, Grace made a plate and brought it to Chris, who stood alone, staring at the pond.

She touched his arm and said, "You need to keep up your strength. When was the last time you had something to eat?"

"Thanks for buying all this food for everyone. I guess I should have thought of that."

"Nonsense," Grace said, one hand still on his arm, the other holding out the plate of food. "You have enough to worry about with your wife gone. This is what neighbors do for each other. Just relax and let us help."

Chris took the plate and ate a steak kebob, perhaps because Grace remained at his side and watched him expectantly.

As that was happening, Victoria caught Mark and Faith Humphrey with their heads tilted together in a hushed conversation. When Faith looked up again, she stared right at Grace.

Handford and Lexi were talking together, not far from the table of food. There was no sign of Craig.

The searchers had nearly depleted the refreshments before they all set off again on the dark trails, relying on flashlights to illuminate their way. The night wore on and fatigue set in. One by one, the searchers departed, starting with Chris's colleagues. They promised to resume searching the following day if Zoey was still missing.

The best they could hope for now was that Zoey had taken off on her own, unaware or indifferent to the commotion she had caused and the hell she was putting her husband through.

38

Chris

Now

Chris had marched through the undergrowth for hours, his eyes scanning the dense foliage for any sign of his missing wife. Zoey was out there somewhere, vulnerable and alone. She had to be. He didn't want harm to have befallen her, and yet he couldn't accept that she had left him intentionally. She wouldn't do that. Not Zoey.

Except, what if he were wrong? How humiliating it would be if she'd left him! So many of his new coworkers were here, having taken most of the workday off to help with the search. What would they think? Chris grimaced. He didn't care what they thought. Even if Zoey had left him, he could make peace with that, eventually, as long as she was safe.

As night fell, and the haunting sounds of forest wildlife intensified, Chris pictured Zoey out there alone, and it was almost impossible to keep his tears at bay.

Before the searchers left, he'd rallied enough to thank his colleagues for coming all the way to Mountain Meadows. He'd also thanked his new neighbors, the Mullers and the Nelsons, who he hadn't met until the search. They'd all been great so far, though he realized Connor Rhodes hadn't been with them.

Chris trudged back to his house in a light-headed daze. Grace had convinced him to eat a few things, though he couldn't remember for the life of him what he'd put in his mouth. His appetite had disappeared the moment he realized Zoey was missing. Never had he felt anything as terrible as the soul-crushing helplessness gripping him now.

As his house came into view, it only saddened him more. It was Zoey's dream house, but without her, it was just an empty shell.

Partway up the rotting stairs, he stopped. His dogs were already looking out the windows on either side of the door, barking at his arrival.

Chris stared down. Mud coated the center of the newish doormat. Had it been like that before, and he just didn't notice? He could have sworn the mat was clean the last time he looked down. Zoey had been working so hard to get the house in good shape. He'd tried to do his part to keep it that way. Even though it was a doormat, he'd gone out of his way not to wipe his shoes on it after their walks.

Before going inside, Chris dialed Detective Sullivan. "Did you send officers back to my house today while we were searching the woods?"

"No," the detective answered. "Why?"

"Oh, um, I was just wondering."

"I'm going to have to call you back, Chris," Detective Sullivan said. "I've got someone on the other line."

Chris didn't mind. His heart leaped as he rushed to turn the door handle, thinking Zoey might have come home, but the house remained locked. That didn't matter. Zoey had a key. Once he was inside, he found a bit more dirt on the foyer floor. He ignored the dogs as he hurried through the house. On the kitchen counter, a small stack of mail was now spread across the counter.

He ran into Zoey's office shouting, "Zoey? Zoey!"

The top drawer of Zoey's desk was partly open. Her notes across the desk's surface. Zoey never left drawers open, and she kept her papers and the mail in neat little piles.

"Zoey!"

Chris tried to calm down, telling himself the police had searched the entire house looking for clues. Perhaps they hadn't returned things to the way they'd found them. He couldn't remember.

He went from room to room, and all were empty, but the door leading down to the basement was slightly ajar. Chris and Zoey kept that door closed because they didn't want the dogs to go down there. Had the police forgotten to close it all the way, and he just hadn't noticed until now? Or was Zoey in the basement?

With a lump of excitement filling his throat, Chris reached for the door handle. His pulse quickened as he descended the creaking stairs. The basement was a maze of dark, unfinished rooms with cement floors.

"Zoey?" he called. "Are you there?"

The basement was empty, but as Chris scanned the space, something just didn't feel right. Had Zoey come home and then left again? Or had a stranger entered their house? And if so, what were they looking for?

39

Zoey

Then

Zoey's fingers strummed an anxious rhythm on the surface of Steve Johnson's former desk. Her urgency escalated, pulsing in her chest with each passing second of listening to monotonous background music.

Finally, a crackle of static and a voice spoke. "Myron Water Labs, how can I help you?"

Zoey wasted no time. "I recently had two water samples tested from a pond. I have some questions about the results." She relayed the order numbers from the tests.

"Give me a minute." The sound of typing filtered through. "Okay, I've got the results here. What seems to be the issue?"

Zoey inhaled, organizing her thoughts. "The samples came from my neighborhood pond, which was supposedly treated for algae and bacteria between the test readings. But the test results are virtually identical. What does that mean?"

The technician paused, and Zoey could practically hear the frown in his voice. "That's...concerning. Are you sure the treatment occurred?"

"As far as I know, yes," Zoey replied, as doubt crept in. "My dogs got sick after the supposed treatment. I need to understand what's going on."

"Well, if it was treated, and the contamination hasn't improved, the treatment wasn't effective. The best solution would be to dredge the pond. Have it drained, clean the basin, and then refill it."

"It's a large body of water," Zoey said.

"It's really the only other way to deal with the problem. You either keep treating and testing or dredge it. I can give you the names of a couple companies that specialize in the work, if you'd like."

Zoey jotted down the information. "Thank you. Oh, wait. What made the pond contaminated in the first place? If I have it drained or dredged as you call it, what prevents it from happening again?"

"I can't answer questions specific to your pond, ma'am. It depends on a lot of things."

The line went silent, leaving Zoey to grapple with the task ahead. She typed an email to Grace.

To: Grace Fairchild

Subject: Reevaluation of Pond Treatment

Hi, Grace,

I hope this message finds you well.

Following up on the recent treatment of our neighborhood pond, I conducted a second set of water tests after my dogs again became sick after swimming in the pond. Unfortunately, the results show no improvement in water quality. Attached are both test results for your review. Given the unchanged levels of bacteria and algae, could you provide the contact details for the company responsible for the treatment? I suggest a more thorough approach—draining and cleaning the pond—to ensure our community's safety.

Thank you. Your assistance in this matter is highly appreciated.

Warm regards, Zoey

Zoey hit send. The email's polite tone felt like a betrayal of her true feelings, but she knew the stakes. Sharing her frustration would be social suicide—a sure way to make enemies of her new neighbors.

40

Grace

Then

A few days after Zoey sent the first email, Grace's lips twisted into a sneer as her gaze darted across the screen, reading yet another message from her least favorite neighbor.

To: Grace Fairchild

Subject: Reevaluation of Pond Treatment–Message 2

Hi, Grace,

Please see the email that I sent last week, dated 10/24, regarding the pond water.

I contacted a company about draining the pond because it's necessary. I now understand the neighborhood moves slowly in these matters, and I'd prefer not to wait. If you could just forward the name of the person or the company I should speak with, that would be great.

Thank you in advance.

Best, Zoey

Grace's back stiffened and she tapped her foot with an impatient rhythm on the Sersen carpet. The audacity of the note was staggering. The presumption. The disregard for how things worked in Mountain Meadows.

Compelled to share her outrage with someone, because that's what she did when upset, Grace jammed her finger against her phone, dialing Craig. The call went to voicemail. So as not to sound frazzled, Grace forced a calm into her voice, collecting herself before leaving a succinct summary of the issue with Zoey.

She called Faith next, expecting a little commiseration, or at least a sounding board.

"Is this about the fundraiser?" Faith asked.

"No, this concerns our neighborhood. You won't believe what Zoey Hamilton intends to do."

Faith's response was less than enthusiastic. "Do I want to hear this? Do I need to?"

Undeterred, Grace plowed ahead. "She wants to dredge the pond, and she thinks she can circumvent the entire process."

"Is it because she doesn't know the process? Did you tell her how it works? Does she know she should present her case to the HOA for approval?"

Faith's apparent sympathy for Zoey annoyed Grace. "You're missing the point," she snapped. "Zoey dared to insinuate we—more specifically, I—operate at a sluggish pace. Clearly, she's oblivious to the standards I've established here."

Cutting Grace off, Faith asked, "What makes you think she's specifically targeting you?"

"Who else, Faith? I'm the one who has been helping her. But before she attempts to 'save' our neighborhood, perhaps she should address the dilapidated state of her own home. It's an eyesore."

As Grace gathered ammunition to further disparage Zoey, her phone buzzed with another call. Craig getting back to her.

"Do you have Zoey's phone number?" Faith asked.

"I don't know her phone number, and I have to go," Grace said before hanging up on Faith and accepting her husband's call.

"I just listened to your message," Craig said. "Who is this person?"

"I told you, the woman who moved into Steve Johnson's former home."

"Just tell her no. The neighborhood shouldn't use community funds to drain the pond. It's not meant for swimming."

"I know, but it's not about the cost. That's not the issue here. It's about her attitude and the way we do things—"

Craig interrupted, saying, "Look, Grace, I'm at work. I can't have this conversation now. Can you handle this on your own?" He sounded unusually angry with her.

"Of course I can," she said, surprised at his tone.

Craig hung up without saying goodbye, leaving Grace alone with her seething frustration. She wasn't opposed to having a clean pond. Grace liked everything clean and in order. What she didn't like was Zoey taking over.

After pouring a glass of wine, Grace settled into a chair, determined to concoct a plan to get Zoey Hamilton back in line.

41

Zoey

Then

An icy-cold chill gripped 6613 Mountain Meadows Road and seeped into Zoey's bones. The inspection report mentioned nothing about an ineffective heating system, but now, when the temperatures had dropped and they needed heat, it had stopped working.

Alone in the house, Zoey wore her fleece-lined clogs, sweatpants, a cardigan, and under that, a long underwear top she'd bought for a ski trip a decade ago. She felt like a little old lady who was perpetually cold.

In search of a fix, she descended the creaky stairs into the basement, where the air was even colder than the rest of the house.

Goosebumps prickled her skin as she ventured through the dark rooms. The basement made her think of Steve Johnson and the man cave he'd once wanted. It was hard for Zoey to wrap her head around the fact that no one knew where he was. Maybe he'd never left. What if he was hiding behind a door in the back of the basement right now?

Don't be ridiculous, she told herself. She looked back toward the staircase, wanting to make sure the door remained open, and a shaft of light filtered down.

A shiver rocked her body, and not from the cold. Her eyes darted to the dark corners, and she held her breath, listening for any strange sounds.

Tucked away in a corner, the heating unit emitted a dull hum. Zoey moved closer to inspect it, hoping for a simple solution. Her gaze fell upon a cardboard box in the corner. It wasn't a new one she and Chris had used to transfer their own belongings. This box had been there for years.

Curious, Zoey kneeled down and pulled the object toward her. She blew away the layer of dust coating the surface and lifted the lid, revealing a tall stack of papers. She sorted through the first few. Legal documents. They must have belonged to Steve Johnson.

A single sheet of lined notepaper between the others caught her attention. The paper had figures and question marks scrawled across its surface, accompanied by a handwritten plea: *Find out what happened!* Whoever wrote the message seemed to be puzzled by the figures.

The paper reminded her of the one she'd discovered inside her desk. She took the newfound page upstairs and compared the figures on each. They were the same.

Again, it occurred to her the paper might be evidence. She snapped an image of each document with her phone. After a few minutes of consideration, she called a non-emergency police line. She wasn't sure who she should speak to or what response to expect, but she hoped relaying what she'd found might somehow shed light on what Steve Johnson had done and where he was hiding. Maybe it would help dispel the shadows lurking within her home.

42

Zoey

Then

Zoey's phone remained frustratingly silent. No return call from the HVAC repair company. Not a peep from the police about the mysterious handwritten documents Zoey had sent them. Likewise, her inbox contained no response from Grace about the HOA.

The gas logs she'd purchased sat in their boxes, mocking her inability to start a fire with the quick press of a remote. She eyed them now, her jaw tensing. To hell with waiting on someone else. With the persistent cold inside the house, she planned to take matters into her own hands.

Legs crossed, she settled by the hearth and selected the shortest video tutorial on her phone. She zeroed in on a handsome older man in flannel who showed her how to arrange the logs she'd gathered. In the next video, a gorgeous silver-haired woman talked Zoey through lighting the tinder.

Zoey struck a match, holding her breath as the tiny flame licked at the bundle of newspaper. Smoke hazed the air, but no fire caught.

She tried again, and this time the logs crackled to life. The flames danced, mesmerizing yet precarious. One wrong move and everything could go up in flames. Yet as the fire continued to burn, a new sense of purpose took hold.

Zoey was done with relying on others to fix her problems. She was tired of waiting for responses, solutions, and, above all, for the elusive feeling of control to return. This time, she'd handle things herself.

"I arranged to empty and clean the pond," Zoey told Chris when he got home.

"The neighborhood approved it?" Chris asked, eyeing the plate of food covered in tinfoil she'd left out for him.

"Not exactly. I haven't spoken with them. They were supposed to have treated the problem, but did they? Do we trust them? It will be easier for me in the long run if I make sure it gets done. If we have to pay for it, I'm sure we'll get reimbursed. I mean, it's important. They have to take care of it."

"Not sure it will be that easy, Zoey. The HOA might have to take a vote before they agree to something like this. How much money are we talking about?"

"It's a lot, but we'll get it back. This is really important to me. I miss seeing our dogs swim. I want them to go in the water without getting sick. And I thought we had the money."

"We do have money, but it has its limits. As soon as we find someone to do the house repairs, someone we're comfortable with, we have to take care of them. And fertility treatments can be expensive. Very expensive."

Zoey's face dropped.

Chris sighed and softened his tone. "If we need the treatments, I want to be prepared. Look, if it was our pond, in our backyard, that would be one thing. But Zoey, it's not our pond."

"But it's one of the reasons we moved here. And now we can't even use it?" Zoey asked, her bottom lip quivering.

"I know, and I know this is important to you, and you're upset. But it's not really about the pond, Zoey. It's not. Can you see that?"

Confused, Zoey stared at him. "What else would it be about?"

"Come here." Chris brought her into his arms. "Consider everything we're going through. We've completely changed our lives. You've put your career on hold. There's so much to tackle with the house. We're anxious about starting a family. Susan is still harassing you. God, as I'm saying it aloud, it sounds like too much already. I've been working really long hours. I haven't been around or with you as much as I want. So many things are happening that are out of our control. In all this chaos...maybe it seems like the pond is the one thing you can fix. But your focus on it might be turning into an obsession." His voice was gentle as he asked, "Do you see what I mean?"

Zoey leaned into his shoulder, her breath hitching as she fought back tears. He was right. Things were a mess. She felt lonely. Useless. She was becoming irrationally fixated on something she couldn't have, just like Susan. A bitter thought crossed Zoey's mind—was Chris drawn to women who spiraled into obsession? No, Zoey would not let that happen.

"You might be right," she sniffed, determined to rise above the situation and not let it consume her. The idea of mirroring Susan's path in any way was a fate she desperately wanted to avoid. "It does kind of feel like I'm losing my grip on things."

"I'm sorry. But it will all settle. Let's take a step back, pitch the idea to the neighborhood. See if we can get their support and funding. That way, we don't have to worry about if and when they'll reimburse us. Okay?"

Zoey sighed. "I might've jumped the gun. I already scheduled a company to drain it."

"Call them back and put things on pause until we talk to whoever we need to talk to."

"Okay. I will. I'll call them in the morning."

Chris hugged Zoey tighter and whispered into her ear. "I can think of something that might make you feel better." He planted gentle kisses on her neck, moving down toward her collarbone and the spot where his lips felt almost irresistible. Smiling, Zoey pulled away to take his hand and lead him up to their bedroom. His dinner would have to wait.

43

Zoey

Then

Zoey swiveled from side to side in her chair, gazing into the soot-laden fireplace she needed to clean. If she did nothing at all today except feed her dogs, no one would notice. It hardly mattered if she stayed in bed all day and didn't shower again.

Last night with Chris had been great, but now that he was at work and Zoey was alone again, she felt very much the same. Lonely. Frustrated.

Her husband's words haunted her, challenging her focus. *It's not really about the pond.* Maybe he was right. It wasn't just the pond. Now, rather than moving forward, Zoey obsessed about everything else that was wrong. The list of problems Chris had rattled off yesterday expanded in her mind. Her neighbor, snooty Grace Fairchild, was sending strong vibes that Zoey wasn't welcome. A shortage of handymen had stymied their repair efforts. Progress on the writing front inched along like a snail. But worst of all, her attempts to become a mother had resulted in yet another failure.

All her goals and expectations were reasonable. Yet each one kept slipping through her fingers.

Zoey looked down at her phone, and her frustration hit a new high. Susan had just sent another email. As usual, it came from an address Zoey didn't recognize. A Gmail account with a random mix of letters and numbers. She clicked the message open, her heart quickening in anticipation of what she'd find. As always, the message was curt, but this one was different.

No one wants the pond drained so your filthy dogs can swim in it. Stop pushing back or you'll be sorry.

A sudden, icy chill made Zoey feel feverish. How could Susan possibly know about the pond? Either she was listening in on Zoey's conversations or had hacked into her emails. There was no other way for Susan to know ...unless Chris had told her. Nausea rose from Zoey's stomach. Had Chris betrayed her trust by sharing her problems with Susan?

He had seemed so certain Susan wasn't going to bother them anymore. But he was wrong. Now, with this latest message, Zoey had reason to be angry with Susan *and* Chris.

Zoey knew better than to respond. Countless times she'd been warned engaging with Susan would only worsen matters. Yet Zoey had been holding back since this all started and look where it had gotten her. Susan took breaks but refused to quit, only digging deeper and coming closer. Well, enough was enough, something Zoey should have realized long ago. She refused to cower in silence any longer. At last, she fired back a scathing response.

You're nothing but a sad, desperate loser. You're beyond pathetic. I know all your dirty little secrets. If you threaten me again, you're the one who is going to be sorry.

Even as Zoey's finger went for the send button, she knew she shouldn't, but she pressed it anyway. The impulse to stand up for herself was over-powering, and it felt good to do it. She awaited a response, glaring at her phone, preparing to unleash all the pent-up anger that had simmered beneath the surface for far too long.

The minutes stretched on, and no response came. Zoey waited a bit longer before typing another message.

I've had it with keeping quiet about your despicable behavior. I have all the evidence I need to expose you as the sicko you are. You're going to see how it feels to be humiliated in front of your friends and family.

Zoey remained glued to her phone for half an hour, her muscles tense, her forehead tight as she awaited Susan's reaction. But Susan never responded. Zoey's only message came from Chris, telling her he would be home later than expected, yet again.

Later that evening, Chris arrived home looking exhausted, with dark circles under his eyes, his powerful stride replaced by a weary shuffle. Still, Zoey didn't hesitate to share the latest onslaught from Susan as he entered the kitchen.

"Did you tell your ex- fiancée that I'm having issues coping with our new house and the move? Is that how she knows about the problem with the pond?" Zoey's pitch rose as she spewed questions in a torrent of frustration. "What else did you tell her, Chris? Does she know I can't get pregnant? Because I'm sure she'd love to hear about that! It would fill her sick soul with joy, wouldn't it?"

"What? Zoey...no. I didn't tell Susan anything. I don't share anything about our personal life with her or anyone else. I would never. What's gotten into you?"

"If you didn't tell her, then she either hacked my emails or bugged our house somehow. At this point, I don't even know what's worse." Zoey shook her head, shifting her weight from one foot to the other. "Why won't she just get over it and leave me alone?"

Chris lifted his hands, fingers spread. "Okay, calm down. Now you're sounding paranoid. Let me see your phone."

Zoey thrust it at him. "This isn't the first time she's made a comment about the dogs. She might be the reason they got sick. Maybe the pond was never even the problem."

Chris frowned as he read the messages. "Wait, you responded to her?"

"Yes, I did," Zoey said, making no apologies for finally telling Susan off. In fact, how dare Chris focus on the fact that she responded rather than Susan's relentless harassment.

Chris let out a loud sigh as he set his computer bag down. "Let me take care of this." Rubbing his temples, he walked back outside. Zoey watched from the window. He paced around the front yard, frowning, phone to his ear. He was talking to Susan and didn't want Zoey to hear the conversation, or he wouldn't have left the house.

When he came back inside, he said, "Susan swears she's innocent."

"Innocent? After all she's put me through?"

"That's not what I mean. She insists she didn't send the last message."

"And you believe *her?*"

"It's not about believing her over you, Zoey. I saw the message you got. It just didn't come from Susan."

"Yes, it did! She knows our new address, and she's watching and listening to me! She's not going to stop until I'm dead, and you don't seem to care! You're just worried about poor, crazy Susan getting into trouble!" Zoey turned on her heel and stormed up the stairs. "How can this get any worse?!"

Behind her, Chris called, "Zoey, don't run off," but she kept going.

44

Zoey

Then

Chris had sent an apology text. Zoey had ignored it.

She yearned for just one thing in her new life to fall into place, as it should.

Finch looked up at her, his big round eyes hopeful. He wagged his tail, asking for food, a walk, or to chase a ball a few hundred times.

Zoey tried to shake away her negative thoughts. Nothing good could happen under the weight of her dark mood. She needed to clear her mind. A walk in the fresh air might do the trick. She leashed up Finch and Wren, grabbed her phone, and headed out the backdoor, locking it behind her.

Her mailbox hung open. Someone had placed a folded blue notecard inside. Zoey opened the note and read it.

Hi, Zoey. This is your neighbor, Faith Humphrey. I don't have your email, but I heard you were looking for the contact for our HOA. The company is called Hawthorne Management. Their number is 314-891-0036 and email is Hawthornemanagement@gmail.com.

I'm sorry you didn't have it until now. Hope you are well. Any chance you and your husband could come over for a casual dinner on Saturday night? If not this week, then next Saturday also works for us. It will just be me, my husband Mark, and our daughter Lexi.

Faith had included her email and phone number at the bottom.

Zoey pocketed the note. She appreciated the dinner invitation, though she wasn't going with Chris and pretending to be a happy couple. Not until he agreed to call the police about Susan. At least, finally, she had the HOA information.

In hindsight, it never should have taken so long to get what she needed. It had been a mistake to correspond only with Grace, who had clearly complicated the matter. Zoey didn't know why, and she no longer cared. To hell with Grace Fairchild.

Not wanting to squander another minute, Zoey called the neighborhood's management company. At the beep, she left a message explaining the situation in Mountain Meadows, emphasizing the health hazards posed by the pond. She added the possibility of legal repercussions should the issue go unaddressed, particularly if harm befell an innocent child. She attached links to the articles she'd found about pets and people becoming fatally ill from swimming in contaminated water. But Zoey didn't cancel the pond drainage. Not yet.

The pond cleaning company hadn't set a firm date, mentioning it might be a week or more before they could get out to Mountain Meadows. Now that she'd contacted the HOA and informed them of the cost, maybe they'd grant a quick approval, and she wouldn't have to cancel.

With her dogs leading the way, Zoey took the path from her backyard. When they reached the pond, Finch and Wren clamored toward the water, eager to plunge in.

"Not today. But soon," she told them, with a trace of bitterness. She would not give up until the water was safe enough for them to swim.

The dogs kept pulling, Finch whining in desperation, as if Zoey didn't understand his longing. She understood, and it made her angry. The water was a dangerous biohazard and no one else seemed to care except her. They should care. Everyone who lived in Mountain Meadows should care.

With a conflicted glance at the water, teeming with algae and bacteria invisible to the naked eye, she moved past, toward a trail that crisscrossed the woods.

As Zoey marched along beneath a thick canopy of towering pines, the woods grew denser, and the familiarity of her surroundings blurred. She stopped at a fork in the path, each direction equally unfamiliar. The shadowy trails and trees suddenly all looked the same. She could no longer see mountain tops through the forest. A sinking feeling set in as she realized she might be lost. Anxiety gripped her as she pressed forward, hoping to stumble upon a familiar marker.

A premature darkness had settled over the trails. "A storm must be coming," she muttered, willing herself to stay calm as panic clawed at her nerves. She didn't want to get stranded in the woods amid thunder and lightning. A check of the weather app on her phone proved useless. She had no signal. Had Zoey and Chris not been arguing, she would have told him she was headed for the trails. He'd know where she was should anything happen to her. Now, it wasn't possible to call anyone or send a message.

The wind had strengthened, and the branches swayed. One tree emitted a creaking sound similar to her front door, but louder, longer, and more foreboding. Zoey scanned the forest, praying a tree wasn't about to fall and crush them.

She could turn around now and try to retrace her steps, or she could keep going. Seconds ticked away as she remained in one spot, deciding, her dogs by her side, the woods growing darker.

Desperation propelled Zoey to keep moving, following her dogs. She wished she knew if they were leading her deeper into the unknown or toward the safety of her neighborhood.

The tension in her shoulders lessened when she spotted a painted white square on a tree trunk. She walked with renewed purpose, eager to escape the looming storm.

Zoey relaxed even more when she came around a bend and could make out a corner of the gazebo's green roof in the distance. Not much further and she'd be out of the woods.

A figure draped in a long black raincoat appeared at the end of the trail, face concealed by a hood. Zoey squinted at the mysterious silhouette advancing toward her.

Her fear returned.

45

Victoria

Now

"I've got all our dogs in the car. I've got water for them. You ready to go?" Ned called from the garage.

"Yes. I'm coming."

As Victoria pulled her hiking boots on, her phone buzzed with an incoming call from Payton.

"Something just came in that needs to be included with the Steve Johnston file," Payton said. "It's two handwritten documents. They're not anything that would move the case forward, but I thought you might want to know."

This information surprised Victoria. Someone else was thinking about the Steve Johnson case now? "Who sent the documents?"

"A woman named...hold on, I'm checking..." The sound of Payton typing came through the line. "Her name is Zoey Hamilton."

Victoria let out an incredulous gasp. "Wait. What? Zoey Hamilton is my missing neighbor, the one I told you about."

"Oh, wow. Seriously?"

"Yes. When did she call?" Victoria asked, crouching to lace up her boots.

"Four days ago."

"That was the day before she disappeared. But didn't you say the documents just came in?" Victoria asked, heading through the kitchen.

"What I should have said was the documents just found their way to the correct file. Zoey sent scanned copies. Whoever took her call and accepted the evidence did nothing with it for a few days. The additional evidence just sat on a computer somewhere."

Victoria straightened, looking around the room to make sure she had everything she needed for the hike. "Did anyone follow up with Zoey?"

"Looks like no one did," Payton replied, a note of apology in her voice. "It was before I picked up the case. But I'm looking at the two handwritten documents now. I don't think they warrant any follow up, actually. They're nothing critical. Just wanted you to know."

"Thanks for telling me. It could be relevant to whatever happened to Zoey."

Ending the conversation, Victoria grabbed her water bottle and headed into the garage.

"You all set?" Ned asked.

"Yes. I'm ready, but I'm just going to make one more call." From the passenger seat, she contacted Detective Sullivan and told him about the papers Zoey had found. "They aren't critical evidence of anything, according to my colleague in forensics accounting. But it's the timing that concerns me. Zoey calls this in, and then she disappears. It's a reason to consider that Steve Johnson's disappearance might be the key to finding Zoey."

"Agree. Especially since Chris's ex is no longer a suspect."

Victoria's eyebrows shot up. "She isn't?" She gestured for Ned to start driving, and the SUV began to roll out of the garage.

"The LAPD located Susan," Sullivan said. "She's been tormenting Zoey for years, but she's not responsible for Zoey's disappearance. Susan has an alibi for the past week."

Victoria frowned as she snapped her seatbelt into place. "For the entire week?"

"She's currently checked into a psychiatric facility. Part of her recovery is admitting to wrongdoings. She admitted to everything except for the last threatening message Zoey received."

Victoria leaned forward, her free hand gripping the armrest. "What message?"

"The one that came the day before Zoey disappeared. It was the reason Zoey and Chris were fighting. The message made her think he was sharing things about their new life in Mountain Meadows. Hold on, I've got it here. I'll read it to you." The line went quiet for a moment, filled only by the hum of the SUV's engine. Victoria placed her hand over Ned's. Then Sullivan's voice returned. "This is the message. No one wants the pond drained so your filthy dogs can swim in it. Stop pushing back, or you'll be sorry."

"Another threat? If Susan didn't send it, who did?"

"I'm working on that. We're tracing the IP address."

Victoria's gaze drifted to the passing scenery, her mind racing with questions. "What was Zoey pushing back against?"

"I don't know, but I'll find out."

As Victoria ended the call, she exchanged a meaningful look with Ned. They couldn't afford to let another lead slip through their fingers. It was time to uncover the truth about the shadowy situations in Mountain Meadows.

46

Grace

Now

When Grace got home from Pilates and lunch, everything appeared to be in order. The children were at school, followed by lacrosse practice, and Craig was busy working. Grace could have poured herself a glass of Chardonnay and reclined with her feet up, except for one thing. She couldn't stop thinking about Chris Hamilton, whose wife was still missing, and what he was doing that very minute. His body, his face, even his voice kept popping into her mind. The man was undeniably attractive, even carrying the weight of his current stress. She found his vulnerability appealing.

While at the club, Grace had instructed the chef to pack a gourmet meal for Chris. Now seemed like the perfect moment to bring it to his house and find out how he was doing.

In the Hamiltons' yard, the bird feeders were still up. Grace had half a mind to tear them down herself and stash them in the nearest trash bin. She wanted to, and yet she would never stoop to such low-life criminal behavior. But with Zoey missing, Grace could hardly insist Chris remove the birdfeeders now. She sighed, not knowing how much longer she'd have to endure them.

There was a blue Subaru parked beside the Hamiltons' garage. Yet when Grace rang their doorbell, no one answered. Rather than returning home, she left the packaged meal on the porch and continued her walk.

Mountain Meadows Road didn't have sidewalks. A deep ditch ran down each side of the road to catch the runoff water that poured down from the mountains after heavy rains. Grace had to move off the pavement and onto the Hamiltons' front yard as a large truck approached carrying some sort of construction equipment. Another truck followed close behind, this one carrying an excavator on a flatbed.

Grace frowned as they passed. Despite the sign at the end of the road that said *Private Road, No Through Traffic,* people still made wrong turns and had to drive through the neighborhood before turning around.

Pivoting at the intersection of the main road, Grace headed home. A flock of noisy black birds flew overhead. She wondered if Zoey's feeders attracted them and if they'd pass over Grace's house, defiling her patio furniture with disease-ridden droppings.

Grace realized the trucks had not turned around and come back down the road as she'd expected. They were still somewhere inside the neighborhood. Concerned, she kept walking but found no sign of the trucks near the Nelsons or the Mullers.

Mountain Meadows' stringent bylaws stipulated all work must occur between seven am and five pm. Any use of heavy-duty machinery required a permit and advance notice to residents. Grace bristled at the flagrant disregard for protocol. What if she'd planned an elegant soirée, only to have it ruined by the cacophony of unauthorized construction? The very thought of such discourtesy made her blood simmer.

She continued to fume as she approached her neighbors' properties, checking first at Connor's house, then the Hamiltons'. The trucks weren't at either home.

The package of food she'd left for Chris was still on his porch, making her wonder where he was and when he would come back.

A dull throb began to pulse behind Grace's eyes. The stress of the last few days was taking its toll. She massaged her temples, but the ache only intensified. She needed to lie down and take some pain killers before this turned into a full-blown migraine. With one last glance down the street, Grace headed home, promising herself she'd get to the bottom of this truck situation once she felt better. Self-care always had to come first.

Hours later, when a few pills had taken the edge off her headache, Grace emerged onto her screened-in porch.

A faint mechanical hum came from somewhere in the back of the neighborhood. Determined to uncover the source, Grace checked her reflection, brushed her hair, reapplied her lipstick, and set out to investigate.

The sun dipped low on the horizon, and the shadows of trees stretched across the road as Grace hustled toward the common area. The mechanical noises grew louder. Suddenly, she had a bad feeling about what she might find. "Oh no. She did not. She did not," Grace muttered aloud. Her pulse quickened as she thought of Zoey. But how? Grace tried to stay calm. She didn't know for sure what was happening. Not yet.

When she reached the back of the neighborhood, the trucks were there. Their enormous tires had carved deep tread marks out of the soft earth. A giant hose made a loud sucking sound as it trailed off a truck and into the pond.

Rage exploded inside Grace's chest like fireworks. Planting her hands on her hips, she marched toward a man in overalls with a cigarette dangling from his lips.

"No. No. No. You cannot drain this pond!" she shouted. Even at its loudest, her voice barely cut through the sound of the pump's engine and the squelching water.

The man took a languid drag from his cigarette, his expression calm, indifferent to Grace's boiling fury. "The pond has a bacteria problem. We're gonna drain it today and clean it up tomorrow."

Grace's eyes flared with hostility. "You need to stop right now. Turn off the pump. No one signed off on this!"

He glanced down at her, his gaze dismissive as he blew out smoke and flicked away the ash. "Yeah. The neighborhood did. You'll need to take it up with them." His tone suggested she was nothing more than a trivial inconvenience.

"I am the head of this neighborhood," she hissed, her eyes narrowed to slits. "And I did not approve of this."

The worker shrugged. "I'm not interested in the politics of your neighborhood. We already got our deposit and I'm just doing my job, ma'am."

Unyielding, Grace stomped over to another worker, waving her arms in a determined motion. "Stop what you're doing."

Dismissing her with an odd look and a wave, the worker continued his task.

Aghast at being ignored, Grace got right in his face, shouting, "Stop draining the pond!"

The pump let out a prolonged and grotesque gurgle as it ceased operating.

Finally, Grace thought.

The water level had plummeted, reducing the pond to a nearly empty shell with a giant murky puddle at its center.

The man in the overalls pointed to the water.

At the bottom of the pond, a strange formation of grayish-colored stones lay suspended in the muck. Grace moved forward, craning her neck to make out the details in the twilight.

As the sight sharpened into focus, realization hit her like a slap to the face. It wasn't merely a pile of rocks. At the top of the pile, the smoothest, most easily identifiable object was a skull. A very human-sized skull. Decayed clothing kept the rest of the bones together and partially obscured the skeleton.

Grace's instincts whispered, then screamed, telling her to turn away, to run, but a stronger, invincible force kept her rooted in place, eyes glued to the morbid discovery. Voices shouted around her.

"There's a body!"

"Holy crap! Ain't found nothing like this before."

"Oh, no," Grace murmured, in a daze. Her mouth opened again, but nothing came out. Time blurred as she stood in a suspended moment of horror, only snapping back to reality when a man yelled for someone to call the police.

Grace spun around and fled to the nearest path. Heart pounding, breaking into a sweat, she ran down the trail, muddying her shoes, not stopping until she'd reached her house, where she slammed the door behind her and locked the deadbolt.

47

Victoria

Now

It was dark by the time Victoria got back home, noticed the commotion, and reached the pond on foot. Vehicles filled the circle where she and Ned had parked only four days ago, the first time they'd helped search for Zoey. Yellow police tape cordoned off the path to the pond. A young cop stood by the trail entrance, his arms crossed and legs splayed.

Victoria had come prepared. She lifted the FBI lanyard from her neck, showing it to the rookie cop. He nodded as she ducked under the perimeter.

"What's going on?" she asked.

"Some workers found a dead body in the pond."

Victoria hurried down the trail and past the gazebo. She remembered finding the leashes there and staring at the pond, wondering if Zoey had fallen in. Victoria had dismissed those thoughts when Chris assured her Zoey could swim. Sullivan must have found something that told him otherwise. Something that made him search beneath the water. What had she missed?

Seeing the almost empty pond surprised Victoria. The basin resembled a gaping, muddy crater. An evidence team had set up lights around the shore. Two of the beams converged on a collective point of interest—skeletal remains. Was it Zoey? She'd only been missing a few days, and these remains were mostly bones. Yet there were many ways to desiccate a body and hasten decay.

Victoria moved closer, her eyes on a dark gray rectangular object, the edges and sides sharper and more pronounced than any of the rocks in or around the pond. The object came into focus. It was a cinder block. A rope weaved through an opening in the block, connecting the heavy weight to the skeletal remains.

This death was no accident, but intentional. Murder or suicide.

Victoria spotted Detective Sullivan leaning against a dark sedan. She wove around other officers to reach him. Light from a nearby cruiser cast a bluish-gray sheen over his face. Even with that deathly hue, he looked more alive and energetic than when she'd seen him yesterday, as if this new development had invigorated him.

Sullivan straightened and raised his brows when he saw her. "Agent Heslin. Interesting neighborhood you live in."

"Unfortunately." Victoria blew out her disappointment with a sharp exhale. "What do you know?"

"The remains are male."

She felt some relief with the news, but wanted to be sure the information was accurate. "You're certain? How?"

"Yes, we're certain based on the size and what's left of the clothes. There's a man's belt on the pants. Been underwater at least a few years is what we're currently thinking. Checked the pockets. No wallet. No ID."

"How did you know there was a body in the water?"

Sullivan folded a stick of gum into his mouth. "I didn't know."

"Then why did you have the pond drained?"

"That wasn't me. I spoke with the men who did the work. They don't have information about the person or persons who hired them. I'll get that when I have a chance to speak with their boss." He nodded to acknowledge an officer walking past them, then offered Victoria a piece of gum.

"No, thank you. You should contact Chris tonight. Before he hears about the discovery and jumps to conclusions, someone should let him know it's not Zoey. Spare him some agony."

"I will," Sullivan answered. "I have things to wrap up here first. Do me a favor, would you?"

"What?"

"The workers told me someone made quite the scene while they were working earlier. A woman was yelling at them to stop. She took off when they found the body. Whoever it was, she didn't want the water drained. Can you find her for me?"

48

Victoria

Now

Victoria slipped back under the yellow crime scene tape and headed down a trail. As the glare of lights diminished behind her, she turned on her flashlight. The temperature had dropped several degrees since sunset, leaving her chilled in her jeans and light sweater.

On the path ahead, a figure hurried toward her.

Chris entered the beam of her flashlight, his face filled with fear. He hadn't shaved in days. A dark shadow surrounded his jaw. "I saw the lights. All those police cruisers. What happened? Is it Zoey? Did they find her?"

"No. It's not Zoey."

"It's not? You're sure?"

"I'm sure. They found a corpse, but it's not Zoey."

"You're sure?" he asked again.

"Yes. The remains are male."

"Oh, thank God. Thank God." He leaned over, hands on his knees, and took deep breaths. "How did they find the body? Were they looking for Zoey? Is that what happened? Did they think she might have drowned?"

"Detective Sullivan is at the pond now. Go talk to him."

Chris looked torn. He turned from Victoria to look down the trail toward the common area, then swung his head back. "Sullivan is supposed to be helping, but he's not. He's gone through the timeline of my day again and again, like he expected me to get confused and tell him something different. Zoey and I had a fight, but it wasn't a big deal. We were trying to get pregnant. We wanted a family. Zoey and I love each other. But Sullivan thinks...he thinks I might have taken her."

"Why would he think that?" Victoria asked, wanting to hear Chris's version of the story.

"My ex was harassing us. Sullivan found phone calls from my phone to hers and maybe he thought I was having an affair. I explained I was telling Susan to leave us alone. Zoey wanted me to call the police, but...I don't know. Maybe I should have."

"Is that the only thing he's focused on with you?" Victoria asked, knowing there was more.

Chris frowned. "Someone said Zoey got into my car the day she disappeared. Not my car, exactly, but the same make and color. But it wasn't me. I wasn't home that day."

"You were at work all day?"

Chris nodded. His eyes holding her gaze.

"You never left?"

"I left to do a few errands. I was gone for about an hour. A little over an hour."

"Did anyone see you leave and come back?"

"I don't know. There's a record. I had to swipe a card to get in and out of my parking lot."

Victoria's next question could exonerate Chris or leave him as a potential suspect. "How far is your office from here?"

"About twenty-five minutes."

Victoria studied Chris, letting him do the math and realize the gravity of his situation. Ten minutes might be enough time to make someone disappear.

Chris dropped his head back and let out a loud groan. When he finished, he faced Victoria and said, "I can't believe this is happening. I wish we'd never moved to this damn neighborhood. People disappear here. There are dead bodies in the pond. You have any idea how screwed up that is? I hate this place!"

"Go see Detective Sullivan," Victoria repeated. "It may not seem like it, but he is trying to help you and so am I. We will find Zoey."

Chris hesitated. He sighed. Eventually, he left, walking toward the pond.

Continuing down the path with her flashlight, Chris's outburst replayed in Victoria's mind. At the moment, she shared his sentiments. She wasn't too fond of the troubled neighborhood, either.

"Victoria?"

She whipped around. Chris had doubled back on the path and was coming toward her again.

"Yes?"

"What about you? Are you helping, too? Helping to find my wife."

"Yes. I am."

"Good. I understand you've found missing people before. We need your help. Zoey and I. I was so upset a few minutes ago, thinking they'd found her, I forgot to tell you...Zoey wanted the pond drained and cleaned. She was waiting for the HOA to approve it. Do you think that might have something to do with her disappearance?"

49

Victoria

Now

U nder the carriage lights in the Fairchilds' foyer, Grace appeared pale, her jaw set in a tight line. "Back again so soon? Is this an official visit, or are you still just a concerned neighbor?" She lowered her eyes to the FBI lanyard draped around Victoria's neck.

"Both. Until we've figured out what's going on in Mountain Meadows. You were at the pond earlier today while it was being drained, weren't you?"

"Yes. I went for a walk and heard the racket. I was there when they discovered what appeared to be a corpse."

"It was."

"Oh, my God. I thought so. Do they think it's....do they think it's Zoey?"

"No," Victoria answered. "The remains are male."

Grace looked surprised, but then seemed to find her voice. "It's absolutely horrible and frightening. So close to home. I walk around that pond. So do my children." Grace turned and headed deeper into her home, beckoning for Victoria to come along. "Let's talk inside. I'll make drinks."

From the scent of liquor emanating from Grace's breath, it wasn't her first drink of the evening.

Victoria followed Grace into the sleek kitchen. She opened a glass cabinet stocked with premium spirits.

"I heard you tried to stop the pond from being drained. Why?" Victoria asked.

"Care for a gin martini? Or perhaps vodka?"

"I'll pass, thanks. I'm more interested in the pond situation."

With a slight tremor betraying her composure, Grace poured a clear liquid into two glasses, preparing drinks despite Victoria's refusal.

"Grace?" Victoria asked.

Setting a glass before Victoria, Grace finally spoke. "Protocols, Victoria. There are protocols. No one approved the drainage work. Zoey Hamilton must have taken it upon herself. She's been complaining about the pond water since her arrival."

"So, you were aware Zoey wanted the pond drained and cleaned?"

Grace nodded.

"Did you know there was a body in the pond?" Victoria asked, studying Grace's reaction.

Grace froze, her glass inches away from her lips. She lowered her drink with a deliberate slowness. "Are you really asking me that question?" Her voice had climbed an octave.

Victoria returned Grace's fierce gaze with one of her own, but she kept her voice calm. "Yes. Is there a problem with answering?"

Grace scoffed. "This may not be official business entirely, as you say, but I'm not certain I should answer such a question without having my attorney present."

Victoria held her silence, letting it stretch between them. She used the weight of expectation to her advantage, forcing Grace to fill the void.

"We've known each other since we were children. Our parents were close. My mother only has the best things to say about yours and was devastated over her tragic death. Really, Victoria?"

"Really," Victoria answered, unwavering.

Grace exhaled with a sharp force. "Of course, I had no idea. Why would I? How could I?" Grabbing the decanter, she poured herself another drink and downed it in quick gulps.

"Who else knew about Zoey's plans to empty the pond besides you?"

"Several people were aware of what she wanted to do. Faith, for one. I confided in her, partly seeking advice, partly because Zoey's impatience and insistence were becoming unbearable. As I told you, there are proper channels for these things. I also contacted our HOA representative. His name is George, if you don't already know. But it's Zoey who told people about the issue. She had discussions about the pond with numerous individuals outside our community. Water testing facilities. Pond maintenance companies. Who knows who else? She might have told every single person in the neighborhood, for all I know."

The implications were clear: Zoey's plans had circulated widely and might have fallen into the wrong hands. And yet, the information didn't necessarily need to travel far to reach someone with malicious intentions. Someone who, perhaps, didn't want the pond to give up its secrets.

50

Victoria

Now

A large whiteboard with notes and timelines dominated one side of Detective Sullivan's office and served as the focal point for information on Zoey's case. Seated by the display, wearing a sports coat with jeans, Sullivan handed Victoria a report.

"What's this?" she asked.

"Coroner's report. We got the confirmation on the body from the pond. It's Steve Johnson. Perfect match to his dental records."

"Wow. That was fast."

"I called in a favor. Said it might impact Zoey's case. A forensic anthropologist measured the rate of decomposition, aquatic insect activity, and the condition of the remains. All of it points to approximately five years underwater."

Victoria opened the file, scanning the contents. "Five years. That's when he supposedly disappeared. Instead, he's been in Mountain Meadows all this time."

"And millions of dollars might remain hidden in an offshore account until the end of time because no one but Steve knows where it is."

"Someone strangled him," Victoria said aloud as she scanned another section of the report.

"Yes. Fractured hyoid bone. Then the killer tied a cinder block to the remains. Crude but effective. It worked."

Victoria considered the implications. The presence of the block ruled out the possibility of an accident. The broken hyoid bone now made suicide extremely unlikely.

"He was murdered," Sullivan said. "The question is, by whom?"

"The report lists no other bone trauma. No gunshot wound. No evidence of a head injury. That suggests a considerable amount of force was needed to subdue and strangle him, and to dump his body into the water. It's likely his killer was also male."

"Right. Though the killer could have drugged him first. You're lucky you moved here after he disappeared or we'd be investigating you, too."

"Had I known there was a cadaver in the pond, I might not have been so taken by the neighborhood. But listen, did Chris tell you Zoey wanted the pond drained?"

"Yes, and I confirmed she paid the deposit for the work. As far as her husband knows, she never suspected there was a dead body under the water, and neither did he. The pond contained toxic algae and bacteria. Not sure if a decomposing body contributed to the issue or not, but the water was contaminated. That was Zoey's sole reason for wanting the pond drained and cleaned."

"And whoever killed Johnson would have a good reason to prevent that from happening," Victoria said, stating the obvious.

"It's a private pond in the back of a neighborhood. Not many people know it's there, which makes your neighbors the primary suspects for Johnson's murder. Particularly the woman who was out there shouting and waving for the workers to stop."

"Could be someone who works in the neighborhood. There are a lot of options there. Most residents have services coming in and out on a daily or weekly basis. But I agree with you about Grace Fairchild. Her behavior makes her look very suspicious."

Victoria shared her recent conversation with Grace and explained Grace's objections to the pond being drained—the matter of "protocols."

Sullivan raised his brows. "You believe her?" he asked, leaning forward and resting his elbows on his desk.

"I'm not sure." She believed Grace was confident and self-righteous enough to lie straight to someone's face and do a good job of it.

Sullivan nodded. "Well, I'm working the cases as if they're connected now, and I hope they are. I'd hate to think these are just random incidents. But if there is a connection, it doesn't bode well for Zoey's well-being."

Rising from her seat, Victoria silently agreed, though she was still intent on finding Zoey safe and sound.

Victoria left Sullivan's office, thinking about Mountain Meadows and how one neighbor's death might have led to another's disappearance.

51

Zoey

Now

A pitiful whimper escaped Zoey.

Where am I?

What happened?

Her mind lurched from one fragmented thought to another in a fog of confusion. A gag covered her mouth. She could only breathe shallow gasps through her nostrils. Steady pain hammered her skull, pounding in sync with the throbbing inside her bound wrists and ankles.

The dark space had no windows, but it was climate controlled, not too hot nor too cold. It smelled clean. She detected a lemon scent, maybe a disinfecting product. Occasionally, weird noises came from the floor above her—a mechanical whirring and sporadic thuds.

Why would someone take me? What's going to happen next? Is Chris looking for me?

She tried to piece together how she ended up in this nightmare. Her desperate attempts led nowhere. Nothing was clear. Nothing made sense. It was all disjointed and vague.

Amidst her terror, it was a tiny relief to find her clothes still on. She wasn't seriously injured as far as she could tell, though her muscles screamed from being tied up.

She writhed against her bindings; the friction rubbing her skin raw. The more she panted and struggled, the more her head hurt. There was something on her arm, something that didn't belong there, causing a tight sensation on her skin. It wasn't large. A square-sized shape, an inch or two on each side. A bandage?

Who did this? Was it Susan? Did she go from slander and threats to physical violence?

A door opened behind Zoey, the noise so soft and smooth she might have missed it if there had been anything other than silence and darkness around her. She craned her neck to turn around, but couldn't see who had come in.

Shafts of light came through the open door, allowing her to see more of her surroundings. A cement floor. Not plain but polished and tinted to look industrial chic or modern. A large plush sofa against one wall. Built in cabinetry against another. An enormous television. No personal items or decor.

Even in her groggy state, pure terror coursed through her veins. Every cell in her body screamed with a primal urge to flee, yet she could do nothing more than crane her neck toward the footsteps approaching from behind her.

Was this the end? Was she about to be killed? Tortured? Tears cascaded down her cheeks and over her gag. A convulsive shudder wracked her body.

The footsteps stopped right behind her. The sound of quick breaths reached Zoey's ears, mirroring her own fear. She cringed, bracing herself for what was to come.

Her captor snarled. "What the hell am I going to do with you?"

The words floated to Zoey's ears, muffled and distant, as if she were underwater.

Suddenly, she felt a sharp tug on her arm as the foreign object ripped off her body. It left behind a stinging sensation, quickly replaced by the pressure of another material being pressed against her skin.

The room seemed to spin. Every muscle in her body relaxed involuntarily and her thoughts dissolved. Her eyelids grew heavy, drooping shut as if weighted down.

She was floating, untethered from time and place, until she succumbed to nothingness.

52

Victoria

Now

The scant facts surrounding Steve Johnson's disappearance replayed on a maddening loop in Victoria's mind during the drive to meet his wife. For five agonizing years, Sarah had clung to hope, only to have it cruelly extinguished by the discovery of her husband's body. Victoria's chest tightened at the thought of half a decade suspended in limbo, frozen between dreading the worst and desperately wishing for his safe return.

The FBI's inadequate initial investigation was partly responsible for Sarah's torment. Now they had a second chance to uncover the truth, pursue justice, and perhaps offer her a semblance of closure. Victoria gripped the steering wheel, fresh determination steeling her resolve.

The journey stretched for over an hour along country roads. Brilliant fall leaves lined the route, a fiery kaleidoscope of reds, oranges, and yellows vivid against a dreary, steel-gray sky.

From the moment Sarah Johnson came to the door of her modest two-story home, Victoria sensed the woman's resentment.

In the living room, Sarah sat motionless on a well-worn sofa, her eyes fixed on a spot somewhere beyond the room's walls. She clasped her hands tightly in her lap. Sarah had just turned fifty. She looked much older.

Victoria took a seat across from her. "I'm so sorry for your loss."

"You're too late," Sarah said, her words tinged with bitterness.

Everyone dealt with grief differently, and Sarah might have good reason to be disappointed with law enforcement.

"Steve was a good man," Sarah continued. "We'd struggled in the past, financial troubles, medical bills... but we'd just gotten back on our feet. I was about to start a job teaching high school science. We had plans, dreams." Tears streamed down her cheeks, but her red-rimmed eyes blazed with anger. "Tell me this. Is it normal for the police and the FBI to screw up so badly? Right from the beginning, they just believed he was guilty. I even heard an officer say Steve was an attorney, and most attorneys are crooked."

Victoria's anger rose at the way law enforcement had handled the initial investigation. So poorly, it didn't make sense unless parts were missing from the file. "We have another opportunity to find out what really happened. Can you please tell me anything you remember about the days before Steve disappeared?" she asked, her pen poised over her notepad.

"I wasn't home. I was visiting my sister. Steve told me he had a work emergency. That was at night, and the last time I heard from him."

Victoria chose her words carefully. "What can you tell me about The Magnolia Estates Fund?"

"Nothing you can't read about online. Steve never talked about work issues because of attorney-client privileges and because he had a hard-fast rule about not letting his work spill over into our marriage. Unfortunately, I was never aware who he worked with or how he got involved with Magnolia Estates. I tried to find out but couldn't get answers once the investigation started."

Victoria tilted her head, her gaze intent on Sarah's face. "Steve was an investor in the fund, wasn't he?"

"No. Not really. Not like the other investors. We didn't have the money for extra things like that. Our next priority was to fix up our house. It needed a lot of work when we bought it."

"Then...how did Steve get involved?"

"He was initially brought in to help with a few legal issues. The problems kept coming. As payment for his services, we were given a land parcel in Magnolia Estates. He thought he'd be able to sell it for a good amount once the houses were built. That's all I know. If only he hadn't gotten involved," Sarah continued, her voice a mix of sorrow and fury.

Victoria reached out, placing a comforting hand on Sarah's. "I promise you, Mrs. Johnson, I want to find out the truth about what happened to your husband."

"What about the black Range Rover? Did anything ever come of the tip?" Sarah asked. "Someone claimed they saw Steve getting into one. It would have been the same day when he stopped responding to my calls and texts. The day he disappeared. There are a lot of black Range Rovers out there, but a man on our street had one. I asked him myself, but he denied even being in town when Steve disappeared."

Victoria had seen nothing in the FBI's case file about Steve getting into a vehicle. "Do you know who saw him?"

Sarah shook her head.

Another anonymous tip, perhaps. Maybe the police didn't consider it credible. Connor Rhodes drove a black Range Rover now. But did he have it when Steve disappeared?

Victoria said goodbye to Sarah and headed back to her car. Many loose ends were left dangling all those years ago. This time, Victoria vowed, things would be different. Questions about what happened to Steve Johnson demanded answers. Victoria had to make sure those answers came in time to help Zoey.

53

Victoria

Now

Ned had beaten Victoria home from her visit with Sarah. His SUV was in the garage. The moment she stepped through the back door, three of her dogs bounded over, tails wagging furiously in greeting. She secured her gun in the safe before one of them knocked it loose.

Noise filtered to her from the kitchen, a drawer opening, followed by the dull thud of it closing. Ned looked up as she entered. His face brightened upon seeing her. "Just got back from the clinic," he said, as if the scrubs he still wore weren't a telltale sign of how he'd spent his afternoon. "I was hoping you took some time to relax today."

Victoria managed a slight smile as she set her keys on the counter and told him where she'd been.

"Is that going to help find Zoey?" he asked, carrying a large Tupperware container of homemade dog food to the counter.

"It might."

"Any new leads?" he asked.

"Not yet. Not that I'm aware of."

Just like that, the mood in their kitchen turned solemn. It gave Victoria a moment to appreciate what she had—her partner was alive and well at home. A luxury neither Sarah Johnson nor Chris Hamilton could claim.

The heavy silence stretched until Ned finally cleared his throat. "Dinner thoughts? Because I was thinking we could try the new pasta recipe I bookmarked."

She mustered another half-smile, squeezing his arm in silent gratitude. "Sounds perfect. But let me power through some work first."

"Go ahead. I'll make dinner."

Before heading to her office, Victoria helped him feed the dogs. The gentle clinking of bowls and opening of containers filled the kitchen. The sound usually summoned a chorus of eager barks and thumping tails, but only three of the dogs showed up to wait expectantly for their dinner.

Victoria's brow furrowed. "Where are the rest of them?" That's when she realized the entire pack hadn't rushed to greet her when she'd come in a few minutes ago. Even if they'd been in the yard, they usually raced inside through the dog door at the sound of her car, and none of her dogs ever wanted to miss a meal.

Panic edged Victoria's voice as she went out into the backyard, calling for her dogs. Those calls were met with silence.

She had a bad feeling when her phone rang.

"It's Grace. There was a dog in my yard a minute ago, running through my flower beds. I think it's one of yours—white with brownish spots."

Victoria felt another wave of fear settle over her as she pictured sweet, goofy Oliver. "Thank you for calling, Grace. We'll be right there."

Grace let out a huff. "It's not here anymore. It already ran off."

"Okay. Did you see which way he went?" Victoria asked.

"No. Sorry."

Victoria turned to Ned. "Somehow, they got out of the yard."

Ned cursed, already heading to the back door.

They didn't have time to ponder the hows and whys; they had four dogs to find. Grabbing leashes, treats, and a can of sardines—irresistible to their greyhounds—Victoria and Ned rushed outside.

Fortunately, Mountain Meadows Road had minimal traffic. At least one dog had headed deeper into the neighborhood rather than toward the main crossroad, and they usually traveled in a pack.

Greyhounds had thin skin, easily torn if they ran through the woods or nipped at each other. That's why they wore muzzles at the racetracks and when they played together. The dogs were vulnerable and yet they also posed a danger to smaller animals because of their strong prey drive. If anyone in the neighborhood had an outdoor cat, it would become a target the moment the greyhounds spotted it. Victoria wasn't sure what the dogs would do if they caught an animal, and she didn't want to find out.

Before Ned and Victoria reached the far end of the backyard, she saw a gate was open. When they got closer, she spotted the large rock preventing it from closing.

Ned looked furious as he scanned the adjacent path. "What the hell?"

Victoria felt as if she'd just received a gut punch. Someone had trespassed on the private trail leading to their property, unlocked the gate, and intentionally propped it open.

A phone rang again. Victoria checked her pocket, but this time, it was Ned's.

He listened, then said, "Thank you. Can you try to grab them?" He turned to Victoria. "That was Chris. Three dogs are at his house. Let's go."

They sprinted to Chris's house, neither speaking. When they got there, Chris had corralled three dogs on his porch. Myrtle limped, Oliver had blood on his legs, and Izzy's sides heaved as she panted, but all three seemed thrilled to see their owners.

Victoria told Chris about the gate.

"That's horrible. Well, glad I could repay the favor and for all you're doing to help," Chris said, as he and Ned set out to catch one more dog.

At home, Victoria cleaned Oliver's cuts and then paced the house. When Ned returned with Godiva, Victoria could barely contain her relief.

Ned unzipped a bag of his veterinary supplies. "Godiva needs a few stitches, but otherwise, she's okay. I found her on Connor's back porch. She probably got tired and wanted to lie down somewhere."

As Ned treated the dogs' minor injuries, he voiced what they were both thinking.

"That was strange. Someone intentionally let our dogs out. Who would do that? And why?"

54

Grace

Now

G race pursed her lips in distaste as one of Victoria's greyhounds raced across the grass and stopped to sniff in the flower beds. Honestly, was it too much to ask for a little common courtesy from one's neighbors?

Grace let out an exasperated sigh. She supposed she ought to make Victoria aware her dog was running amok. It was the neighborly thing to do, though it interrupted Grace's current plans. Her neighbors kept proving to be utterly exhausting.

After calling Victoria, Grace got back to her own business. She stood at the top of the basement stairs, one hand clutching the banister, and called down to her husband. "Craig, darling, I need to talk to you."

After a prolonged silence, Craig's muffled voice floated up. "What is it?"

"Please come upstairs so I don't have to shout." Rarely did Grace venture into the large basement, not since the children had outgrown the play-room. Nor did she *need* to go down, since they had a wine storage room upstairs as well. Tucked away in a corner of the basement was a panic room she couldn't recall ever entering, though she supposed the hope for all panic rooms was that they remain unused. Unlike Grace, Craig frequented the basement room with the bar and television whenever he wanted time to himself, which was increasingly often.

Craig finally emerged, trudging up the stairs with a full glass of scotch in hand.

"I'd like to talk to you about this." Grace thrust a glossy brochure for Lakeside Estates at him. "My father was asking me some questions about the development. During the conversation, he mentioned most of the lots were still available."

Craig barely looked at the brochure. "Not all of them."

"Just how many have sold?"

"Three," Craig said before taking a few generous swallows of his drink.

Grace's eyes widened in disbelief. "Three? But that's... how can only three lots have sold?" She lowered her voice. "Is it because of what Steve Johnson did?"

"No."

"Then how could this have happened? Is there a group blocking the development? Is it the location?"

Craig swirled the ice in his glass. For a few seconds, the clink of cubes filled the tense silence. "It's not any of those things. I'm doing everything I can, Grace, but I can't control the market. The demand isn't what we were told to expect in our last market analysis. Interest rates are up. People are holding on to their money or investing it elsewhere right now. It's just a down phase."

Grace stared at him, her brow furrowed. "All right, but what I really don't understand, the reason I'm confused, is because when I look at the pamphlet, it says there are only two lots left."

"Well, yeah. Obviously, that's a marketing tactic."

Grace wasn't sure what to say. "Perhaps I should be more involved in what you're doing from now on. I put a brochure in the welcome basket I gave the Hamiltons when they moved here, though I doubt they can even afford a vacation home. But I was trying to help you. I could do more of that."

Craig downed the last of his scotch, avoiding Grace's questioning gaze. "While I appreciate your offer to help, it's not necessary. I'm on it. I'm working on adjusting our sales strategies and offering incentives to potential buyers."

Grace couldn't understand how he could be so calm about something so important—their financial well-being. She tried to keep the panic from creeping into her voice. "Okay, well, when were you going to do those things? Because if sales continue like this, won't it affect our finances? After Magnolia Estates, and what happened with Steve, I assumed the success of Lakeside Estates was critical."

"It is. We need the lots to sell. We need people to start building. In the meantime, our financial situation is fine. We're fine."

Grace tilted her head, eyes narrowed. "Really?"

Craig held up his hand, counting off on his fingers with exaggerated patience. "You just bought a new car, redid the kitchen, and pre-paid for a spa retreat with the cosmetic surgeon. I also saw you booked a trip to Italy."

"Yes, I forgot to tell you about the trip. We haven't been there since we took the children when they were young. I thought it would be nice for all of us."

Craig nodded, slowly. "When have you ever had to worry about money, Grace?"

"Never. That's the point. I certainly don't want to start now. Not at my age."

"You don't have to. I'm on top of everything, and I'll find a solution. I always do." He turned and went back down to the basement, leaving Grace alone, a little confused and unnerved by their conversation. With all that was going on in the neighborhood, she didn't need this extra source of stress.

55

Victoria

Now

Now that her dogs were back and Ned was tending to Godiva's wounds, Victoria could focus on other things. She fired up her laptop and found a message from Payton with the requested information. A list of the investors in the Magnolia Estates project.

Victoria's gaze sharpened when she scanned the list and familiar names leapt out at her: Mark and Faith Humphreys. Connor Rhodes. Three of her current neighbors had put money in the development and then lost their investments. Were any of them angry enough to murder Steve?

Remembering the tip Sarah mentioned, Victoria accessed the DMV database. Five years ago, Connor Rhodes had indeed owned the black Range Rover he had now.

As an investor in the Magnolia Estates Community, could Connor have taken matters into his own hands upon discovering Steve's betrayal? Was Connor capable of strangling the person who had wronged him? If he were guilty of criminal actions, wouldn't the FBI have uncovered evidence of his wrongdoing in the initial investigation? They might have, *if* they'd conducted the investigation in a thorough manner, which they had not.

If Connor was responsible for Steve Johnson's murder, was he also responsible for Zoey's disappearance?

Victoria was deciding on her next steps when Chris called.

"I found something I need you to see."

"What did you find?"

"I have to show you. Just come. Hurry." His breathless reply carried new urgency. "I'm in Connor Rhodes' backyard."

"What are you doing there? Is he with you?"

"I found something when I was here, helping to corral your dogs. I came back to check it out. Please. Hurry!"

The line went dead before she could probe further.

Victoria rose from her chair. She still didn't know what was going on, and she didn't want anyone else getting hurt.

"I have to go," she said, giving Ned a brief overview of the call from Chris as she grabbed her keys once more and headed out.

Ned looked worried. "I'm almost finished with Godiva's stitches and then I can go with you."

"No. It's okay. Take your time and finish up. I'll be fine. I should be right back."

"Okay," he said. "Be careful."

She unlocked the safe by the door, grabbed her gun, and hurried into the garage.

On the drive, she had time to wonder what Chris had found that required an urgent visit to Connor's house at night.

Victoria parked her Suburban a short distance away from Connor's property, her instincts screaming at her to approach with caution based on the suspicions she now harbored. She walked through Connor's yard as if it was a common property, neither using the trees as cover nor announcing her presence. The moon cast long, haunting shadows across the ground, turning tall bushes into lurking figures. As she rounded the back of the house, someone emerged from the shadows.

"Over here. This way," Chris called.

She followed him deeper onto the property.

Chris stopped beside a tarp covering a large mound. He flicked his flashlight on. "Look what I found under here."

Bright lights burst on all around the house, cutting through the darkness.

Connor Rhodes stood on his back deck; his silhouette framed by the floodlights. "I've already called the police! Get off my property now!"

"It's me, Victoria Heslin," she yelled back.

Connor moved toward them on his deck. "What the hell are you doing in my backyard?"

"Did you really call the police?" Victoria asked.

Connor hesitated before answering. "No. But I was about to."

Chris emerged from the shadows and stormed toward Connor. "What have you done with my wife? What did you do to Zoey?"

Connor held his ground. "Whoa, buddy. I told you I don't know where your wife is."

Victoria rushed to get ahead of Chris and hold him back. He was in a desperate state, and he might have a weapon. "Chris, let me handle this, please."

"He's the one who dumped a body in the pond," Chris yelled. "He did it. And he must have done something to Zoey to stop her. He must have known she was going to drain it."

"That's absurd. None of that is even remotely true." Connor tossed his head back as if he were laughing. "You need to calm down, buddy. You're out of your mind right now."

"Look at this," Chris shouted. He veered off, out of Victoria's grip, heading toward the piles of building materials. Crouching near the ground, he pulled back the tarp and shone his flashlight on what lay beneath—cinder blocks, dozens of them.

56

Victoria

Now

The wind gusted through the trees, amplifying the tense scene playing out behind Connor's house.

"What's going on? What did you find back there?" Connor shouted.

Ignoring Connor for the moment, Victoria tried to reason with Chris. "Anyone can have cinder blocks."

"Yeah, but not everyone who has them lives near a pond with a dead body tied to one," he shot back.

"This is not how we handle potential evidence, Chris. You need to go home." She worried the cinder blocks would be inadmissible because of the way they'd discovered them.

"Do I need to call the police?" Connor shouted.

"Yes!" Chris yelled back, his voice low and powerful. "Tell them to get over here now and search every inch of your home."

"Look, I don't know what you're talking about, but I haven't done anything wrong," Connor said. "Get a hold of yourself before you say or do something you'll regret."

"Let me handle this," Victoria told Chris. "I'm going to talk to Connor. Go home for now. Please."

"He might have Zoey," Chris shouted. "What if he does?"

Victoria placed her hand on his arm and felt tremors coursing through his body.

Chris stared at her. "I'm not sure who to trust right now. You could all be in on this together."

"You can trust me, Chris. I'm a federal agent and I didn't move to this neighborhood until after Steve disappeared."

Chris let out a long breath. Muscles quivered in his neck. "If he hurt her, I will..."

"I know. Let me take care of this," Victoria said.

Chris stared at her a few seconds longer before his gaze swung to Connor. Finally, Chris left, each step heavy with torment. Victoria understood the feeling. She could empathize with his rage. She was prepared for him to spin around and return at any second, but he kept walking. She watched him until he disappeared into the darkness.

Victoria considered telling Ned what she was doing and decided not to. If the situation turned dangerous, she didn't want her fiancé walking into it. Instead, she sent Detective Sullivan a quick summary of the situation before approaching Connor and entering his house.

———

Inside his spacious kitchen, Connor's tone contrasted with his shouts from only moments ago. "Would you like some tea? I have a special blend of Jasmine Pearls. It's soothing, and I think that's what we need right now."

Victoria nodded, all her senses still on high alert.

Connor pressed a button on a sleek contraption that boiled the water. He moved with a certain grace and deliberateness as he fetched a clear glass teapot and an ornate tin. He carefully measured the tea on a spoon.

"The thing about Jasmine Pearls," he said, his attention moving from Victoria to the tea, "is that you need to give them time and space to unfurl."

He poured hot water over the leaves. "The water should be just the right temperature, steaming but not bubbling."

A floral aroma filled the kitchen as the pearls slowly opened and the leaves unfurled inside the teapot. The process seemed to have a calming effect on Connor, and Victoria seized the opportunity to press him.

"Just how mad were you at Steve Johnson when he made off with your money?"

Connor stared at the tea leaves before he answered. "Yesterday, when I learned his body was in our pond, I was surprised. That transcended any anger I might have harbored back then. But in all honesty, I'm not sure I ever felt any intense anger toward Steve. What would it get me?" Creases formed across Connor's forehead as he carefully placed the lid on the teapot. "We have to let the tea steep now. It will only be a few moments."

"You weren't angry about losing hundreds of thousands of dollars?"

"About two hundred thousand, to be exact." He fetched two cups from an overhead cabinet, setting them down with a soft clink on the countertop. "I've lost money on investments before. There's always a risk."

"But embezzlement? That's not the type of risk people usually factor in, is it?" she asked.

"No. It's not. That sort of thing rarely happens outside of the movies. I was out of the country when everything went down. Came back to find a neighbor on the run, which is what everyone thought, and my investment vanished. I believe my initial reaction was disbelief. I wondered how anyone could think they would get away with such a thing."

Connor poured the pale, golden tea into two cups and pushed one toward Victoria. "It's ready," he said, offering a small smile.

Victoria reached past the offered tea for the one behind it. Warmth spread into her palms as she grasped the cup, waiting for Connor to take a drink before she did the same.

"You don't trust me, do you?" He looked hurt for an instant but smiled before taking several sips of his tea.

Victoria stayed silent, prompting him to continue.

"Magnolia Estates seemed doomed soon after I invested. There were legal battles, cost overruns. The project started bleeding money on law-suits." Connor lifted his eyes skyward and sighed. "Steve was almost a saint with how he tried to salvage the project. Charged next to nothing for his legal work, so the costs didn't eat right through the development's fund. I always thought he took the money as compensation for his efforts, for all the hours he put into trying to save that development, and I can't say I blamed him. My real issue was with the Fairchilds."

Victoria tried not to let her surprise show. "The Fairchilds? Why?" she asked, leaning in slightly.

"They're the ones who roped me into investing, promising big returns once the community was developed. Grace came over with a brochure, talking the place up like it was going to be the most wonderful new com-munity on the planet. Craig was supposed to be overseeing the funds, ensuring our investment was safe. The way I see it, his negligence was as bad as the theft."

"I just read over the FBI's files on Steve Johnson's case. The Fairchild name isn't mentioned anywhere."

"Really?" He laughed. "I assure you it was their development. But I'm not surprised they managed to get their names scrubbed from the records. Wouldn't want to scare off future investors with such a colossal oversight on their hands. But how would they...ah...I know how. Grace's father,

George Stanford. He was the governor then, and he's never had my vote. That man will do whatever it takes to make things go his way. He could have bribed someone, even the FBI. Granting favors and promises to erase names from records, limit an investigation, all to ensure his daughter and son-in-law were no longer associated with such a disaster."

It was certainly possible, but Victoria refrained from offering an opinion on Connor's statement. If the Fairchilds had indeed managed to cover their tracks, she wondered just how deep their deception ran.

Connor's gaze hardened. "I took the write off on my taxes and tried to forget about the loss, but it's the reason I want nothing to do with the Fairchilds. Funny thing is, no one ever questioned me regarding the investment or what I thought of the situation."

"Not the police? Not the FBI?"

"No one. Guess they either had more important matters to deal with or, like I suggested, Governor Stanford swept the whole fiasco away." Connor took another sip of his tea. "I've told you the truth and I have nothing to hide, but I think I better give my attorney a call, just in case."

Victoria nodded. "Yes. I think that's in your best interest."

She was determined to get to the bottom of the matter with Steve Johnson, and even more pressing, she was desperate to help locate Zoey. Victoria wouldn't spare anyone, no matter how much she might like that person, not until the full truth was exposed.

"Are you going to try your tea?" Connor asked.

"Thank you very much, but I'm just not thirsty right now." Like Chris, she still wasn't sure whom she could trust.

57

Victoria

Now

Victoria left Connor's house, processing the information she'd just gathered from him about the Fairchilds' involvement in Magnolia Estates. As she walked, she dialed Detective Sullivan, knowing he'd pick up even at this odd hour. She told him about the cinder blocks in Connor's backyard and the tip from Sarah Rhodes regarding a black Range Rover.

"Connor lost a lot of money because of Steve. That's a motive for the murder. As we speak, I'm sure he's calling his attorney. Can you get a warrant, then get an evidence team to his address? Have them compare the blocks in his backyard to the one found with Johnson's remains."

"I'll get on it."

Victoria also told Sullivan what she'd learned about the Fairchilds. "I need to talk to them and hear their side of the story."

"I'd meet you there, but I can't right now."

Victoria shifted in the driver's seat, ready to get out of the vehicle. "I can handle it."

"Agree. Anything else?"

"Yes. We have to watch Chris. I'm worried he's feeling increasingly helpless, and he suspects Connor is guilty of something. The last thing we want is for him to go vigilante on us."

"I'll check in with him."

"Okay," she said, her hand on the door's latch. "I'll update you later tonight if I learn anything worth mentioning."

Leaving her SUV where she'd parked in front of Connor's house, Victoria headed down the road to see the Fairchilds. The wind blew dried leaves across the pavement, and above her the branches of an oak tree swayed and scraped against each other. As Victoria walked, she called Agent Payton Jennings and left a message.

"Hi, Payton. I need a favor." Victoria explained what she'd learned from Connor. "When you have a chance, can you search for information on the Fairchilds? Anything pertaining to their involvement with Magnolia Estates or other neighborhood developments."

Victoria's running shoes barely made a sound on the stone walkway as she approached the Fairchilds' front door. Since her visit three days ago, someone had replaced the yellow mums with rust-colored flowers and green and white gourds. The new autumnal display reminded Victoria time was marching on, and yet they still hadn't located Zoey. Each passing day diminished their chances of finding her alive and well. The urgency of the situation bore down on Victoria with renewed intensity.

Squaring her shoulders, Victoria rang the doorbell. She waited, scanning the darkened windows for movement. After a prolonged silence, she tried again, peering through the beveled glass panels. The house appeared empty.

As she turned to head back, a few drops of rain fell, and she thought of the umbrellas she'd left behind in her SUV.

Another SUV was coming down Mountain Meadows Road toward her. The Jeep Wagoneer slowed as it approached and pulled up to the curb. Victoria waited as the back door swung open. The Fairchilds' teenage son climbed out wearing a sports uniform with a backpack slung over one shoulder and a lacrosse stick protruding from the top.

The SUV drove off, and the boy walked toward her.

"Hi. We met the other day when you skipped practice to help search the trails. Handford, right? I'm Victoria."

Handford's eyes narrowed as he looked her up and down, a smirk tugging at the corner of his mouth. In that instant, he looked very much like his mother. "Yeah. I know who you are. The famous FBI agent. Didn't expect you to be so..." He trailed off, apparently unable to find the right words to articulate his thoughts, and settled for a dismissive shrug.

Victoria held his gaze, undeterred by his suggestive tone, though it was a little disturbing coming from a kid. "Are your parents at home?"

Handford swung his backpack to his other shoulder and crossed his arms over his chest. His smirk disappeared. "Why? You think they did something?"

She was a little surprised by his question but didn't let it show. "I just need to speak with them."

Handford seemed to consider this as the cold rain fell harder around them. "Nah, they're not home. And I don't know when they'll be back. They're with my grandfather. You have questions about the dead body? Or the missing lady?"

Victoria felt a chill that had nothing to do with the rain and everything to do with the boy's casual reference to Steve Johnson and Zoey. "It's about Magnolia Estates."

"Never heard of it," Handford said.

"Okay. I'll come back." Victoria offered a tight smile.

Handford headed toward his house as Victoria jogged back to her Suburban and got inside. Raindrops drummed on the roof and against the windshield. The windows fogged as she replayed the conversation with the Fairchilds' son in her mind. With one former neighbor dead and one missing, Handford didn't seem very concerned.

Her phone buzzed. Payton's name flashed on the screen. Victoria answered immediately.

"Hey, I got your message," Payton said. "I'm sorry to tell you this, but you can't proceed with an investigation involving the Fairchilds or their immediate family members. Not now."

Payton's statement set off alarm bells. She wouldn't say that unless there was already an ongoing investigation, and the FBI didn't want anyone else to interfere with it.

"I'm looking at them as persons of interest in Zoey Hamilton's missing person case," Victoria said.

"Do you have solid evidence they're involved?"

"I'm working on it. Not enough for a warrant yet."

"Either way, don't breathe a word of this, but Craig Fairchild is the son-in-law of George Stanford, the former governor."

"I know. What about it?"

"We've been gathering evidence against the former governor for over a year. We have what we need to arrest him, but we want to make sure we have enough to put him away."

The governor again. The pieces were falling into place a little faster. Maybe Connor was on to something with his theory.

"I hate to hinder your investigation," Payton said, her voice softening. "I know the missing woman lives in your neighborhood, but we need to handle this situation carefully or we could lose over a year of work. You understand, right?"

Victoria sighed. "Yes, I understand. I need to tell the detective working on Zoey's case."

"Just make sure he knows what is at stake. I'll keep you posted," Payton said. "And be careful, Victoria. You may be a federal agent, and they may be your neighbors, but that family clearly thinks they're above the law. They wouldn't hesitate to punish anyone who crossed them."

The line went dead, leaving Victoria alone with the rain and her swirling thoughts. One thing was clear: even if the Fairchilds had nothing to do with the problems in Mountain Meadows, it appeared they weren't completely innocent.

58

Victoria

Now

From her vantage point near Connor Rhode's house, Victoria could see across the street to the Humphreys' residence. Movement flickered in her periphery. A figure emerged from the side door. Victoria grabbed the binoculars she kept in her car for work. It was Mark, dressed in a long, black trench coat.

What was he up to sneaking around outside in the rain? Why the obvious attempt at discretion?

If Mark and Faith were investors in Magnolia Estates, they had also lost a significant amount of money. Victoria had just as many reasons to suspect them of killing Steve as she did Connor and the Fairchilds.

Victoria gripped her binoculars as Mark swiveled his head, scanning the area with an undeniable air of secrecy. Satisfied he wasn't being watched, he hurried out of sight behind the privacy fence at the side of the property.

Victoria's instincts screamed a warning. This was more than a late-night stroll. Throwing off her seatbelt, she exited the vehicle, leaving her umbrella behind in case she needed to use her gun. She followed the fence line, sticking to the shadows cast by the large oak trees. In the back of the Humphreys' yard, the door to a small barn stood open.

From inside the barn, Mark grunted. When Victoria peered in, he was handling something large, with an irregular shape, concealed under a thick blanket. The object resembled the curled-up form of a human body.

Victoria stepped forward. "Mark, it's Special Agent Victoria," she said in a no-nonsense tone, using her official title and holding her service weapon by her side.

He whipped his head up, eyes wide. "Whoa! You startled me." He held up his hands defensively, lowering the heavy object and letting it lean against the side of the barn. "What are you doing here?"

"What is under that blanket?" Victoria asked, her muscles tense, her entire body alert.

"This?" He looked down at the lumpy form. "It's...Oh...I can see what it looks like, but it's not what you think."

"Show me. Slowly."

Seconds ticked by as Mark stared at her. Slowly, he turned and pulled the blanket away from the object.

Underneath lay a gleaming hunt seat saddle on a wooden stand.

"Lexi's birthday is next week, and we had this saddle custom made for her. Faith picked it up, so I hadn't seen it yet. I just wanted to take a peek before Lexi opened it."

Victoria's mouth went dry as she lowered her weapon, and the adrenaline drained from her body. Lexi's upcoming fifteenth birthday. Of course.

Victoria managed a tight nod. "My apologies for following you in here and startling you. I don't make a habit of spying on my neighbors, it's just, with Zoey gone, things are a little different now. I was across the street and saw you sneaking out."

"You were perceptive," he said, grinning. "That's exactly what I was doing. I didn't want Lexi to follow me out here and ruin the surprise. Guess I need better tactics, huh?"

Even as the innocent explanation registered, prickles of doubt persisted. In Victoria's line of work, she couldn't accept anything at face value. Trust was a luxury she could ill afford right now, not when a missing woman's life could be at stake. In her determination to find Zoey, she viewed the entire neighborhood through a dark lens. One where no one was above suspicion.

59

Zoey

Now

Z oey drifted into consciousness through a thick, painful fog. Something was wrong, terribly wrong, but her thoughts were groggy, slipping away from her even as she tried to collect them.

Her body felt foreign—heavy, constricted. A cold wet sensation had spread between her legs, and the stench of stale urine filled her nostrils. She'd wet herself. But how? The smell—acrid, foul, humiliating—suggested hours, perhaps days, had passed in this horrible state.

Disjointed recollections flickered in and out of her head. She remembered waking up in the strange room before, then...nothing. Just a black abyss of lost time.

She tried to move again, a surge of desperation giving her strength, but she couldn't get up. Fear overwhelmed all other thoughts. Her arms and legs were still bound, her skin burning where the restraints bit into her flesh. And she still didn't understand why she was there, who had done this to her, or what was going to happen.

A door opened behind her. Fear formed an icy lump in the pit of her empty stomach as her mind lurched toward horrific possibilities.

"Why are you doing this? Please, let me go!" she screamed, but the words came out garbled and indecipherable under her gag.

The person behind her kept approaching. An arm came toward her face.

Shivering with fear, she braced herself for an assault. Instead, she felt a sharp sting as the intruder ripped the gag from her face.

"You can scream all you want, but no one will hear you," her captor said. "Just answer my questions, and this can all be over for you."

Over how? Zoey didn't think her captor would allow her to walk out of there alive.

"Tell me how you found out," her captor demanded.

"Found out what? I don't know what you're talking about."

"How did you know what I did?"

Zoey was confused, still thinking about Susan and her threats. Susan must have paid someone to do this.

"Just tell me how you learned about the pond."

The pond? What did the pond have to do with anything? "I have no idea what you're talking about. I really don't."

"You had the pond drained."

"I was going to. It was contaminated. Is that what you mean? Because if you think I did something, you must have the wrong person."

"So now you're lying? Not so brave and threatening anymore, are you? You should have listened to me."

"I don't know what you're talking about!"

"Who else did you tell?"

"Tell what?" She sobbed. "I didn't tell anyone anything. I have nothing to tell. Whatever you think I know...you're mistaken. I promise. I haven't done anything wrong. Please, let me go."

"You can sit there and stew in your own filth some more, but your time is running out."

Her captor pressed a new gag over her mouth and ripped the patch off her arm. Another patch replaced the old one. It must be delivering drugs into her system. That explained the time lapses. She had to resist, to stay awake. She'd never get away if she couldn't stay conscious. But how? She dipped her chin toward her shoulder, trying to push the patch off. She twisted and strained against the bindings. The chair groaned beneath her, but her efforts proved useless.

The edges of her consciousness blurred, her brief lucidity fading fast. A powerful tide gripped Zoey, tugging her toward a sea of darkness. She hoped her pounding heart and adrenaline might win over, but it was impossible. The world slipped away again as the drugs pulled her under and held her there, extinguishing the last flicker of her awareness.

60

Victoria

Now

Victoria settled into the passenger seat of her Suburban as she and Ned headed down their long driveway, going out for a quick dinner.

"Do you have the address for the taco place?" he asked.

"I'm on it," she answered, eyes on her phone. "Was it Tacos for Life? Something like that, right?"

"Hey, there's Grace and Craig."

Victoria snapped her head up and caught the black Mercedes S-class gliding down Mountain Meadows Road. "Change of plans. We need to follow them."

Ned raised his eyebrows. "You want to tail the Fairchilds?"

"I've got a feeling about this. And if I'm wrong and they're just going to dinner, I'm sure wherever they're heading is worth checking out."

Ned hung back, trailing the Fairchilds at a distance until they pulled up to a new restaurant called Zoros on the outskirts of the city.

The valet attendant opened the passenger door for Grace, who stepped out in a black cocktail dress. Wearing a sports coat, Craig handed his car keys over and the couple disappeared into the restaurant.

Ned opted for the parking lot behind the establishment. "A client mentioned this place last week. It just opened. I'd love to try it, but we're not dressed to go in."

They wore comfortable shorts and t-shirts they'd put on to walk their dogs earlier. Fine for the order-at-the-counter taco place, but not for Zoros.

Victoria hesitated only briefly. "I have this hunch about Grace and Craig, and I really want to go in and talk to them here. We'll be fine as long as we look confident. Look like we belong, and no one will say a thing. I promise." She leaned forward and pulled a sweatshirt on to conceal the weapon at her hip.

Inside, the young hostess swept an appraising gaze over them. "I'm sorry. Zoros is reservation only, and we're completely booked for the next few days."

Victoria clasped her hands together. The movement made her sweatshirt ride up, just an inch or two, but enough to expose her weapon for a second. The hostess hadn't missed it. She looked horrified, either at the sight of Victoria's gun, or the fingertips Victoria had lost to frostbite.

Just as quickly, the hostess's expression shifted, and her eyes lit up. "You're Victoria Heslin, aren't you? I'm so sorry, I didn't recognize you at first. Oh, and you're Ned, right? The veterinarian from Flight 745."

"That's us." Ned smiled, just barely, to be polite. His memories of what they had endured and who they had lost were not fond ones.

"I'm sorry. We really are booked but let me see what I can do," the hostess said.

Victoria spotted the Fairchilds. "Our neighbors are here, and it looks like there's room for us at their table, so if you wouldn't mind having two more chairs and place settings brought over, we would really appreciate it. I'm sure they'd love to have us."

"Of course, right away," the hostess replied.

As they approached the Fairchilds' table, Grace's eyes narrowed to slits, though she recovered with a tight smile.

"We saw you come in and wanted to say hello," Ned told them.

Victoria made a show of looking around. "What a wonderful spot. I can see why it's become so popular."

Grace assessed their appearances, starting from the top and moving downward. "You're a little underdressed."

"We know," Ned said. "We weren't planning on staying, but then we saw you two. Now that we're all here, do you mind if we join you? Or is this a private celebration?"

Victoria appreciated Ned's cooperation and made a mental note to thank him later.

Craig straightened in his chair and said, "Please, join us. I'll get someone to bring more chairs."

That's when two servers in uniforms appeared with the extra seats Victoria had already requested.

Victoria stepped aside to make room. As she moved, her elbow caught Grace's purse and knocked it to the floor.

"Oh, I'm so sorry," Victoria said with a practiced embarrassment. She crouched, gathered the scattered items, and returned the bag to Grace.

Grace grinned. "Did you and Ned have a few pre-dinner drinks at home?"

Victoria only laughed. The last thing she wanted was to have dinner with the Fairchilds, but this was important, so she took a seat. Fortunately, Ned seemed comfortable in nearly any situation.

A server arrived to take their drink orders and recite the daily specials. When he left, Grace asked, "Any updates on Zoey's situation? We simply can't stop thinking about the poor woman."

"Nothing new to report, I'm afraid," Victoria answered.

"Well, at least we know one thing. She's not taking an extended swim at the bottom of the neighborhood pond," Grace said.

An awkward silence descended. Craig's face drained of color before he let out a hollow laugh and barked, "Jesus, Grace...that's in poor taste."

Grace waved a dismissive hand. "Oh, I don't mean anything by it. It's just none of us really got to know Zoey in the short time since she moved in. Nor do we know about the state of the Hamiltons' marriage. I'm sure it's difficult when they're so different."

"Different, how?" Ned asked.

"You know. All I mean is chances are good Zoey returned to California doing whatever she does with her birdhouses..." Grace trailed off with an artful shrug.

"I don't think so," Ned said. "I'm sure you heard, we found the Hamiltons' dogs loose the day after Zoey disappeared. Their leashes were in the gazebo."

Grace grinned again. "*Your* dogs were loose, and you and Victoria appear to be just fine."

"Our dogs got out of our yard because someone propped open our gate and let them out," Ned said.

Grace flashed a peculiar smile. "Really?"

Victoria nodded. "It's true, and I'm going to find out who did it. You know, I'm in touch with the detective working on Zoey's missing person case. He's ruling out suspects, but he feels strongly that if something happened to Zoey, someone in our neighborhood is responsible."

Grace leaned closer, her eyes shining. "Connor Rhodes," she said with relish. "I'm telling you, if anyone did something, it was him."

Craig shifted in his seat. "Can't say I know Connor well. He keeps to himself. He's a loner. And my work keeps me pretty busy."

"Since you mentioned Connor," Victoria said, not missing the subtle tension around Grace's eyes. "Last night, he told me you two brought him in as an investor for a development called Magnolia Estates. Apparently, it was before I moved to the neighborhood, or I imagine you would have shared the opportunity with me as well."

Craig cleared his throat. "That was a long time ago. No sense in talking about past opportunities. We have some new ones though, if you're interested. Lakeside Estates comes to mind. It's gorgeous."

"I have a family home at Lake Lucinda, but I'm always open to exploring options." Victoria didn't need or want a vacation home, and most luxury developments would never permit her menagerie of animals.

Grace beamed. "Wonderful. I'm so glad we might be able to help you, though before we make any promises, we'd better check to see how many sites are left. They're going so fast. We'll double check and if there are still possibilities, I'll deliver the materials to you tomorrow myself."

"Thanks. Also, just a heads up," Victoria added, lowering her voice, "I heard there will be house-to-house searches in our neighborhood soon."

Grace ran her nails through her hair, pulling it over one shoulder. "Really? They must be desperate, then. But surely they'll need warrants?"

This time it was Victoria who shrugged. "I'm not sure what they found, but it must be something significant."

A server filled the wineglasses and Craig steered Ned into a conversation about sports.

No one lingered over the dinner. Victoria thought the Fairchilds were serious drinkers, yet they never ordered a second bottle of wine.

"The food was great. That's the one positive thing I can say," Ned told Victoria once they were outside.

"Yes, it was. You don't like them, I take it?"

Ned hesitated. "They're not my favorite people. That's all I'll say."

"Not mine either. I want to drive, okay?"

"Be my guest. It's your vehicle. What was that bit about the police searching all our houses? You didn't mention that before," he said once they were inside the SUV.

Victoria started the engine. "Because it's not true. I made that up to rattle them. We need to get back to Mountain Meadows before they cover their tracks."

Ned's eyes widened. "And do what? I mean, what do you think they'll do?"

"They'll get rid of evidence related to Zoey's disappearance or Steve Johnson's death. If my fib struck a nerve, they'll destroy anything incriminating the second they're behind closed doors."

Victoria steered the SUV around a curve. "Hold on tight," she said with a glint in her eye. "We might just get a break in these cases."

61

Zoey

Now

Zoey's eyes fluttered open to the now familiar sound of bumping and whirring above the ceiling, a grim reminder of her current reality.

Chris must be frantic looking for her. He had to be. But would he find her? Where was she? How far from home? She didn't know how long she'd traveled when she was unconscious, before she woke up bound and gagged. She could be anywhere now, any house with a windowless basement room. What if she was hours away from civilization? Maybe in a remote cabin deep in the woods.

Choking back a sob, Zoey tugged and squirmed against her bindings. The knots were tight, the ropes unforgiving, and they held firm. She thought of animals caught in traps, willing to gnaw off their own limbs for freedom. The way she was tied, that was an impossibility, but the mere thought made her shudder. No matter how desperate she became, there was no escape.

She longed for her ordeal to be a terrible nightmare. One she would wake up from soon, in her own bed, safe and comfortable next to Chris. If that happened, she would be eternally grateful and appreciative of her life.

Before her abduction, she'd been slowly drowning in unhappiness and a series of disappointments. Nothing had seemed to go her way since the move. Over the last few days, pure terror had changed her perspective, reframing everything. She realized she'd taken her freedom for granted.

Compared to this nightmare, her previous solitude was paradise. All her frustrations with the house seemed trivial now. She was truly alone in captivity, aside from the visits from her captor who kept demanding answers her fear-addled mind couldn't provide. She only wanted to escape and get back to Chris and her dogs, and she wasn't sure those things would ever happen.

A door opened behind her again. Zoey tensed at her captor's return.

"How did you find out about the body in the pond?" the voice demanded.

"What body? Whose body?" she asked through her tears. "I don't know anything about a body."

"This is your last chance to tell me. You're running out of time."

62

Victoria

Now

The last rays of the setting sun cast shadows across Mountain Meadows Road as Victoria dropped Ned off at their house. She continued to the Fairchilds, walked up their front steps, and pressed the doorbell without hesitating. The chime echoed ominously through the quiet evening air. If Craig and Grace were already inside, they must have driven straight home from the restaurant at breakneck speed. Someone would do that if they had an urgent reason to hurry, though it was also possible Craig simply loved driving fast.

Grace appeared in the entryway, gripping the door frame. She still had a full face of makeup, but she'd changed from her dress into a beige cashmere sweater and designer jeans. Victoria's suspicions wavered. If the Fairchilds had been in a panic to hide something, would Grace have taken the time to change her clothes?

Victoria scanned Grace for signs of distress or hurried actions. Every gleaming hair on her head was smooth and in place. Nothing about Grace suggested a frantic attempt to conceal any wrongdoing. Victoria wondered if she'd misjudged the situation.

Grace greeted Victoria with a cold smile. "Back so soon? Perhaps we should schedule a standing appointment."

Victoria ignored Grace's chilly reception. "After you left, I found something of yours on the floor. It must have fallen out of your wallet. I wanted to bring it by before you missed it."

From her pocket, Victoria produced the driver's license she'd palmed earlier from the contents of Grace's purse.

Grace gasped and reached for the laminated card. "My license! I didn't know it was gone. The last thing I want to do is deal with the bureaucratic nightmare of the DMV. There is truly nothing worse."

They regarded each other in the doorway, the air thickening with unspoken tension. Victoria hoped Grace would invite her inside for a drink. If not, Victoria had a plan.

"We had such a good time at the restaurant. I don't feel like going home yet," Victoria said.

"Really?" Grace asked. "I notice your fiancé isn't with you. Having troubles in your relationship already?"

A sound from within the house, a muffled noise, caught Victoria's attention. It emanated from somewhere below them. The basement? Was Craig down there getting rid of incriminating things as fast as he could, thinking a search was imminent?

Grace stiffened. "I'm sorry, Victoria. Now really isn't a good time. We just got home, as you know, and I have things I need to take care of."

"What was that sound?" Victoria asked.

"Sound? Oh. What you're hearing is the furnace. We have someone coming to do a tune-up next week."

Victoria wasn't convinced. She didn't think she'd heard heating, pipes, or an appliance. She was pretty sure she'd heard a person down there.

Only a second passed before she heard it again. The same ambiguous noise.

"You must be hearing Craig in the basement," Grace said.

Victoria locked eyes with Grace. "It sounded...odd. We should check on him."

Though Victoria left no room for argument, Grace wasn't accustomed to being told what to do. "I didn't hear anything unusual. I'm sure Craig is on the couch watching a game."

"No. I definitely heard something strange." Victoria imagined Craig getting rid of evidence. She had to get down there to find out for sure. She strode toward the single door between the foyer and the kitchen. "Does this lead to the basement?"

Grace cringed as if she'd just stepped in something terrible. "Yes, that's the door to the basement. If you insist on going down there, go ahead. But there's nothing wrong."

Victoria gripped the doorknob and turned. It opened with a soft click.

As they descended the stairs, the noises grew more distinct.

The stairs ended in a spacious room with a pool table, a giant television, a bar, and couches.

Victoria scanned the space and the doorways. Only two doors were closed. She gestured to one. "What's in there?"

"Our downstairs wine storage."

Victoria crossed the room. "And this?" she asked, near a door with a numeric keypad and a glowing red light.

"The panic room. Thankfully, we've never had a reason to use it."

Victoria tried the door, but it was locked. "Enter the code."

"I'm not sure I remember it." Grace stepped up to the keypad and punched in a six-digit code, then tried the door. It remained secure. "I thought that was it, but it's not. Must be something wrong with the lock or the code. It's happened before. I'll have to call someone to look at it."

Victoria didn't move from her spot beside the door. "Try again."

Grace frowned. "You know, Victoria, you're crossing a line here, making demands in my home. I think if I told people, your father would be mortified."

"I heard something that worried me, Grace. Please try again."

Victoria had probable cause to justify her search, but there would be less need for damage control later if she maintained her pretense of polite concern now. If she were wrong, she could handle any embarrassment that might follow. She was only being a concerned neighbor.

Grace made another attempt at entering the correct code. When she finished inputting the numbers, an electronic beep emanated from the mechanism. A green light came on.

"Go ahead. Please, open the door," Victoria told Grace.

63

Victoria

Now

The door to the panic room cracked open under Grace's hand. In that exact moment, all the overhead lights flickered out, plunging the basement into darkness.

"What just happened?" Grace sounded surprised.

Victoria went for her gun. "Get the lights back on."

"I will, as soon as I find the switch. I can't...I'm not sure where it is. And, oh my God, what is that terrible smell?" Grace asked.

The room emitted a stench like a reeking alleyway. Guttural sounds came from only yards away, raising the hair on the back of Victoria's neck. Something was lurking there.

A door opened in the back of the room, exposing a sliver of pale light and a whisper of fresh air.

Victoria adjusted her grip on her gun.

Finally, Grace located the switch, and light flooded the room. Victoria caught a fleeting glimpse of movement at the back door, a leg disappearing as the door clicked shut. Yet it was the harrowing scene in the center of the room that held her attention.

Zoey Hamilton was bound and gagged, her eyes screaming silent pleas for help. Dark stains saturated her clothes.

Grace's eyes were wide at the sight of Zoey. "What the—What are you doing here?" Grace exclaimed.

With the gag covering her mouth, Zoey couldn't answer.

Victoria positioned her back against the wall. "Get in the corner, Grace, and then don't move a muscle."

Grace did as she was told, stammering, "I...I don't get why she's here. I didn't...this is as much a shock to me as it is...This is insane!"

"Zoey Hamilton?" Victoria asked to confirm the woman's identity.

Zoey nodded, her glassy eyes conveying terror and confusion.

"Did Grace do this to you?" Victoria asked.

Zoey shook her head.

"Are you sure?" Victoria watched Zoey's and Grace's reactions closely.

Zoey nodded.

"I told you, I don't understand what she's doing here!" Grace shouted. "It doesn't make sense. This is preposterous. It can't be happening."

Covering the room with her weapon, Victoria got her phone out. "This is Special Agent Victoria Heslin. Request immediate backup and ambulance at 6615 Mountain Meadows Road. I've located Zoey Hamilton. A suspect in her abduction just fled the scene. Please dispatch units immediately to establish a perimeter and sweep the area."

Victoria took slow, deliberate steps toward the center of the room, ensuring a clear line of sight to both doors. She dared not lower her gun. With her free hand, she grabbed a corner of the tape covering Zoey's mouth and yanked it off.

Zoey gasped and drew in her first unobstructed breath. "Can I... can I call my husband?" she cried. Her voice sounded raspy from disuse.

"Soon," Victoria assured Zoey while keeping Grace within her sight. "Who did this to you?"

Tears streamed down Zoey's cheeks. "A man. I'd never seen him before he took me. He's kept me drugged." Her frightened gaze darted to Grace. "Why are you here? Where are we?"

Victoria answered, "This is Grace's house. You're in her basement."

Grace stood frozen in the corner, wringing her hands, then clutching at the wall behind her. She looked sickly pale; the color having drained from her face. Her eyes looked as wide and shocked as Zoey's. Her lips parted as if to speak, to deny or explain, but no words came. Only the strained rasps of Zoey's labored breathing filled the room.

64

Craig

Now

Fear and regret consumed Craig as he sprinted through his house, raiding the bedroom safe and grabbing the emergency supplies he'd stashed away, including a Colt Python revolver. Stuffing a suitcase, he replayed every bad decision he'd made leading up to the one he was making that very minute.

A fleeting thought crossed his mind as he raced down the stairs, taking them three at a time—could he stay and face the consequences, lawyer up, perhaps salvage some semblance of his former life? Zoey was still alive. He hadn't killed her. He'd barely hurt her. With a good team of lawyers and his father-in-law's help, he might get out of this.

No, he couldn't. This was bad. Fleeing was his only option.

Before leaving, Craig swiped Grace's treasured Munch painting from her office wall. The image of the screaming man had always bothered him, but the painting was worth a small fortune. He wouldn't get its true value by selling it on the black market, but it should bring in more than enough for him to live on, as long as he didn't have to provide for Grace as well. If only he'd sold the painting years ago.

From the day Victoria had moved onto his street, Craig had a bad feeling. Her presence had haunted him. Fortunately, she'd kept to herself. Grace and Victoria hadn't socialized or become friends. Over the last few years, along with everyone else, Craig had read about Victoria in the news. She had built an impressive reputation with the FBI, but it was almost as if she didn't really live in Mountain Meadows. Craig rarely saw her. Not until Zoey went missing.

Five nights ago. Had it only been five nights ago?

He'd had to move fast, before Zoey destroyed everything. When he saw her walking on the trails, that was his opportunity to stop her before she drained the pond and ruined his life.

He'd stood over Zoey in a panicked frenzy, every nerve ending firing, his body trembling so hard his teeth clattered. He'd knocked her out. For a long time, she hadn't moved, but she was still breathing. He wasn't sure if he was relieved she was alive, or if everything would have been simpler if she wasn't. No. Craig had needed Zoey alive. He had to understand what she'd discovered and how.

He'd taken her to his basement and tied her up in the panic room. No one ever went in there except him. Grace called it claustrophobic. His children had better places to hang out.

Rifling through Zoey's backpack, he found her phone and her husband's text about leaving work soon. A frenzied idea sparked. Craig could buy himself time by sowing confusion. He typed out an ambiguous response. *I'm with a friend. Don't worry.* It was best he didn't give the friend a name.

Craig hit send, his heart pounding.

Later, he used a version of one of Grace's excuses. It popped into his head because he'd heard it so often. *I'm in one of my moods. Feeling a bit overwhelmed and need some me-time. Don't trouble yourself waiting for me.*

While he still had Zoey's phone, he'd sifted through her camera roll. Mostly he saw dogs, birdhouses and bird feeders, until he zeroed in on two of the most recent images, photos that proved Zoey knew more than she was telling him. She had handwritten lists with the exact dates and amounts of money that disappeared from Magnolia Estates. Craig didn't know how she'd found the information.

While everyone in the neighborhood was searching for Zoey, he'd used her keys to get inside the Hamiltons' house and look around. He didn't know what evidence he'd expected to find, and he'd found nothing.

Zoey's presence in his basement had gnawed at him relentlessly. She couldn't stay down there forever. For days, he'd tried to dull his paranoia with scotch as he searched for a solution. When Victoria mentioned the impending house searches at dinner, he went straight home to get rid of Zoey. But he was too late.

Victoria had come down to the basement with Grace. Craig hadn't stuck around to find out what happened next, but they must have discovered Zoey.

He had anticipated that possibility, with Victoria poking around the neighborhood. He couldn't say exactly why he'd let her dogs out of her yard. To distract her, he supposed. Maybe to punish her. It hadn't helped.

All his dirty secrets were about to get dragged into the light.

He couldn't hesitate now. As the garage door lifted, he bolted out in reverse, the Mercedes' tires screaming against the pavement. He kept watch in the car's mirrors, expecting Victoria to come after him any second.

He made it all the way down Mountain Meadows Road with no one tailing him. If he could just make it to the highway, he'd have a good chance of disappearing. Going way over the speed limit, he shot past the location where, four nights earlier, he'd hurled Zoey's phone deep into the woods.

As he tore along Bailey's Gap Road, each passing mile was a desperate bid to escape the consequences closing in on him.

65

Victoria

Now

Victoria's heart pounded like a drum as she sprinted to her Suburban. She flung open the driver's door and leaped onto the seat. The engine roared to life. She spun the vehicle around and sped off in pursuit.

"He's driving a black Mercedes S-class sedan. I'm going after him," she told Detective Sullivan.

"Good, because we've got enough to arrest him, even if you hadn't just found Zoey. I was about to call you. We were finally able to trace the last email Zoey received. The one she thought was from Susan Cruz."

As she listened to Sullivan, Victoria scanned the road ahead for the Mercedes. Craig's car was built for speed and handling, and he had a head start. At least she was equally familiar with the dark and winding roads. "Who sent the email?"

"Craig Fairchild."

Victoria recalled the message. *No one wants the pond drained so your filthy dogs can swim in it. Stop pushing back or you'll be sorry.* And Zoey had responded, telling him to leave her alone, and she was about to expose all his secrets.

Victoria turned the corner, caught sight of the Mercedes' taillights in the distance, and increased her speed.

The Mercedes swerved. For a moment of uncertainty, Victoria's breath caught in her throat. She didn't want Craig to die in a high-speed chase.

Not when she and other investigators had so many questions and he alone might have the answers. When his car corrected and kept going, she let out the breath she'd been holding.

Victoria didn't have a siren on her car, though she didn't expect Craig to stop if she did.

She reported again to dispatch. "Suspect traveling south on Bailey's Gap Road. I'm in pursuit."

As Victoria's Suburban barreled through another sharp curve, she couldn't shake the haunting image of Zoey's terror-stricken face and the repulsive stench of unwashed body. The disturbing scene flashed into her mind, along with the grisly sight of Steve Johnson's remains from two days ago. Her once idyllic neighborhood had transformed into a rendition of hell. She couldn't let the person who appeared to be responsible escape. Still, she struggled to close the distance.

Each time the road ahead straightened for a bit, Victoria pushed her vehicle harder, fueled by the need for answers. Had Craig abducted Zoey to prevent her from draining the pond? Had he killed Steve? If so, why?

Around the next bend, two massive bucks stood in the middle of the road. With lightning-fast reflexes, she yanked the steering wheel left. Her Suburban veered off the pavement. Branches clawed against the vehicle's sides, wood screeching against metal as she plowed through dense underbrush. Careening back onto the road, she narrowly avoided a collision with an oncoming car.

The other driver's horn echoed behind her as she pushed down on the gas pedal and kept going. Ahead, the Mercedes' taillights beckoned, then disappeared around another turn. The highway juncture was only a few miles away.

"Suspect still heading south on Bailey's Gap Road and nearing the highways," she reported. "I need backup coming north."

Victoria pushed her SUV to its limits around the treacherous curves.

Craig's brake lights flared as he lost control on a sharp turn. The Mercedes careened sideways, slamming into the guardrail with a thunderous crunch of twisting metal.

Gritting her teeth, Victoria jerked the wheel hard right. Her tires screamed in protest. The frame shuddered as she forced it sideways, trapping Craig's Mercedes between the guardrail and the Suburban.

Craig bolted.

Gripping her gun, Victoria jumped out and sprinted after him.

She didn't know if Craig could outpace her, though he seemed determined to try. This was where all her endurance runs with Ned might pay off.

"Stop!" she shouted.

Craig had run to the end of the field and into the woods. Crunching through the underbrush around natural obstacles, she closed in on him.

"Craig! Stop!" she shouted again.

The thump-thump-thump of a helicopter approached as they headed deeper into the woods.

Craig stopped running. He'd reached the edge of a ravine. There was nowhere else for him to go.

The helicopter's powerful beam cut through the darkness, trailing over the woods until it hovered, spotlighting Craig in a giant circle of light and illuminating his wild appearance. He had a gun aimed at Victoria.

"You don't understand," he shouted, his entire arm shaking.

Victoria kept her voice steady despite the chaos. "It's over, Craig. Drop the weapon and surrender."

For a moment, he wavered, and the gun dipped slightly. A dark look crossed his face. He fired four times. Victoria dove, dodging the gunfire. When it stopped, she took aim from the ground and fired twice. Her shots hit their mark.

Craig's weapon fell from his grasp as he clutched his shoulder.

Victoria raced toward him. She lunged for his gun, kicking it over the culvert before he could fire again.

Craig wasn't giving up, but Victoria didn't want to shoot him again. She couldn't risk him dying. He elbowed her in the cheek, the blow sending a sharp jolt of pain into her face and down her neck. Another blow slammed her chest, knocking the wind from her lungs.

Ignoring the pain, she barreled into Craig's wounded shoulder. The impact sent them both tumbling to the ground.

Craig's face contorted in a mix of agony and fury as Victoria wrestled him into submission and secured handcuffs around his wrists.

"You have no idea what you've done. You're going to be sorry," he spat, hanging his head.

Gripping his arm, she forced him to his feet and marched him toward the road. A growing swarm of police vehicles with flashing blue lights awaited and officers rushed toward them. Victoria pulled her badge out from under her sweatshirt and held it up. "I'm FBI. I called it in. Victoria Heslin."

An officer took in the blood staining her face and clothing. "You're hurt."

"No," she said. "I'm a little cut up, but not shot. I'm okay, but he's not."

"I didn't do anything," Craig shouted.

The police surrounded them and whisked Craig away. Victoria walked to her damaged Suburban, the adrenaline from the chase ebbing. Her cheek throbbed where Craig's elbow had made contact. Her face, neck, and arms stung where she'd gotten cut by branches.

She watched as the police loaded Craig into an ambulance. Victoria wouldn't get her answers tonight, but they were one step closer to unraveling the truth behind the dark events in Mountain Meadows. This time, she wouldn't stop until they exposed every last secret.

66

Craig

Five Years Ago

C raig stood by the neighborhood pond, his anxiety mounting with each passing moment. The area, so quiet and isolated in the falling darkness, did nothing to calm his nerves. Steve's insistence on meeting face-to-face had set off alarm bells.

Steve arrived in his Volvo, parked it, and walked toward the pond. As he got closer, his disappointed, serious expression confirmed Craig's worst fears. There was no escaping the difficult conversation that lay ahead.

"I'm going to get right to it," Steve said. "I looked at the Magnolia Estates Fund this morning. Imagine my surprise when I saw there was almost nothing left."

"Steve," Craig began, attempting to sound calm and take control of the situation, "I don't understand why you're—"

Steve held up his hand. "You and I are the only ones who could access those funds, and I know I haven't touched them." Steve shook his head and a look of pure disgust settled on his face. "I've completely waived my standard fees, which, as you know, would have otherwise inflicted substantial financial losses on the project. I'm trying to save this development so when we get the green light, we can proceed. After all that...after all I've done to protect the investment account, I find out it's gone."

"The builders wanted deposits, or they were going to walk."

Craig shook his head. "That's not true. I checked with the builders. I checked with everyone associated with the development, everyone waiting on payments. I did that so I would know what was going on before I talked to you. The money is gone because you took it. Jesus, Craig. What were you thinking?"

Craig couldn't remember much about what he was thinking when he borrowed from the fund. Just a little at first. Then more. He needed the money. Originally, he imagined he could replace it. The more he took, the less likely that would ever happen. Once he'd taken most of it, he might as well take it all.

"I'm going to put the money back," Craig said, knowing it was impossible.

Steve continued, voice low but determined, "Good. I don't know what's going on with you financially, but it's not your personal fund to use as needed, you know that, right? I mean, if I reported this, it could land you in jail for a long time."

Craig nodded. Magnolia Estates was one of his many development projects. That's what he'd led others to believe. Except it wasn't one of many. There was only one other community development project underway, and it wasn't doing well. The lots weren't selling, and Craig had zero income coming in. Meanwhile, he and Grace spent like there was no tomorrow. She had to have the newest and the best of everything, and as soon as she had something, she claimed it was passé and needed replacing. And it wasn't Craig's fault he also loved and appreciated the luxuries of life. He couldn't help that their new boat cost a small fortune, though he'd compromised by purchasing one costing far less than the one he'd really wanted.

"Right now, I'm the only one who knows the money is gone," Steve said. "I haven't told anyone. If you put it back now, I promise you, that's how it will stay. The matter will stay between us, and I'll take it to the grave."

Craig's gaze dropped to the ground, his fingers clenching and unclenching as he battled the fear and debilitating shame that was sure to get much, much worse if anyone else found out what he'd done. "I'll need some time, Steve. I don't have the money right now, but I'll have it soon." A few weeks, he was thinking. Then, when that time came, he'd have to beg Steve to keep silent for a few more months. The thought of it made Craig cringe. He didn't enjoy begging. But what choice did he have?

Steve's voice hardened. "You have to find the money. Sell your new boat for starters. And I'm sure you could get at least a few million for your house here. I think we can cover this up for another week, hopefully."

"A week?" Craig stammered as his heart raced, pounding a panicked symphony inside his chest. Maybe he'd have a heart attack right now. If he died, he wouldn't have to figure a way out of this situation. That sounded pretty good at the moment, a sure way to make his problem go away. And really, he didn't have to pray for a heart attack. Suicide was always an option. But there was one giant obstacle—Craig didn't want to die. He loved his new boat, his beautiful house, daily rounds of golf at the club, his limited-edition Bentley. He loved his life, except for the awful situation unfolding right now.

Steve reached his hand out and touched Craig's arm. "If you're going through some sort of rough patch financially. I get it. I've been there. You must have friends or family who can help you."

Craig gulped. There was always his father-in-law, though he might not have much in liquid assets. But the humiliation that would bring...it was too much.

"Put the money back by the end of the week and I promise you, I'll never breathe a word of this. But beyond that, it's my legal obligation to report it."

There was no way Craig could replace the money in a week. If only Steve hadn't found out. If only Steve wasn't involved. If only he didn't exist. Suddenly, Craig had another idea. Adrenaline surged through his veins. If he hesitated, he might talk himself out of it. It needed to happen now. This was his chance. Perhaps his only chance.

In one swift, ruthless motion, he tackled Steve, knocking him backward. Kneeling on his chest, Craig wrapped his arms around Steve's neck. He squeezed and squeezed. Steve thrashed and fought for his life, but he was no match for a much larger man fueled by the terror of losing everything.

When Steve's body became motionless, Craig finally let go. All was quiet around them. Sweat rolled down his temples. He gasped for breath, hyperventilating as his panic rose.

He'd solved the problem of how to execute the theft, but now he had a bigger problem—how to get away with murder.

67

Craig

Five Years Ago

Craig's chest heaved as he stared down at Steve's lifeless body. What had he done?

His hands wouldn't stop shaking as he grasped Steve's collar, dragging the dead weight across the grass toward the woods. Every nerve was aflame with panic, his head swiveling in the dark. What if someone was walking nearby? What if they saw?

No, no one would be out here at this hour. The trails were deserted. But his mind still raced with images of being caught red-handed, surrounded by police, his life ruined. He squeezed his eyes shut, struggling against a rising tide of hysteria.

Think. He had to think! People got away with this kind of thing all the time. There were entire shows dedicated to unsolved murders. As long as he played this right, he could be one of those guys who slipped through the cracks.

A frenzied plan took shape. If he framed Steve for embezzling, made it look like he ran off with the cash, there would be no corpse. No murder. Just a white-collar criminal who went on the lam.

Craig's heart continued to pound and sweat dripped from his pores as he committed to the scheme. Yes, this was the way. It could work. It had to, because he had no other choice now. He'd gone too far to turn back. He could pull this off.

He rifled through Steve's pockets and grasped the keys to the ancient Volvo parked nearby. Craig's first idea was to stuff Steve's body in the trunk and leave the sedan at the airport's long-term parking lot, making it look like Steve had skipped town. But that wouldn't work. He should definitely leave the car at the airport, but the body needed to disappear.

Craig paced back and forth. He had to get this right. He had to bury Steve's corpse deep underground. A shovel—that's what he needed, and he didn't own one. He couldn't buy one without attracting suspicion, nor could he ask to borrow one from a neighbor. Craig wasn't known for doing yard work of any kind.

Something splashed out of the water, and Craig jerked his head toward the sound. Ripples spread over the pond's surface. Just a fish or an animal.

Another demented idea took shape. No one used the pond. It was just there to look interesting. If he could weigh Steve's body down, conceal it on the bottom...

In a flurry of manic energy, he gathered every rock he could find, stuffing them into Steve's pockets. It wasn't enough. He needed something more substantial to ensure the corpse never resurfaced.

He thought of the guest house Connor Rhodes once planned to build in his backyard. The cement and cinder blocks were still there, and Connor was never home. Craig could sneak over and grab what he needed.

He concealed Steve's body in a tangle of brush and limbs to keep it temporarily hidden. With one last paranoid glance over his shoulder, Craig hurried off into the night. Maybe, just maybe, his plan would work. As Steve had pointed out, only Craig and Steve had access to the money. With Steve missing, all signs pointed to him as the one who stole it. Anyone who compared the two men would see Steve as the one with money troubles.

Steve had a run-down house, an ancient car, and a dowdy wife. Appearances mattered, and Craig's life was in great shape.

After locating a rope in his garage, Craig found the perfect item across the street behind Connor's house—a cinder block no one would miss.

Back at the pond, he threaded the rope through the block's holes, securing the other end to Steve's belt loops.

Craig stripped off his own shoes, pants, shirt, and sweater. With a series of grunts and snarls, he hoisted Steve to the side of the pond. Thank God Steve wasn't a big guy.

Craig lowered the corpse into the water, then plunged in, grimacing at the thought of filth and bacteria clinging to him in the cold depths. He'd always avoided ponds, except to walk around them on golf courses, but this had to be done. Clutching the block to his chest, he pulled Steve's body behind him, partly buoyed by the water.

Mud sucked at his bare feet with each labored step, a grotesque sensation. His muscles ached. The water rose to his chest, then his neck. Not quite at the center, but close enough, he released the block. With a sickening squelch, the dark liquid sucked Steve under.

Craig dragged himself out of the pond and collapsed on a nearby bench. The pond's surface had returned to an eerie stillness.

That night, he left Steve's car at the airport's farthest, least used parking lot, one with no cameras. He took public transport to the city, then an Uber home from his office. Sinking back against the cloth seats, he wondered if he'd pulled it off. The true test was yet to come.

68

Craig

Now

At the police station, Craig slumped against the cement wall of his holding cell. The smell of unwashed bodies and cigarette smoke permeated the air. He could hardly believe they'd locked him up like a common criminal. In the cell across from him, an inebriated older man with long, matted hair and filthy clothes sat hunched over with his head in his hands.

It was Grace's fault. She was the catalyst, the driving force behind his desperate actions. Everything he'd done was for her. Grace believed they had a magical, infinite wellspring of money, a never-ending supply. Every day brought a new desire—a bigger this, a more luxurious that. Something was always too old or too dated. She seemed to live in constant fear their lives weren't perfect enough.

Grace was always too much. Yet he believed that somehow, he could bridge the gap between them. Fill it in by being more and doing more. And for a long time, he did. They were not just okay; thanks to his efforts, they had thrived, at least on the surface. In truth, she'd pushed him to the brink. Her constant needs made him feel like a hamster on a wheel, forever chasing an unattainable goal. Craig knew their life had spiraled out of control, yet he couldn't bear Grace or her family viewing him as a failure. More than once, he had considered leaving her and imagined the sweet relief it might bring. Instead of succumbing to that fantasy, he'd made deals with the devil.

The man across from him looked up. He stared at Craig, then yelled at the top of his lungs, "They're coming for us! We have to get out of here!"

The drunken man's screams turned hysterical, filling the cramped space with a sense of utter madness. Craig covered his ears, though he wanted to scream, too.

Inside the holding cell, Craig couldn't stop thinking about the night he'd killed Steve, and what happened next. The details played out in his mind like scenes from a horror movie. After disposing of Steve's corpse and all the evidence, Craig returned home. He'd crept in through the back door, hoping not to wake anyone. In a daze, he'd stripped off his clothes in the laundry room, stuffed them in the washing machine, and tried to figure out how to get the damn thing started. When he walked out wearing only a towel around his waist, there she was. Grace. The last person he wanted to see right then.

Grace stood with her thin arms on her slim hips. He'd come close to telling her the truth and unburdening the weight of his sins. But as she scanned him from head to toe, her steely gaze more powerful than any brute muscle, the fear of losing everything had kept him silent.

"It's three in the morning. Where have you been?" She held up a hand before he could answer. "If you're having an affair, Craig, so help me God, I will destroy you."

She was her father's daughter through and through. Rage and disgust coursed through her veins. She believed Craig was cheating on her. The notion was almost laughable. If only infidelity were the extent of his transgressions.

It all became real in that moment. The sickening realization had washed over him like a tidal wave. He had crossed a line he could never uncross. But he wasn't a cheater. He was a killer.

Craig strode past Grace without meeting her eyes, heading straight for the bar and the crystal decanters gleaming on the shelf. He poured himself a tumbler full of whisky.

"What is going on?" Grace's voice sliced through the air like a sharp knife.

"Give me a minute," he mumbled, swallowing the fiery liquid in a few gulps.

Grace's eyes never left him. She stood there, demanding an explanation with her silence. This was his first test. If he could fool her, he was golden. And if not...

Craig poured another drink, the liquid burning a trail down his throat. "I have some bad news," he finally uttered, locking eyes with Grace.

"What happened?"

"It's about Magnolia Estates."

Grace lashed out with, "Again? Who blocked it now? Who else wants to prevent it from moving forward?"

"That's not it. It's the money." Craig sank onto the leather couch, though it offered no comfort. His body remained a rigid vessel of exhaustion and fear.

Grace slowly enunciated her next words. "What about the money?"

"It's gone."

"What do you mean, it's gone?"

"I think...I'm pretty sure Steve Johnson stole it."

Grace's face radiated fury as she processed the information. "You *think* he stole it?"

"He must have. It's the only explanation. And now I can't find him. He took off."

In an instant, Grace redirected all her anger to Steve.

Grateful her fury had shifted, Craig brushed away the tears brimming in his eyes. He felt like he just might outsmart everyone, after all.

But now, as he sat alone in his holding cell, an arm and a shoulder bandaged from Victoria's shots, the painful truth hurt. His reckoning had arrived. No more anonymous tips about black Range Rovers and blue Subarus to confuse the cops. This time, there would be no escape. Unless Grace's father could intervene and make this entire nightmare disappear. Yes, Craig's father-in-law was his only hope.

69

Grace

Now

Grace sat alone in her darkened office with the shades pulled. The physical ache of her humiliation pressed down on her with an unseen weight. With each shallow breath she took, a knot twisted a little tighter in her stomach. She hugged herself, trying to contain the emotions battling inside her.

Her Munch painting was gone. The space where it used to hang tormented her. The work of art was being held as evidence by the police, along with Craig's wrecked car, but Grace could still envision the painting's image with vivid detail. For the first time in her life, she related to the artwork. The anxiety and despair depicted in the screaming figure resonated within her.

Their attorney said the evidence against Craig was damning, and they should aim for a plea deal. The news would spread like wildfire, an uncontrollable blaze that would consume every bit of her once-. Her reputation would crumble, leaving her disgraced and shunned. The whispers would be rampant, a toxic undercurrent of pity and disdain from people she considered friends. Grace could already feel the crushing weight of their judgments, and the unspoken questions about her complicity. They'd wonder if Grace was an accomplice or the world's biggest fool.

After the Magnolia Estates project went bankrupt, and she'd learned Lakeside Estates had only sold three lots, how could she have been so blind to the source of Craig's income? The awful things she'd said about Steve and Sarah Johnson made her grimace in pain now.

Her phone rang. She didn't answer. Her attorneys had instructed her to speak with no one.

If the allegations were true, Craig had harbored secrets so dark they would swallow every bit of light from her existence. He'd stolen millions, murdered Steve, and then framed him. As if that wasn't enough, Craig had abducted Zoey and kept her tied up in the basement. Grace couldn't bear to think about what he had planned to do next. If Victoria hadn't barged into the basement, would Craig have murdered Zoey?

Grace felt a wave of nausea rising inside her. There had to have been clues along the way. Had Grace simply refused to see them?

There was the time Craig had come home past midnight and put his clothes in the washing machine, though she'd never witnessed a single instance of him doing laundry throughout their marriage. She'd imagined he was having an affair and wanted to eliminate the scent of another woman's perfume from his clothes, but he'd denied it. That's when he'd told her about the missing money from the Magnolia Estates fund, and how Steve had taken everything. Was that the same night he'd killed Steve? It must have been. A cold, sickening sensation rippled through her body. She pulled the blanket tighter over her shoulders.

When Grace informed Craig of Zoey's plans to drain the pond, never did she imagine what it would lead to. How could she? She didn't know her husband was a killer who had hidden a corpse in the pond.

The truth was terrible. So terrible. And yet...if it weren't for Zoey Hamilton and her insistence on draining the pond, none of these ugly truths would have come to light. Grace would still have the life she had worked so hard to create. Truly, ignorance was bliss.

Bile rushed up to her throat. Covering her mouth, Grace raced to the bathroom, but didn't make it in time. She vomited in the foyer as she ran.

There was no cleaning crew coming. Grace had canceled them, unable to face anyone. She needed privacy to handle her immense shock, embarrassment, and deep betrayal. Craig was responsible for all that had gone wrong in Mountain Meadows, and Grace hadn't known.

Sitting on the floor beside a pool of vomit, she mourned the life she thought she had, grieving for the woman she was before—the one who believed she had an almost perfect life and she and her husband were beyond reproach. All of that was gone. She was no longer someone people admired and envied. Now, everyone would think of her as the wife of a criminal. A pitiful fool. In the same way she'd thought of Sarah Johnson.

Grace's phone rang. Her mother calling. Grace braced herself for an onslaught of we-told-you-so's, and you-never-should-have-married-him's.

Her mother's voice seemed distant, as if she were speaking in a trance, "Your father was just arrested."

"What?" The words shocked Grace. How could that be? She could barely process her husband's arrest, and now her father?

"I can't talk right now," her mother said. "I'm just letting you know. Don't speak to anyone. Our attorney is on his way. Come to the house as soon as you can so we can prepare our response."

"Why was he arrested? What happened?"

"Not now, Grace. I'll talk to you when you get to the house. Make sure you look presentable. A hat. Sunglasses. There will be cameras, I assure you. But don't wear black. It's not a funeral."

Grace's stomach churned with the news of her father's arrest. Shaken, she turned on the local news in time to see a large group of reporters on the steps of the courthouse, crowding her father's attorney.

A reporter asked, "Why did the former governor have the Fairchilds' names erased from records involving the Magnolia Estates bankruptcy?"

The attorney answered, "We will not comment on any ongoing investigations or allegations. Governor Stanford maintains his innocence and looks forward to addressing these matters through the proper legal channels."

One reporter persisted, her voice urgent. "But what about the charges beyond the Magnolia Estates situation? The Virginia police have arrested the governor on multiple counts."

The attorney's expression remained impassive. "As I've stated, we have no comment on any pending legal matters. The governor respects the judicial process and will cooperate fully. Direct any further questions to my office through the appropriate channels."

Without another word, he strode away from the camera. A swarm of reporters trailed behind him, shouting questions as he descended the courthouse steps. "Was the governor involved in the alleged murder and cover up orchestrated by his son-in-law, Craig Fairchild?"

Her father's attorney entered an awaiting sedan, shut the back door, and drove off.

Grace continued to stare blankly at the television long after the news program ended. Her life would never be the same. As the magnitude of the situation sunk in, she made a silent vow. Grace would not dwell on her mistakes. She would rise above the whispers of pity, disdain, and scandal to reclaim her life as someone stronger and more resilient.

Grace rose from the floor and went to find a mop. Cleaning up the mess was just the beginning of her long road to atonement. But mere contrition would not suffice. She vowed to make Craig sorry for ruining her life.

70

Victoria

Now

"This ended better than I'd imagined it would," Detective Sullivan said. "Gotta be grateful for that."

Victoria's heels clicked against the hospital's linoleum floors as she strode down the corridor beside him, breathing in the smell of antiseptic.

She replayed the sequence of events that had led them here. This was supposed to be the final stretch of her vacation, her chance to do nothing and decompress. If she hadn't been home for the week, she would have been traveling, working long hours. Same with Ned. They would have missed most of what went down in Mountain Meadows. And if they hadn't run by the pond on that first morning, stumbled upon the missing dogs and met Chris, gone to the Fairchilds' house to ask about Zoey, the outcome could have been worse. Victoria was glad she'd had the opportunity to get involved.

The past week was a great reminder of why Victoria had chosen her line of work. It was for people like Chris and Zoey who found their lives suddenly altered by another's callous actions. Her mission was clear: to restore peace where it had shattered, reunite families, and help ensure justice prevailed.

As they entered Zoey's room, Victoria squared her shoulders, pushing her personal thoughts aside. Resting in the hospital bed, Zoey was recovering from a head injury and severe dehydration. An IV line led to her arm, delivering vital fluids, and a cuff monitored her blood pressure on a machine beside the bed. The doctors said she would be fine, at least physically.

Chris sat beside the bed, one of Zoey's hands clutched between his own. Victoria had never seen the couple together before. As she and Sullivan approached, Chris released his grip and adjusted the blanket over his wife. Then he leaned toward her, his lips grazing the crown of her head, and whispered something.

It was obvious how much Chris cared for Zoey, and Victoria allowed their private moment to play out before she stepped forward. "Hi. I'm Special Agent Victoria Heslin and also a neighbor on Mountain Meadows Road. And this is Detective Sullivan."

"It's good to see you safe, Zoey," Sullivan said.

The Hamiltons focused on Victoria's face, taking in the dark bruises there. Craig had gotten in a few more jabs than she'd realized before she took him down.

"You saved me," Zoey said to Victoria. "Thank you."

Regret clouded Victoria's thoughts. "I'm sorry it took us as long as it did."

Detective Sullivan spoke next. "The man who took you, Craig Fairchild, we have him in custody now. He's charged with your kidnapping and assault. Additional charges are pending for murder, embezzlement, and lying to federal agents regarding Steve Johnson's disappearance. The evidence establishing Fairchild's guilt is strong. The judge will almost certainly deny bail, given the violent nature of his crimes and his proximity to you in Mountain Meadows. Twice now, he's proven to be a significant danger to his neighbors."

"He really killed Steve Johnson?"

Victoria nodded. "We still have to prove it, but I'm confident we will."

"And he kidnapped me because I wanted to empty the pond?" Zoey asked, her voice wavering.

"He sent you a threatening email to prevent you from draining the pond. You were getting too close to the truth. When you responded with a threat of your own, to expose his secrets, it gave him another motive to stop you. He thought you'd uncovered what he did to Steve Johnson," Sullivan said.

Zoey's eyes widened. "But I knew nothing about Steve! That message wasn't for Craig. When I responded, I thought I was messaging Chris's ex. She's been harassing and threatening me."

Sullivan gave a somber nod. "We're aware of Susan's history of harassment. Unfortunately, Craig wasn't."

Victoria folded her arms and spoke in a gentle voice. "If you hadn't been so insistent on cleaning the pond, we might not have discovered what really happened to Steve and gotten justice for his wife."

"Your courage and persistence made a difference," Sullivan said. "And the emails between you and Craig will be part of the case against him."

Chris squeezed Zoey's hand.

"Okay," Zoey said. "So I guess all I went through, it wasn't for nothing."

"No, it wasn't. And if you're up to it, we need to get some statements from you," Sullivan told her.

When the interview with Zoey was complete, Victoria and Detective Sullivan left the hospital room. At the elevator, Sullivan pressed the down button, his eyes thoughtful. "Imagine moving into a neighborhood, only to be abducted by your neighbor, a murderer. I doubt the Hamiltons will want to stick around after that."

Victoria shrugged. "I wouldn't blame them if they moved."

"What about you?" Sullivan asked as the elevator dinged, and its doors opened for them.

"Move?" She shook her head. "No. But I think it's time I pay more attention to my own neighbors."

71

Zoey

Now

Zoey entered her house and took a long inhale. Finch and Wren immediately surrounded her, wagging their tails and panting, ignorant of the horror she'd endured. After the Fairchilds' basement and then the hospital, she was grateful to be back in the comfort of her own space. It smelled familiar, like home. She wasn't sure if it had before, but it did now.

Chris hovered beside her, as if expecting she might shatter at any moment. He'd taken time off from work to stay by her side until Kim arrived for a visit the following week.

"I'm okay. You don't have to hold me up." Zoey gave him a reassuring smile and made her way to the couch, sinking into the cushions.

"It's so great to have you home, hon," he said, finally letting go of her arm.

"You have no idea how great it is," she answered, her voice heavy with emotion.

"I'll make us something to eat. Are sandwiches okay?"

"Perfect. Thank you."

"Faith brought a sandwich platter over yesterday, so you could just relax when you got home. So did Grace. She brought dinner, but um, I wasn't even sure if I should tell you."

Zoey grasped Chris's hand, her fingers intertwining with his, and squeezed, a little too tightly. "That was nice of them. I'd love a sandwich now, but I'd like to cook dinner tonight. I'm looking forward to things getting back to normal."

Chris disappeared into the kitchen. Zoey sat alone with Finch and Wren close by, their heads resting on her knees. Stroking their fur, she gazed around the family room. All the things that needed fixing still needed fixing, but they no longer bothered her. It would all get done in time. And if not, that was okay, too. Just a day ago, she wasn't so sure she'd live to do anything else.

Zoey opened her new phone and culled through the emails that had piled up while she was captive. She nearly choked when she saw one from Susan. Didn't the woman know what Zoey had been through? The message had come from Susan's personal email address, not a cryptic anonymous one. Still, Zoey opened it, expecting another barrage of threats. But the message was different this time. An apology.

Susan wrote she had checked herself into a psychiatric treatment facility to get help. She recognized how unwell and obsessive her behavior toward Zoey had become, and she was finally getting the treatment she needed.

Zoey reread the email several times. After years of harassment, months of living on edge, it seemed Susan's vendetta had reached its end.

Zoey typed out a brief response, wishing Susan well on her journey to recovery. No matter how much emotional pain Susan had caused, there were far darker paths, like the one Zoey had experienced in the Fairchilds' basement. Zoey wanted to forgive Susan and forget about her.

A thump and a clatter came from the kitchen. Zoey froze. The hairs rose on the back of her neck and her grip tightened on Finch's collar.

"My bad. Dropped something. All okay," Chris called.

Zoey released a shaky breath, allowing herself to relax once more.

The events of the previous week had left their mark. Unexpected noises made her jump. She wouldn't be walking the trails or going to the common area by herself anytime soon. At least her nightmares seemed to be fading. But sometimes, she could feel Craig's hands on her arm, the tight patch, and the gag over her mouth.

Zoey shook her head, taking deep breaths and willing the sensations away. On the bright side, the ordeal had also ushered in her new perspective. She was ready to face whatever challenges lay ahead with courage and, ironically, a sense of grace.

72

Victoria

Now

The residents of Mountain Meadows, minus a few, gathered inside Ned and Victoria's great room, a space that hadn't seen many guests since Victoria moved there.

Connor Rhodes had arrived first with his partner, John, followed by Faith and Mark, the Mullers, and the Normans. Until recently, all of them had mostly kept to themselves.

The neighbors helped themselves to the appetizers and drinks, exchanging furtive glances. Each of them seemed to assess the mood and atmosphere of the gathering.

At first, no one brought up the charges against Craig Fairchild. No one mentioned Victoria had found Zoey in the Fairchilds' basement.

The Normans gushed about their new grandchild and how exhausted they were after taking care of her for a few days, while Victoria started a conversation with Connor and his partner.

"I'm glad you're here, and I have to say, I'm surprised," Victoria told Connor. "It sounded like you were as much of an introvert as me."

"We almost didn't come," Connor answered. "But I wanted to show my support to Zoey and Chris. God knows they need it right now."

"I think you're right about that."

"Otherwise, it might look like all the terrible things that happened here were everyday occurrences. And they might be in your line of work. Actually, they are, aren't they? But for the rest of us, they never should be the norm."

"Agree," Victoria said.

"Do you think the Hamiltons will show?" Connor asked.

"I hope so," she answered.

As everyone got more comfortable, talk of Steve Johnson and Zoey Hamilton became the main conversations.

"We didn't know. We didn't have an inkling," Mrs. Nelson said, for the third or fourth time.

"Kind of mind-blowing what he did. Still can't wrap my head around it," Mark Humphrey said. "Did you hear Victoria suspected me?" His stern expression turned into a slight smile. "She caught me heading to the barn behind my house to get my daughter's birthday gift and thought I was up to no good."

Victoria's gaze drifted to the door just as the Hamiltons arrived. Chris had his arm wrapped around Zoey's shoulders. It seemed like she had regained her strength. She had a radiant complexion and sparkling eyes.

Chris looked different, in a good way. He was smiling, his clean-shaven face void of worried lines now that his wife was by his side.

After a round of introductions and some small talk, Ned stepped forward, his firm voice cutting through the subdued atmosphere. "Thank you all for coming. Seeing everyone, I think it's a good thing we're together. It's been a difficult time, especially for Zoey and Chris, but here we are." He raised his glass. "To brighter days ahead in Mountain Meadows. To friendships and the promise that nothing like this will ever happen here again."

Victoria added, "To good neighbors."

Smiling, Chris lifted his glass higher. "Here's to knowing your neighbors, being grateful for the good ones, and keeping a sturdy lock on your doors for the rest."

Laughter rippled through the room.

Zoey's eyes swept across the gathered faces. "To a new beginning," she said, her voice clear and steady. "And to the truth always finding its way to the surface... one way or another."

The room fell silent for a beat.

Zoey smiled. "To new beginnings," she repeated.

Some nodded in agreement, others clinked glasses.

Faith embraced Zoey, and Connor Rhodes patted Chris on the back.

Victoria watched it all unfold, a gradual letting go of the weight that had been pressing down on them.

EPILOGUE

B undled in a few layers of clothing, Zoey and Victoria walked past the gazebo toward the trails. A bit of frost sparkled in the shaded areas beneath the trees. New motion-activated lights and security cameras dotted the area. The pond had yet to be refilled, and the empty basin served as an uncomfortable reminder of the awful events that had recently occurred in Mountain Meadows.

"Our guys must be so cold riding in this weather," Zoey said, referring to the grueling bike ride Ned and Chris had started as the sun crested above the mountains.

"Ned loves it," Victoria said. "He's so glad to have someone to ride with."

A few months had passed since Zoey's harrowing ordeal, and in that time, she and Victoria had grown closer. The Hamiltons had insisted on taking Ned and Victoria to dinner. From there, new friendships blossomed.

"If you don't mind me saying so, you seem really happy," Victoria said as they walked side by side, following their dogs on a wide trail.

"I am." A smile played on Zoey's lips. "I wasn't before...you know, before everything happened. To be honest, I was pretty miserable." She gave Victoria a sheepish look. "I didn't have any friends here, and the house was a disaster. My abduction, the entire experience in the Fairchilds' basement shifted my perspective. Nothing like your whole life flashing before your eyes to make you appreciate it and desperately want to keep it."

"I'm so glad to hear that," Victoria said sincerely. "Dealing with that level of trauma, it doesn't always turn out that way. PTSD can make it nearly impossible for some people to move forward."

"I'm not saying it's been easy. I have nightmares, but I am grateful to be alive." Zoey's eyes suddenly sparkled with excitement. "We have another reason to celebrate. We found out we're having a baby!" She could barely contain her grin as she shared the joyful news. "It's really early, and we're not telling anyone yet. Except I just did. I can't help it. I'm so excited!"

Victoria's eyes went wide with delight. "Oh Zoey, that's wonderful! Congratulations!"

"Thank you. We've been trying for so long. It feels like a miracle after everything."

Victoria reached out to squeeze Zoey's gloved hand. "I'm just so happy for you both."

"Thank you. I'm so glad to have someone to share the news with."

Victoria smiled.

"Would you mind if I asked you a few more law enforcement questions for my mystery novel?"

Victoria laughed. "Of course not. After all we've been through, you can ask me anything."

Victoria didn't mind Zoey's questions about profiling techniques and evidence processing. Victoria could see the glint behind Zoey's eyes as she took in each explanation, filing it all away for her novel.

"With DNA evidence, even a tiny trace can be a game changer," Victoria explained, recounting a case where a few skin cells had resulted in a conviction.

"So, even if, for example, the victim's body has been underwater for years? There's a chance forensics could still find the killer's DNA? Enough for a conviction?"

"Absolutely. Modern forensic techniques are incredibly sophisticated at recovering and analyzing DNA from difficult environments. No matter how careful the killer tried to be, there's always a genetic fingerprint left behind. But in cases with an identified suspect, one with the means and a strong motive to commit the crime, that can be enough evidence to convict without DNA," Victoria added, realizing there was nothing hypothetical about Zoey's question.

"Even if the killer has the best attorneys?" Zoey asked.

"Yes."

"And if that type of killer got a conviction, what kind of sentence are we talking about?"

"They'd put the perpetrator away for life. No parole. With what he did to you and to Steve, Craig is going to jail forever. It's what he deserves. Don't worry. It will happen."

"Good," Zoey said, keeping her eyes on the trail winding deeper into the mountains. "Sometimes I just need to hear it, you know, to make sure."

The dogs stopped to sniff something on the trail. When they all started up again, Zoey's questions returned to her mystery novel, unrelated to the harrowing crimes in Mountain Meadows.

Victoria felt a surge of gratitude for her new friend, and a surprising sense of contentment.

Getting to know your neighbors wasn't so bad after all.

NOTE FROM THE AUTHOR

If this is your first time reading one of my novels, you might not know *The Bad Neighbor* is actually the ninth installment in the Agent Victoria Thriller Series. Each standalone book in the series features a shocking crime and an investigation which resolves at the end. Victoria's personal story continues from novel to novel. Book one in this series is called *The Numbers Killer*.

More than anything, I want to thank you for choosing *The Bad Neighbor*. Please consider leaving a review and recommending my book to others. Your support is appreciated more than you'll ever know.

Happy reading!

Sincerely,

Jenifer Ruff

ABOUT JENIFER RUFF

USA TODAY bestselling author Jenifer Ruff writes dark and twisty thrillers, including the award-winning Agent Victoria Thriller Series. Jenifer lives in North Carolina with her family and a pack of greyhounds. If she's not writing, she's probably devouring books or out exploring trails with her dogs. For more information you can visit her website at Jenruff. com

a amazon.com/stores/author/B00NFZQOLQ

f facebook.com/authorjruff

[O] instagram.com/author.jenifer.ruff/

♪ tiktok.com/@jeniferruff.author

BB http://bookbub.com/authors/jenifer-ruff

Made in the USA
Coppell, TX
09 December 2024

42045045R00184